Lin Yu-chun/Irene Lin-Chandler was born in Taipei of Hakka descent. As a schoolgirl, she worked her way through the 'examination hell' of Asian high schools. Fortunately, her father believed his children should get a cosmopolitan education and so, after graduating from Bunka in Tokyo in 1987, she travelled to London to work in the fashion industry, and lived in Camden, Kentish Town and Highgate. Whilst in London she met Jonathan Chandler, and they were married in Taipei in 1989 where they still live with their two daughters. Irene and her husband are both writers and also manage and own an English language school in Taipei. THE HEALING OF HOLLY-JEAN is Irene's first novel and she is currently working on her second, which will also feature Holly-Jean Ho.

Lin Yu-chun/Irene Lin-Chandler was born in Taipei of Hakka descent. As a schoolgirl, she worked her way through the 'examination hell' of Asian high schools. Fortunately, her father believed his children should get a cosmopolitan education and so, after graduating from Bunka in Tokyo in 1987, she travelled to London to work in the fashion industry, and lived in Camden, Kentish Town and Highgate. Whilst in London she met Jonathan Chandler, and they were married in Taipei in 1989 where they still live with their two daughters. Irene and her husband are both writers and also manage and own an English language school in Taipei. THE HEALING OF HOLLY-JEAN is Irene's first novel and she is currently working on her second, which will also feature Holly-Jean Ho.

The Healing
of Holly-Jean

1

Holly swerved past the taxi on the kerbside, mounted the pavement and braked inches from the railings with a satisfying screech, gave the throttle a couple of twists of Nipponese high rev and jumped off the brand-new Yamaha, not a scratch on its gleaming red aerodynamic prow.

She doffed the black helmet and checked her face in the offside mirror. Two jet eyes glistened and sparked. Her second best feature.

A soot smudge on her cheek. Removed with licked finger.

She lingered for an instant's appraisal and concluded: not bad at all considering she'd just been powering through the solid city air this hot and humid morning. She stood up straight, all five two of her. Not bad at all? Bloody miraculous for a face that had spent most of its thirty-four years in the same grungy neck of north-west London.

Her best feature? Skin like a two-week-old's. Like fresh *tofu*. Ming porcelain.

Not fair, Marika complained; it's the Oriental genes. Lucky sod.

Holly smiled at the memory of last night's revels at the wine bar. Overdid the aquavit. Again.

She unlocked the seat, extracted the heavy chain and padlock, and secured the bike. A gaggle of young Japanese girls passed by. Their bird-like warblings pleased Holly. Tourists. It was Thursday. Camden Lock wasn't too mobbed. At the weekends you either got out in advance or stayed imprisoned.

From the rear-mounted pannier she hefted the bags from Sainsbury's. They were jam-packed. One visit a week to that asphalt atoll in the middle of Camden where the old bakery used to be was enough. Across the cobbles, up the iron steps, juggling the bags and fumbling with the key, whistling loudly.

The heart-warming yowled reply came, and seconds later her closest companion bounded up with his odd undulating dexterity – three-legged GiGi, her neutered Siamese tom, always so happy to see her. As usual his single front leg failed to brake in time and he tumbled in a heap. He righted himself and rubbed his hindquarters round her ankles, yowling, where's my breakfast?

'Morning, Hopalong.'

The phone was ringing inside.

She dumped the bags on the table and looked at the wall clock. Eleven. Mother.

'*Ni ga ma?*'

Bang on time.

'Hi, Ma.'

'Where you been?'

'I stayed over at Marika's, just been to Sainsbury's.'

'*Ai-yo*, you had a proper job, you'd get up at a proper time. Why you quit—'

'Yes, Mother,' Holly interrupted. 'How's your back?'

'Still moving.' Mother paused. '*Shao-lan*, Little Orchid – '

Uh-oh, thought Holly, when Mother starts Little Orchid-ing . . .

' – now that your father's not with us—'

'Mother,' she said firmly, 'I'm not moving back. You're only ten minutes away. This is my work, my home. You'd better get used to it.'

The usual litany in gutter Hakkanese – dog-fart neighbours, flatulent DHSS monkeys, copulating corner-shop cow. And as usual Holly decided against a syntactical rendition of the ancient language and prised her mother off.

Immediately the phone rang again.

'Miss Ho?' Hesitant, female, middle-ageish, Chinese but not Cantonese.

'Who's this?' asked Holly.

'Can speaky Chineess?' Possibly Fukienese, definitely distraught.

'*Ker-yi*,' Holly said, switching to Mandarin, the mother-tongue for all Han.

'I know your mother, Ho Tai-tai, you too, when you were a baby, you come to my shop many times. Wang Ts-ting's.'

'Yes, I know. Hello, Wang Ma-ma,' said Holly, gently. 'What's the problem?'

'My daughter, Su-ming, she has run away from home.' The woman began sobbing. 'Can you help me, please?'

3

'How old is Su-ming?' asked Holly, keeping her voice calm.

'Fourteen years old.'

Holly's spirits sank. A fourteen-year-old Chinese girl runaway. Another case of acting as go-between for the Street and the law.

'I'm so frightened,' wailed Wang Ma-ma. 'Nowadays, London is an evil bad place!'

'When did she . . .?'

'Yesterday. She didn't come home from school. *Ai-yo!*'

As was polite custom, Holly waited while Wang Ma-ma displayed her grief aloud. Meanwhile, she thought. Normally, she would go down to Gerrard Street herself. Chinatown people rarely liked to leave the area. But today she was expecting visitors, and Minty, the painter who lived next door, her part-time assistant, payment in cash please, was working on a new canvas. Which meant he'd be unstable for a week. Unstable being a euphemism for out of his head. There was also a pile of work here to get through.

Wang Ma-ma took a breather, and Holly broke in and explained carefully that she would have to come up to the office by taxi. Right away. No delay. She gave Wang Ma-ma the Camden Lock address, made her repeat it in her broken English twice before she was satisfied a taxi driver would comprehend.

'And bring a photo of Su-ming. The most recent. You understand?'

'I understand,' said Wang Ma-ma. 'Thank you, thank you, Miss Ho. You're a good woman.'

4

Holly sighed. Great start to the working day. Got to get a move on. She wasn't ready to think about a fourteen-year-old Chinese girl's chances on the streets of London just yet.

The answer-machine message light was blinking; she pressed the button and began to stack her groceries.

Whirr. Click. 'Archie Ross, Computex, nine twelve a.m. I'm messengering over some stuff. See what you think and call me back. And, Jonesy, don't lose it.'

Fuck you too, *Rossy*. She dumped her french sticks in the bread bin.

Whirr. Click. 'Margot here. Something's come up. Free tonight? Kettner's at eight. See you.'

Holly scratched her neck, thinking, then enjoyed the feeling so much she went into a full-blown skull massage with both hands.

Getting to Soho by eight would mean giving aikido another miss. Tommy Chen would be pissed off, what with the tournament coming up. Also she'd promised Marika and the gang she'd be at the wine bar for Sue K.'s slides of Lofoten.

But Margot she needed. Yowl. Yowl. Yowl.

'*Ai-yo*, all right, all right, GiGi!' she yelled at the nagging Siamese. Distractedly, she hacked some chunks off the hanging chorizo and dropped them on GiGi's plate. He snarled and scoffed. Loved his chorizo, did that cat.

Whirr. Click. 'Uh-uh. Uh-uh. I've got my purple tentpole out and it's red-hot and throbbing. Uh yes, yess—'

Holly leapt to the machine and stabbed the fast

forward. That was quite enough of *that*.

She stood a moment, her hands shaking. Used an aikido breathing exercise. Centred.

Phew! Six months since she'd moved in and this was her first heavy breather. That wasn't bad, it was bound to happen sooner or later, she said to herself. It was inevitable, really. God, how depressing. What had happened to the lovely morning she'd savoured along with Marika's fresh-roast coffee?

Then she was struck by a thought: she had the sorry idiot on tape, it might help trace him. She made a mental note not to scrub the perv clean. The doorbell was buzzing.

She spoke to the intercom. 'Who is it?'

'Special delivery for a Ms Jones. Got the right place?'

'Certainly have.'

Another voice broke in. 'De sign-wraiter, missus. Me com up now?'

'Come one, come all,' said Holly, pressing the lock-release.

She looked around. The place was a tip. The table was strewn with toppled groceries, GiGi's saucer of cream-crusted milk had overturned, presumably in the throes of chorizo ecstasy, and she hadn't even taken off her black Lewis Leathers jacket. No wonder she was hot.

She admitted the despatch rider who clumped by in oil-reeking boots and dropped a heavy manila envelope on her table. Holly handled the proffered ballpoint pen and smeared clipboard gingerly, thinking, germ zoo.

''Ere, that ain't Jones,' observed the biker, peering at her signature through long greasy tresses.

'You're right, it's Ho.'

''s your problem, innit?'

'It is,' said Holly equably.

The man shrugged, sniffed and swallowed disgustingly, straightened his straggly moustache with oily thumb and forefinger and left, mumbling 'You'll be lucky, mate,' to the Rastafarian sign-writer who now appeared in her doorway.

Quite a spectacle, this lad. Koh Samui T-shirt, a cummerbund of squared black abdomen and off-putting genitalia-delineating spandex biking shorts. Dreadlocks up in a tottering Carmen Miranda pegged with bamboo. Mirrored Lennon granny shades.

He was a vision of somewhere else, somewhere Holly wanted to be. Someplace where the cool ocean fanned the whispering palms . . . She blinked, shook her head. Weird morning.

'Al'right, missus, where you wan' fe de sign I wraite?' He held a paint-spattered ladder over one shoulder and a huge canvas bag in his hand.

Holly indicated the big window. The one which looked out onto the open cobbled area of Camden Lock. Using a marker and a clean sheet of paper, she wrote the words: 'HOLLY-JEAN HO AND ASSOCIATES, SOFTWARE INTELLECTUAL PROPERTY RIGHTS CONSULTANTS'. There weren't any associates just yet, but you never knew.

They discussed colours, the Rasta pulled out a chart and after a brief debate Holly chose purple shadowed with silver.

'Dat boss, missus!' the Rasta concurred.

From his bag he found a mirror, placed it on the paper. 'Check de sign backwar', missus,' he explained. 'Al'right I paint fe de window inside? Wedder-proot, dat way.'

'Whatever,' said Holly with a friendly shrug and the man gleamed two silver front teeth, eyes frank, challenging, the ancient reflex to rut. Him and this foxy little lady, alone in the studio.

'You need anything?' Holly asked, her jet eyes instantly hard.

'Coffee, tea?'

The sign-writer stared one more second, blinked, dropped his gaze, and raised his hands in a defensive gesture. He spread out an old bedsheet and, whistling nervously, began his work.

Funny that. It always worked. She could stare men down. Something in her eyes they didn't want to tangle with. Was it her sixth dan in aikido? Or the licensed Gerber throwing knife that travelled in her bag at all times? Or possibly the mace she took on assignments she judged potentially dangerous?

Couldn't be. These things she kept concealed. Until time. And since she didn't subscribe to any *chi-kung* mumbo-jumbo about shafts of concentrated *chi* energy as in those hilarious kung-fu movies, this odd ability in a tiny woman always puzzled her. It certainly came in handy.

She scanned her mail, selecting three from the pile, chucked the rest. She dumped ice cubes three-quarters up a straight pint glass – nicked from the pub the night of Marika's fortieth – filled it to the brim with second-day

Pinot D'Alsace, then carried glass, mail and manila envelope to the old leather sofa at the far end of the L-shaped studio.

She sank down, kicked off her trainers and put her feet up on the trestled slab of varnished pine she called her work station, first carefully nudging away some clutter, under which with luck you'd find her PC, laser printer and fax machine.

Inside Archie Ross's envelope was a flattened design package, two floppy disks and some print-out. The software was called Publish-It, and was a good seller in the lucrative desk-top publishing market.

Holly had a slurp of icy Pinot, then began to examine the packaging, always the place to start.

She pulled open the glued bindings, studied the marginal colour tests. Something rang a bell.

She jumped up and began to rummage through the file pile.

'Ah-ah! Gotcha!' She held up a glossy package called 'Key to Currencies – Currency Trading Made Easy'. Compared the jobs. No doubt about it. Two software rip-offs. Same printer. Of course she'd need professional confirmation, Beth Lawton at the lab would run some laser scan tests, but she'd lay odds it was her old friend, Yeh Industries.

Sammy Yeh, buccaneer, whose legitimate operation churning out semiconductors was based in the government-run, twenty-first-century Hsinchu Technological and Industrial Park, Hsinchu County, Taiwan, ROC, and whose illegal software copying shop operated out of who knew what little pristine factory in the paddy fields.

Holly used the cordless phone and asked the women-only despatch service to come by and pick up the two sample packages a.s.a.p.

She read Ross's accompanying note.

Dear Jonesy,

Heard you'd set up as a piracy investigator. After that amazing stunt you pulled at Micronet, I think you could be onto a winner. My son's teacher was using the enclosed for the school magazine. The bastard who copied it put in a bug, and at precisely midnight, 2 June, all files were replaced by a load of Chinese gobbledygook, no offence intended. See the print-out for yourself. The point is, the very last thing we need is a rumour of bugs in Publish-It. I'll be wanting full legal redress, at least against the European importers. The teacher says he got it at a place on the Tot. Court Road called Intertronics. Archie Ross.

Holly sloshed down more Pinot. 'Cheers, Ross,' she said as GiGi jumped up onto her chest. 'My usual fee, one hundred and fifty per diem plus expenses, plus percentage of loss staunched.' The fact that Intertronics had shut up shop three weeks ago, its owner, one Delvin Barker, gone to ground – it was rumoured with some certainty – in a nice little villa at Paleohora on Crete, was neither here nor there at this stage. That Holly-Jean Ho was privy to this knowledge was another story.

She'd give Ross a prelim right away, then leave it a couple, well, a few days, and call him back with the bad news. Explain the situation, the procedure she'd follow and the fat good it would do him. It would go something like this: the Fraud Squad, a.k.a. the Old Keystonians, would be fully informed. They'd issue a statement that enquiries were proceeding forthwith and in effect do sod all. The Greek authorities would receive yet another complaint about one of their expatriates, a solid supporter of the local economy down there in the sun, and promptly ignore it. Taiwan? Forget it, unless you were American and could get your Congressman to threaten trade sanctions under section Special 301 of the 1988 Trade Act.

Nope, said Holly to the Alsace, as a Brit, Archie, you haven't a hope in hell. UK's diplomatic relations with the Nationalist bastion amounts to a tiny trade office which promotes courses at English Language Schools, issues tourist visas and won't even help with lost passports. About as frocked-up as the proverbial Chinese fire drill. Holly had often dealt with the recently renamed, upgraded British Trade and Cultural Office.

The new name was no joke. The gesture, including the word British in the title, was a big one in the delicate balance of East Asian diplomacy. In fact the Brits were kow-towing as basely as Big China would allow them in their hots for a lick of the Taiwan loot. As for Delly Barker, he'd resurface sooner or later, in another guise, with another scam.

Meanwhile, Archie boy, the reputation of Publish-It goes down the tube. What she could do, she'd explain to Ross, after due consideration, as an extra, just for an old friend, you understand, would be to guarantee a bite on all the consumer watchdog reports aired by the TV stations, warning against the copies and disassociating Publish-It from the bug. Exposure that money couldn't buy – that is to say, financial details to be worked out later.

She finished the Pinot without spot of guilt but went on anyway to justify herself – to GiGi, at least, if not to herself. After all, she reasoned, stroking his cappuccino cheekbones while he purred and dribbled, Computex turned over millions, and Archie Ross's personal stock-holding paid for the polo horses, the Porsche, the rumoured lunchtime long-legged ladies from the model agency. Meanwhile, she'd just be doing her job, and doing it damn well. Uncovering the source of the counterfeiting, preventing further financial loss (hopefully) and, more crucially and far pricier to achieve, salvaging the product's reputation. Her personal networking with the TV stations was one of her hardest earned, but it was a gem and, as such, it cost.

Fair's fair. Face it, the reason she'd quit Micronet in the first place was due to her perception of blatant discrimination in reward for merit. The glass ceiling didn't just hurt when you battered your head against it, it left something stinking which you couldn't wash out of your hair. Besides, times were hard all round, and she hadn't had so many jobs since she set up shop six months ago that she could give it away for free.

Holly-Jean Ho had travelled a long hard road from Ms Jones to here. A road littered with put-downs and slights, racial and genderic. She savoured her freedom, this job, this new life – God, she loved every minute of it. She knew it for the precious, fragile thing it was, and she would do everything within her power, and more, to preserve it.

'Nice speech, Holls,' she said still addressing GiGi. 'Not for nothing were you born in the Year of the Tiger.' But GiGi was fast asleep, purring like a chainsaw.

She checked her three letters. Two were excuses for delay in payment for services rendered, pathetically similar wording. Which meant they were probably using the same software – 'How to Avoid Honouring your Word' or 'Bilking for Beginners'. The other was an invitation to the annual electronics show at Hanover. Whoopee, not.

And now some music, to get her in the mood for work. Not forgetting the imminent arrival of Wang Ma-ma which she wasn't looking forward to.

Using the remote which lived on the sofa, she took pot luck on the already loaded CD. Turned out to be the Red Hot Chili Peppers. Holly yodelled loudly with the crashing opening chords, GiGi sprang off and landed on the stained pine floor, glaring at her, tail erect with indignation.

Holly boogied back to the kitchen alcove, passing the sign-writer who was standing on the second rung of the ladder. Lovely bum, she couldn't help but say to herself.

She filched the last of the Pinot from the fridge, dumped in more ice, finished stacking away her groceries, and toted her glass back to the sofa. To work, girl.

First, those print-outs. Check the significance of 2 June. She unfolded the print-out and took a look.

Holly's comprehension of Mandarin characters was

13

limited to a couple of years of night classes a while back, and what she'd picked up as a kid with Mother before school wiped the slate clean. Luckily this was simple stuff.

Five minutes later, with only one recourse to the Chinese–English dictionary, she read: 'Happy Dragon-Boat Day to all you people out there!'

Dragon-Boat Day, as every Chinese school kid knows (but not every half-Brit, half-Chink school kid in Kentish Town, not unless they're particularly frocked up), falls on the fifth day of the fifth moon of the lunar calendar. You get to watch the Dragon Boat races and eat *tsungtse*, rice dumplings filled with mushrooms, meat, shrimps, wrapped in bamboo leaves and steamed. Glutinous but delicious and incredibly filling. This year Dragon-Boat Day must have fallen on 2 June and some Taiwanese whizz kid in Sam Yeh's workshop thought he'd bug the world.

Quaint, perhaps. Pointless, maybe. A dickhead act of criminal malice, too bloody right!

Bugs were no joke as far as Holly-Jean Ho was concerned. A destructive entity, an incubus silently biding its time in the heart of your personal computer. Ask anyone who'd ever lost an irreplaceable file. They'd tell you just how traumatic it was.

Still, thought Holly, there'd been far more vicious programs encoded in other bugs. Like the one she'd come across the other day, timed for Hitler's birthday and programmed to lay waste the computer's hard disc and render the whole instrument so much useless plastic.

14

Holly shrugged. So the world wasn't a nice place – what else was new? She put the print-out back inside the manila envelope and added it to the mound.

Next, deal with the wanker. She called the operator and explained her problem with Mr Tentpole. She was immediately put through to a specialist extension. The woman on the other end wanted the exact time of the call and Holly gave an approximation.

'Let's see, after Ross at nine twelve, after Margot, sometime later, but before Mother at eleven.' The woman seemed satisfied with that.

'Any chance of catching him?' asked Holly. 'This is both my work and home number. I need to be able to answer calls without worrying about something nasty lurking in the airwaves.'

'Theoretically,' replied the woman, 'the new central-ised logging system should be able to trace the caller.'

Holly mentioned the tape. The woman was delighted – hard evidence if it ever got to court.

Pleased with herself, Holly called Archie Ross to give her preliminary assessment, agree on a fee, and confirm go-ahead. When she got through, Archie's secretary put her on hold for three minutes of New Age drear.

She was about to hang up when Archie came on. 'Jonesy, lovely. Got my package then?'

'Check the letterhead, Ross. The name's Ho.'

'Ah, but you'll always be Jonesy to me.'

'My usual rates plus percentage of loss staunched to be calculated by a chosen CPA.'

'For you, my sweet, I'll forgo the pleasure of haggling if you'll have dinner, say, next Thursday night?'

Holly didn't bother to answer.

'Honeysuckle?'

She put the phone down. Ross was fascinating. The concept of PC and the revolution in gender-based attitudes since the sixties had apparently passed him by unnoticed. If he lived Stateside, they'd have his scrotum in a squeezer.

Weird morning.

The doorbell buzzed. She checked the wall clock. Wang Ma-ma.

It was, sporting two black eyes. Holly led her in gently and sat her down on the sofa. Dropped some Oolong in the pot for Chinese tea and said, soothingly, 'Fancy a nice cuppa Oolong cha, Ma-ma, *hau-bu-hau?*'

'*Sye-sye,* Thank you so much, *Ho Shao-jye,* Little Miss, *sye-sye,*' said Wang Ma-ma, promptly bursting into tears.

Getting the details out of her took forty-five trying minutes. The poor woman was frightened half out of her wits.

As soon as she decently could, Holly got her out of the studio, waited on the street till a cab came along and gave the driver the Chinatown address.

She hurried back inside. There was just time to catch her police connection in the Asian Liaison Crimes Office. ALCO by acronym, alcy by nature, went the old joke. Since the unit consisted of a mere six full-time officers, one BA in French between them, none fluent in Cantonese, Mandarin or dialect, who spent the better part of most lunchtimes in the pub opposite the veg stalls at the far end of Gerrard Street, the joke tended to stick.

Holly, who'd been going to Chinatown since her mother pushed her in a pram, was sometimes asked to act as go-between. Now was such a time.

She reached her contact through his mobile phone. Sure enough, the sound of music and drinking could be heard in the background.

'Mick?' she said. 'Holly Ho here. Need a favour.'

'Holly, light of my life,' said the policeman. 'My favours are yours for the having.'

'Yeah, Mick,' said Holly drily. 'Would you mind putting the following Missing Persons description out? Got a pen?'

'Hold on,' said Mick. Sounds of pub. 'Okay, go ahead.'

'Female, Oriental, fourteen years old, slender build, black hair and eyes, about a hundred and forty centimetres. Name of Wang Su-ming – that's family name first, Wang. Given name, Su-ming. Chinese custom.'

'I know *that*,' protested Mick.

'Yeah, well, it's about all you do know about Chinatown. May I continue?'

'You may do anything you like, Holly, anything at all, just say the word.'

She sighed with exasperation. Boys. Mick Coulson was ALCO's lone BA, six foot six, dark and devastating if you liked that kind of thing, which Holly didn't. She finished off her description of the runaway and Mick said he'd put it out right away.

'When did she split?'

'Sometime yesterday is all the mother knew.'

'Fuck it, she could be anywhere,' Mick said. 'There's

twenty thousand vampires sleeping on those streets. All life's cruddy tapestry.'

Holly knew he was genuinely concerned. Mick Coulson's heart was in the right place. Right for some. Not for Holly-Jean.

'Look, Mick,' she said, 'I'll call Centrepoint, the Chinatown Community Service Switchboard, and as many of the refuges as I can.'

'Attagirl.'

Holly went on, 'Wang Ma-ma will have put the word out on the Street. And I'm having copies of a recent photograph sent to your office, care of you, okay? Anything else we can do?'

Mick thought not.

'You could put a red line under this one,' said Holly, 'just for me.'

'Will do.'

'Thanks, Mick. Owe you one.'

'I'll remember that,' he said. 'Any idea why the kid ran?'

Holly told him Wang Ma-ma's story. The girl's father had come home in the early hours after losing badly at mahjong, out of his head on *mao-tai*, the fiery sorghum spirit. After belting Ma around a bit, he'd climbed into Su-ming's bed, as he usually did on these occasions. This time, however, he wasn't too drunk to perform.

Mick Coulson didn't seem to have anything to say, so Holly put the phone down on him. Basically Mick was a good cop with an impossible job.

ALCO was supposed to be undercover, a plainclothes unit with its ear to the ground in Chinatown. Except they

18

didn't understand a word that was spoken from one end of the Street to the other. The fact that everyone in Chinatown knew the ALCO boys by first name only added to the 'Carry On, Constable' atmosphere. As Mick charmingly put it, 'So we stick out like six erect dicks in a nunnery. It's not our fault no Chinese would be seen dead on the force. Someone's got to do the job.'

Holly reckoned Mick's six-pint lunches assuaged any thwarted ambition, for despite the surface familiarity with the unit, Chinatown wouldn't extend its trust to ALCO. Which was where Holly came in, and had done ever since ten years before when she'd helped a friend of her mother's deal with a summons to appear in court for hygiene offences incurred at her *dim sum* stall. The old woman couldn't speak a word of English, so Holly had led her each step of the way through the legal procedures, thereby earning the trust of Chinatown.

For a mixed-up kid that trust had meant a lot. It did to this day. And still they came to her who by fate bridged two worlds. Both sides gave her their trust, used her to span the abyss of history, of race, to reach out tentatively for the fleeting touch.

Networking, networking – Holly's credo. Only she called it by its proper name, its Mandarin name: *guanchi*. Contacts, influence, relationships, favours owed. Asia's most subtle and powerful tool. Or its most deadly weapon.

But where did that leave Su-ming? Holly asked herself. For a traditional Chinese girl, losing her virginity before marriage would cause unbearable shame. Su-ming's adolescent dreams had gone for ever. Her chances of finding a good husband had been destroyed by the very man she trusted to protect her till the time to be given away. Her life shattered, she had run.

Holly shivered as she pictured Su-ming in the snakepit of London's dispossessed. The New Dark Ages. The wailing and gnashing nineties.

There was no hesitation. Holly made a decision. Then she called all the refuges and homeless services she could think of. That took two hours.

Doorbell again. The despatch for Beth Lawton's lab tests. Holly persuaded the girl rider to do a second job right away – getting a copy of Su-ming's photo to the ALCO office at Scotland Yard and returning the original here. When Holly explained why, the girl was only too happy to bend the company rules.

'I'll tell 'em I got a puncture,' she said and in gratitude Holly tipped her £20.

There were other calls to be made and a fax of some thirty sheets of data connected with a previous case to be sent. It was well into late afternoon by the time she made the call she'd been putting off till last, to Marika, to apologise about tonight.

'Must you, *flykta*? You said Margot depressed you,' Marika complained.

'Not really,' Holly replied gently. 'She's old chums.'

'And vhat are ve, darlink?' demanded Marika, her Swedish accent rising comically.

But Holly knew her best friend was hurt, that she'd have planned as meticulously as ever the party in the huge apartment above her famous Islington wine bar. There'd be superb food, fine wine and flower arrangements

20

everywhere. Beautiful music. And good, dear company. Everything just so. Very Swedish. She was truly sorry to be missing it.

'Ve're effen starting the new Gravadlax, I've been marinating vone whole veek just for tonight.'

'Hey, that's below the belt, Marika,' said Holly, making light. 'You know I can't resist your Gravlax.'

'I von't forgive you.'

'Oh, come on, Rika,' she reasoned. 'You get me most nights and, besides, I snub Margot Silverman at my peril. You don't get to be managing partner at Simons, Stewart and Firestone, the biggest literary agency in UK, and have the best list of authors this side of the Atlantic by being a lonely little petunia, you know. I need that networking. Plenty of hardback piracy these days.'

'Yoh, you and your netverking.'

She finally soothed Marika and was excused for the evening.

The Rasta was coming on nicely, if ever so slowly. In mitigation, it was damn hot. Which reminded Holly she hadn't eaten all day, no appetite in this sticky funk.

She made herself eat a banana. Margot came with a crowd, and they all drank like fishes. It wouldn't do to get smashed on an empty stomach.

She spent what time remained at her work.

At six in the evening, the despatch girl returned with Su-ming's photo and the receipt from Beth Lawton at the colour processing lab. A scribbled note accompanying the receipt said the analysis would be ready tomorrow. Which just about tied up the most urgent jobs for the day. The rest could go hang.

Holly placed Su-ming's picture carefully in her bag. Drowsy from the Pinot, she put on a Jobim CD, lounged back on the sofa and let the languid music of Bahia harmonise the afternoon heat. She closed her eyes. Just forty zees.

Her olfactory organ woke her with a jolt. Ganga!

She bawled out the Rasta who'd finished his sign and was enveloped in billows of sweet smoke. She was running an investigation agency, she told him. A bust would do wonders for her PR. But the Rasta's obvious pride in his handiwork and his cheerful glazed grin softened her indignation. She had to admit, too, his sign did look 'boss'. Even better from outside on the cobbles. The purple and silver lettering boosted her spirits. She paid him off with thanks and he left with a jaunty wave.

Holly wandered slowly back up her iron steps. The sign marked a completion for her. A stepping stone on the way to whatever lay ahead. A marker of how far she'd left the other life behind.

She paused in the gold evening light. You're gonna make it, girl . . .

Gold evening light . . . Oh no! She was supposed to be at Kettner's by eight!

She rushed inside the studio. The wall clock said seven fifty. No time for a shower. She tore off her clothes, used a damp flannel on her underarms, face and neck, splashed on something from a Body Shop bottle, slid on a Balinese print cotton sleeveless dress and slipped her feet into plain black low-heeled pumps. Her spiky black hair defied control and anyway she'd have to wear the hateful helmet. Grabbed her bag, checked for wallet and cards, keys, stuffed in a selection of earrings, she'd decide which to wear later, and ushering GiGi out, slammed the door behind her.

She made it to Soho by eight thirty, haring through Regent's Park and stopping at the flower seller outside Great Portland Street Tube for a bunch of purple gladioli on the way. She was right, there was a crowd. All well-groomed, successful, wealthy women. Holly switched on a smile.

'Sorry,' she blurted out breathlessly, handing Margot the flowers, 'only half an hour late!'

'Surprise, surprise, Holly late? Never!' drawled Margot.

'Thank God for air-conditioning,' she said, sitting down and accepting a glass of fizz. 'However did we manage without it?'

'We didn't have to,' said someone. 'There didn't used to be a hole in the sky.'

'Now, now,' cried Margot. 'No doomed planet tonight, please!'

Holly exchanged greetings. She knew most of the faces round the table in Kettner's elegant champagne bar. Old friends and acquaintances, a loose group of women she didn't see very often. Some, like Margot, dated from way back – Camden School for Girls days. Mostly they were a bunch of high-achievers, wealthy from marriages or careers, and Holly hadn't always felt comfortable with them. But tonight, for some reason, she felt at ease, aided no doubt by the never-ending flutes of Cramant Cremant from the three silver ice buckets.

Indeed it was a fun evening. A change from Marika's wine bar. Besides – she recognised the reflex – it was dripping with *guanchi*. At one point she held the floor with a hilarious and slightly embellished tale of computer piracy and shenanigans which ended with everyone hysterical. She passed round her business card.

'Holly-Jean Ho? Whatever happened to Deirdre H. Jones?'

'Weirdry Deirdre!' someone sang. Her nickname at Camden.

There was an awkward silence, all eyes on Holly.

She looked round at their expectant faces, very slowly raised her glass and said, with a sardonic smile, 'That was someone else altogether.'

Everyone cheered, and she saw Margot nodding approvingly. After that, the evening seemed to speed up, getting ever more raucous until suddenly, smoked salmon curling at the edges, people started to say their goodnights.

Holly found herself with just Margot and a face from the past, Jenny Ravensdale, owner of the highly lucrative chain of Ravensdale English Language Schools strung along the south coast from Brighton to Torquay. Jenny had been a close friend at Camden. They'd lost touch over the years. It was good to see her. But socialising wasn't what Holly had in mind.

'So?'

'Let's walk it off,' suggested Margot. 'You're not going anywhere on that bike in your condition, Holly.'

The night air brought a rush, and they giggled and staggered up the streets of Soho, crowded with clubbers and pubbers this muggy summer night.

'Haven't seen you for years,' said Jenny Ravensdale, linking arms with Holly.

'That's because she always piked out on invitations,' called Margot from a few paces ahead. 'Which is what I must do, darlings. Holly, by now you've gathered the motive was to get you two long lost together. Jenny, call me.' She gave an oddly loaded look back as she climbed into a cab.

'She's right, Dee, or should I say, Holls,' said Jenny seriously as they walked slowly on. 'I've often wondered whether you were avoiding me.'

Holly didn't answer immediately.

They were passing the entrance to a pub, a noisy mob of drinkers had spilled out onto the pavement. Luckily the bell was clanging for last orders, and they only got a few half-hearted 'Gerremoffs'.

When they reached the end of the road and turned up towards the square, Holly spoke. 'I don't know, something about the years at Micronet did me in. Everyone told me I was a high-flier. Well, I was. Bloody good at my work, if you want to know the truth. But when men kept leap-frogging me up the old corporate ladder, I started to get shaky. And it went on and on, every year the same, guys with far less experience, qualifications, or achievements got the promotions while I stayed put.' Her heart was pounding. Adrenaline flooded her system, mingling with the wine. No doubt about it, it still *enraged*.

'For a time there,' she continued, 'I couldn't face you lot of success stories. Micronet had stripped me naked – pride, self-esteem all peeled away.'

'You poor thing,' whispered Jenny.

'Yes,' Holly's voice became leaden, hard, 'those bastards beggared my ambition.'

Jenny hugged her closer.

'At one point I started thinking it was because of my mixed blood. I became one of the lads. Knowwha' I mean – nudge, nudge, wink, wink. Touch of the chinky-chonk. Not quite white, if you catch my drift, squire.'

'Dear old England,' said Jenny. 'But surely—'

'Right. The clouds finally parted. Stupid bitch. Nothing to do with being half-Chinese. You could be three-fifths Kazakhstani, for all they cared. Still the wrong gender. You're not going any further, never will, you're not a man. That was the day I gave in my notice.'

'Jolly brave of you,' said Jenny.

'Anger, actually,' said Holly. 'Great motivator, anger.'

'And you've pulled it off.'

'Fingers crossed.'

They were at the far end of Greek Street near the square, quiet now, the streets emptied.

'That anger forged the me you see now,' Holly said. 'Bit jagged around the edges still, but time'll smooth out the rough bits.'

'I sincerely hope not,' said Jenny, with a giggle. 'I like the rough bits.'

Holly smiled back, funny warmth from a long-time-no-see. Nice, certainly; but Holly felt impatient now. Whatever this was about, it had better not be just a

midsummer night's stroll in Soho. She had work to do.
Tonight.

'Besides,' Jenny went on, 'you're quite wrong, you
know. It took a lot of guts to do what you did. And that's
what I see in you. Bravery. Grit.'

'Sweet of you to say so,' said Holly. 'But I'd already
built my reputation in the business. Fact is, I'd just
handled a piracy case when I saw the opportunity
begging for someone to jump in. My father died the year
before and there was a tiny leftover. Enough to get me
started. And here I am!' she sang out, arms stretched
wide, spinning on her toes in the middle of the road. 'Six
months in and I ain't broke yet!'

'Holly-Jean Ho,' chorused Jenny, 'Gumshoe-ess
extraordinaire! Which is why I'm coming to see you
tomorrow, if you've got a free slot.'

Nice waste of time.

2

GiGi woke Holly as usual by nose-butting the window.

She moved a limb. No feeling. Moved another. Nothing. Ridiculous. Any limb would do. Give me some response, body. *Ai-yo!* She had a head on her this morning.

Half asleep, on auto-cue, she lifted herself off the futon, shuffled across the studio floor in the half-light and reached up inside the blinds to open the window and let the cat in.

To the refrigerator. Left turn. Table. Pause, rest, let the throbbing skull subside. Okay. Move on. Refrigerator. Made it. Milk sloshed for the cat. Perrier gulped. Too much. Bubbles up the sinuses. Choke. Cough. Eyes prick and fill. Tongue deflates.

Deep breath attempted. Abandoned. Too dizzy.

Reality? Virtually. At least heading that way.

Wall clock. Seven thirty. Significance nil.

More Perrier, and her focal lenses align. She can see! But what can she see?

Ohmigodfathers.

Standing motionless, the bottle halfway to her lips, Holly

29

sees. At the far end of the studio, on the left side of the futon, face down, fast asleep, her naked body spread to the four corners like a beached starfish, thick raven hair spilled across the pillows, lies Jenny Ravensdale.

Oh dear.

Holly drank more Perrier, sank down on the nearest chair and after an extended blank, began the squeamish task of recall.

It had all started with the decision. The one she'd made yesterday afternoon.

Holly thought about that.

Nope. It wouldn't run in Palooka. Nor Paignton for that matter. As myth it was fine. As chronology it was missing five and a half hours. *And* Jenny Ravensdale.

Holly looked up from her musings, dragged her head slowly round towards the far end of the studio, a vague hope, a prayer even, that it had been just a lucid dream, delirium tremens, a psychotropic flashback, the heebie-jeebies – but no. It was still there. And it wasn't getting any less exquisite.

Holly went to the bathroom, ran her head under the cold tap till she couldn't take any more. Back at the table she tried to put it all together.

The decision had been to spend the night on the Yamaha searching the realms of the homeless. The refuges, the cardboard cities, under the arches, the doorways, anywhere till she found Su-ming. Probably futile, definitely idiotic, but she had to do something. She'd put Su-ming's photograph in her bag that afternoon for that very purpose, lest she got distracted later by Margot or drink.

Then what?

She rewound back to the bike. Still parked outside Kettner's. Jenny driving her mad trying to persuade her to leave the thing there and take a cab, saying she was over the limit, too dangerous for a woman alone at night, on and on. In the end, just to shut her up really, Holly had opened her big mouth and blabbed.

Jenny hit the roof. 'You must be out of your tiny mind!'

'Why? The charity people do it every night.'

'Not alone, they don't.'

Maybe she was right, but what the frock. Besides, they don't come more stubborn or contrary than a Tiger.

The argument ended when Jenny Ravensdale climbed on the back of the scooter and nothing Holly could say would induce her off an odyssey which had lasted till dawn. A fruitless odyssey, it turned out, since they hadn't found Su-ming, or even anyone who recognised the photo. But an educational one. Neither of them was unaware; they were informed, intelligent, morally decent women of the nineties. They simply hadn't been ready for the extent – the numbers, the madness . . . This was Calcutta in London. Except Calcutta didn't have the schizophrenia. By dawn they were numbed, over-exposed and in psychic shock. Wordlessly, they'd come back to the studio and showered the grime from their skins if not from their minds. That they achieved by emptying a full bottle of Metaxa brandy between them.

That was when Jenny had asked for Holly's help. The reason she'd asked for the meeting today.

Holly recalled that conversation verbatim. Anything

connected with her work received full concentration and was instantly logged. She accessed it now.

'There's been a spate of attacks on my students,' Jenny had said, nursing the Metaxa. 'It's always been a problem. Good old xenophobic Britain, people think the neo-Nazis all live in Germany, but go to any resort on the Med. The scum of Europe, they call us these days, and they could be right. But this summer's been by far the worst. It's out of control. Brighton, Bournemouth, Hastings, Poole, Torquay. Over twenty-five incidents. Nearly always involving my Oriental girls. And those are the reported ones. I know there've been others, but lots of girls, like the Koreans, won't report it. Don't want anyone to know about the loss of virginity.'

Holly had nodded in agreement. Su-ming.

'I think somehow the bastards have got hold of this fact,' Jenny said, 'which is why they go for the Orientals. Eleven of the incidents were attempted rapes. Holly, you've got to help.' She grabbed Holly's hand, eyes filling. 'The police can't or won't handle it. They told me rape in this country tops the league in Europe. I feel so utterly ashamed! The girls come halfway round the world on account of me, right?' She slugged Metaxa. Stared Holly down and said, 'Five were gang rapes.'

Holly felt the abdominal stirring of ancient enmity.

'Holly-Jean, I want you to help me nail these bastards.'

Later, Holly asked, 'But why come to me? I'm not a PI. I've no experience of that kind of investigative work. I only handle software counterfeiting.'

To which Jenny replied, 'That's not what I hear.

That's not what I know. You were always a fighter for causes, Holly-Jean. Remember at Camden, the campaigns you organised. Things mattered to you. I reckon they still do. And don't think for one moment we all don't know about your martial arts and the rest. You're a fighter, Holly.' She stood up and walked over to the window. The sounds of Camden waking up filtered through. She turned, her face lit by the dawn light. 'Don't you want to get these scum?'

Holly just stared back into Jenny Ravensdale's beautiful blue eyes.

They'd finished the brandy then and fallen into bed.

Holly shied away from further recall. Too confusing. When it came to the s-word, Holly-Jean Ho was a self-proclaimed oddity.

There'd been a couple of sticky disasters with men early on, including one attempted date rape at college which had left the unfortunate boy with a severed testicle and the end of his rugby career. She'd decided at that point she could do without the hassle. She'd settle for friends, not lovers. She found she generally, but not exclusively, preferred the company of women. Holly-Jean liked to joke about it: for me, physical intimacy means aikido on the tatami.

When she shared Marika's bed, as she had begun to recently, they talked, they kissed goodnight, they slept. Marika hadn't asked for more. Yet. And Holly wasn't ready to address the issue. Yet.

But now, sitting at the kitchen table, her body denied sleep, nursing a hellish hangover, she felt herself blushing, her pulse pounding and her body churning. She knew perfectly well why and it bewildered. Tiny jets of imagery burst forth from her memory of the early dawn. A taste, a cry, a bite, a burning – such a burning . . .

Holly's body became a clamour of remembered sensation. A raft in white-water rapids, caught on the rock of inhibition, the flood racing by, and she fought to free herself, greedily plunged in, embraced the helter-skelter. Slid once more on the satiny curves and magical ridges. Perceived again the precise moment of mutual apprehension, the sharing of a higher place, an elevation she'd never before experienced. Now she felt a gathering, a tidal motion beyond her control, and she shuddered and shook as her body flew, soared up, up, up.

She staggered from the kitchen table, stumbled across the studio, reached the futon, straddled Jenny's soft warm body and bracing her arms against the wall, recklessly rode herself to orgasm, crying aloud, '*Ai! Ai! Ai!*'

She slumped forward, her face buried in the raven strands of hair to hide the tears of release, as Jenny soothed and whispered, 'It's all right, it's all right.'

Holly-Jean floated down to earth in gentle swoops, like stray down from the swan's neck as it flies south for winter. A phrase ran through her head as she fell asleep: 'The amazing utter boundlessness of possibility.'

Was it Auden, Lao Tse, Noel Coward? What did it mean . . .

The two women sat at the table and sipped coffee. They might have stayed all day waiting for one or the other to break the silence but for the sudden appearance of Minty from next door.

He had a paintbrush in his hand, his Medusa-head of riotous curls was spattered with multi-coloured paint flecks. His eyes, dilated huge as twin inkwells, glittered as he said, 'I smell Sulawesi.'

Holly and Jenny cracked up. The tension broke and they burst into hysterical laughter.

Holly said, 'I'll give it a go. Just a day or so.'

Su-ming – she'd keep the pressure on Missing Persons via Coulson. She'd continue to hassle the social services and charities by phone; as for the street, by now Wang Ma-ma would have mobilised the clans.

While Minty and Jenny got acquainted over a fresh pot, Holly packed a bag, sorted out her E-mail, changed her answering-machine message, checked her hard-copy post, performed a derisory filing by elbow. She forestalled her mother by ringing her just before eleven to say she'd be away for a day or so. She promised to call each night.

Ma, for a change, sounded strangely preoccupied. Disinterested, even. Something about Taiwan and a travel agent, but Holly's Hakkanese wasn't functioning too well on no sleep and too much trauma, so she cut Mother off.

Then she called Beth Lawton to delay returning the software packages. Archie Ross could wait.

She called ALCO to make sure Mick Coulson was pushing hard on Su-ming. She described the night's fruitless searching.

'You blood stupid idiot,' he said. 'Brave maybe, but

damn foolish. You realise you could get yourself killed out there.'

'So could Su-ming,' said Holly.

'I know, I know,' replied Mick. 'But I absolutely forbid any more solo shit.'

'Don't wet yourself, Sarge. Actually, that's why I rang. I'm going out of town. Just a day or two. But how about you taking a look for Su-ming yourself? I know it's Missing Persons, not strictly ALCO business, but she's a Chinatown girl. Fourteen years old. Twenty thousand vampires, remember?'

'I'm way ahead of you, Holly-Jean,' said Mick. 'I already have the lads doing the rounds. Get them out of the pub and into the real world for a change. And tonight they're all putting in for overtime. All six of us.'

'Thanks, Mick,' said Holly, and she meant it. 'I knew you'd come through.'

'I'll have a try,' he promised. Then he asked, 'Where are you going anyway? Not often you leave London, is it?'

'None of your business,' Holly told him.

Which left Marika. Holly stared at the phone, and fed GiGi. Stared at the phone, and took a shower. Stared at the phone, and zipped her overnight bag. Was staring when Jenny yelled time to go. Too late. She'd call on the road. Whenever.

Before they left, she made Minty promise to feed GiGi and keep an eye on the studio. She took a last look round. The place was secure enough with Minty along the corridor. There were only the two studios on this floor. And he wouldn't be going anywhere. Not while a painting was in progress. She kissed GiGi goodbye, and that was it.

'Okay, let's go,' she said.

Jenny smiled and said, 'Thanks, gumshoe.'

They took a taxi over to Margot's office at Chelsea Harbour where Jenny had parked her car after driving up from the country.

It was a bit awkward at first. Holly discerned unspoken accusations floating in the air of the huge office overlooking the Thames. It was a place of power she couldn't help but envy, with its enormous desk and the framed letters to Margot from famous authors.

She looked around while Jenny and Margot spoke together in undertones. The photos taken with the legends. Margot and Gordimer, Margot and Graham Greene, and one that really interested her, Margot and a glorious Indian face.

'Is it Narayan?' she called.

Margot looked up from her confab at the desk. 'You're right,' she said, obviously impressed. 'A rare picture.'

'He's got to be one of my all-time favourites,' said Holly.

'Mine too,' said Margot briskly. 'Right, let's celebrate. I knew I was right in suggesting you to Jenny.'

Oh really? thought Holly-Jean. First she'd heard about Margot's oar. She might have known. Margot Silverman had always been a compulsive control freak. The great manipulator at Camden School for Girls, playing life as though it was a board game, shifting alliances and relationships, in command of everything and everyone around her. Or so she liked to think. Holly knew she'd not changed since those days. If anything she played God more than ever, for in her work she wielded enormous influence over other people's lives.

Holly pictured the dashed hopes of the writers who traipsed in and out of this room, or the incredible elation that would follow the signing of a contract. But Margot was not unkind, there was no malice in her games. It was just her. The way she was formed.

Still, Holly reminded herself, with Margot, there was always a point to everything. She never wasted a mic of energy. Bit like the Chinese.

'Lunch,' announced Margot, pressing a button and telling her secretary to hold the fort. 'Then you must be off on your quest.'

Holly picked over the sumptuous meal at the Conrad Hotel courtesy of Margot's expense account. She contributed little to the conversation, blaming her lack of appetite on the events of the previous twenty-four hours and her general lack of sleep. But in fact her mind was alive, churning with spaced energy. For now that she'd made her mind up to take on Jenny's case, she was anxious to be on her way.

'How come you did suggest me to Jenny, Margot?' asked Holly. 'After all, I'm hardly qualified, and there are loads of experienced investigative agencies to choose from.'

Margot paused for a moment, toying with the stem of her glass. 'You know, I can't quite recall. Somebody or other mentioned your name in connection with something or other. Now, who was it?' She screwed up her

eyes in concentration, and Holly knew she was lying.
'Ah, I think it was when I was in Hong Kong last
month . . . Or maybe it was Lucca – you know anyone in
Tuscany?'

Ha ha, Margot, you silly frock.

'No?' Margot sighed. 'Sorry, darling. It's gone. Anyway, all I know is, when Jenny called up in a terrible
state, your name popped up. Out of the blue.'

'Fancy,' said Holly.

'Now, darlings, let's toast,' said Margot, raising her
glass. 'I wish you every luck in finding these beasts.'

They clinked.

'But, Holly, sweet, do please, please take care. You're
heading into dangerous waters. It's dreadfully worrying.'

'Thanks, Margot, but I'm used to watching my backside, remember?'

'I do, I do,' she beamed.

Finally the meal was over and they made it to Jenny's
Range Rover in the Chelsea Harbour underground car
park.

'Just a minute!' called Margot, toting a parcel across
the concrete ramp to the parking space.

What now? thought Holly.

'This is for you, Holly-Jean. It'll come in handy on the
job, so to speak. Count it as a permanent loan, a gift, a
whim.' She paused, handing over the package. 'No,
perhaps it had better be a favour owed. You never
know.'

Holly took the present, glanced inside. 'Why, thanks,
Margot, that's really kind of you. I'll give you a call when
I've figured how to use it.'

'Do that, darlings, and do take care!'

They waved goodbye to Margot, promising to keep her well informed.

She wasn't a bad sort really, thought Holly, but she couldn't banish the feeling there was a lot more to the Silverman-Ravensdale relationship than she was privy to.

They went speeding over the Thames, through south-west London and were on the M3 by mid-afternoon.

'What's the mystery gift?' asked Jenny, skilfully plying the Range Rover at ninety-plus down the central lane, using the fast lane only for overtaking. An old-fashioned but correct practice, rapidly dying out.

'Fantastic, actually,' said Holly, extracting the sleek, black toy. 'The very latest mobile phone, Microtel's state-of-the-art, top-of-the-line, etcetera. Seen it in the catalogues, never been able to afford one. Look, it's wafer-thin.'

'A mobile phone. Oiksville.'

'As an accessory, loathsome,' agreed Holly. 'Wouldn't be seen dead with one strapped to my belt like some North Circular Road cowboy. However, as I always say, I'd rather be on the information highway driving a Porsche than standing on the hard shoulder with my thumb stuck out.'

'You're the clever one, aren't you?'

They reached Jenny's home in the New Forest in the early evening but extra-wired from lack of sleep, Holly persuaded Jenny to press on to Bournemouth and get a look at the Language Centre, the headquarters of the whole South Coast operation.

They arrived at seven thirty and spied on an evening class. A mixed bunch of teenagers, half European, half Asiatic, stared uncomprehendingly at a bearded man talking earnestly about Stonehenge, Druids and mid-summer's eve.

Holly refrained from commenting. She didn't want to say anything that might upset Jenny. But outside the classroom, it was Jenny who bemoaned the lack of decent ELS teachers.

'They're either in Japan, Korea and Taiwan making fortunes, or somewhere nice lotus-eating,' she complained.

They wandered out into the summer evening. The school was a Gothic extravagance, a famed hotel in Edwardian seaside days, with extensive lawns ringed with ancient yews, giant cedars and all manner of shrubs. The gravel drive was pristine. The parked Range Rover looked like an ad for Martini.

Holly launched into song. 'Anytime, anyplace, any-where.'

Jenny Ravensdale, her beautiful face looking drawn, yawned, and said, 'Enough, already. Surely, Holly-Jean, you're ready for a decent dinner and bed.'

'Oh, I do like to be beside the seaside,' Holly sang on. Something in the sea air was getting to her. 'Do the brassbands still play tiddly-om-pom-pom?'

Jenny sighed and smiled, held out her arms. Holly didn't fall into them. Not likely. But she gave Jenny her best smile. Meant it, too.

'I suppose since I'm paying for your services, you'd better earn them,' was Jenny's wry comment as she drove Holly round the seafront.

Bournemouth had been the scene of four of the attacks so far this summer, including the most recent – one of the gang rapes. Jenny pointed out the places where the assaults had occurred. Two had happened on the beach. The others in the backs of vans parked along the promenade. All the girls involved had spent the earlier part of the evening at one of the many discos along the seafront.

'A girl would have to be crazy to go for a walk on any beach at night, on her own, anywhere in the world,' said Holly. 'I'm surprised you don't warn them.'

'They didn't, and I do,' said Jenny sharply. 'It's a fundamental rule of the Centre, posted everywhere connected with our activities. Unaccompanied students are not to visit the beaches after dark. Females not in less than groups of four or more.'

'Oops,' said Holly.

'They're lured down there, don't you see?' said Jenny. 'The police weren't about to be forthcoming, but I happen to be friends with the Chief Constable and he was most cooperative. I was given a discreet look at the reports. The scenarios seem to be similar in a lot of the cases: the boy comes on all charm and gentlemanly. The perfect Englishman, was one girl's description. He gets the girl on her own, away from her friends, out of the clubs for a stroll, just for a minute, he promises, to see the stars, buy fish and chips – "an authentic English experience" – etcetera, etcetera. Meanwhile, his accomplices are ready with the van or by the steps to the beach. It's over in seconds. One minute walking along hand in hand, the next, a blanket over the head and bundled off into a nightmare.'

'Accomplices? These are always gangs?' asked Holly.

'Apparently, yes,' said Jenny. 'Nearly all the assaults have been by groups rather than individuals. The descriptions the police have logged are all pretty similar. Short, neat hair, the odd earring but nothing flashy, Levis and trainers. Gentlemen, they said.'

'Rule out your ravers, then,' said Holly. 'They're covered from head to toe in Day-glo. Besides, they'd be dancing out of their heads on speed and Ecstasy. Ravers are generally a harmless if chaotic lot, but hardly charming English gentlemen. No, it sounds to me more like grown-up skins, bovver merchants. Any mention of discreet or removed tattoos?'

Jenny sighed, shaking her head. 'Not that I recall.'

'Right, I'll check that. How about the other schools? Where are they, Brighton, Torquay?' Holly pressed on. 'Same sort of thing? A group rather than an individual?'

'I couldn't get those reports in detail,' said Jenny. 'But from what the girls have said before flying home, yes. Pretty much along the same lines.'

'They're connected, aren't they?'

'Look, Holly, dear,' said Jenny, her face clearly showing signs of extreme fatigue as they passed a polymer reproduction of a Victorian bandstand. 'I'm an incredibly busy woman. That's why I've asked for your help. I just haven't had time to get really involved. Nor do I want to. Avoiding it, if you like. Of course, people would say my motive is financial. If this carries on, no one'll want to come and learn English here, but also I feel terribly guilty. I really do. These girls come halfway round the world because of me and then . . .' Her voice distorted. A frog in the throat, the oddly perfect description of the thoratic spasm caused by sudden overwhelming emotion.

'Don't be silly, Jenny, you're not to blame yourself for the work of a bunch of patently evil bastards,' said Holly. 'Look at you. You're wearing yourself out. It's not surprising. Running that one place back there would be enough for most people, let alone a whole chain of schools. Leave this dirty mess to me. That's what I'm here for, right?' Then she added, 'One thing though, we'll need to run through all the details in the morning. Then I'll be out of your hair. Promise.'

They drove on slowly, Holly's eyes scanning the promenade.

'Ice cream!' she exclaimed, pointing through the wind-screen at an old-fashioned ice-cream van. 'It's been years since I've had an authentic seaside ninety-nine.'

Jenny braked, turned to Holly and, smiling through her tiredness, said, 'The way I feel about you right now, Holly-Jean Ho, I'd probably strip off and walk naked into the sea if you asked me.'

Holly jumped out of the Range Rover and ran along the promenade to the ice-cream van.

Bournemouth tasted good. Fresh salty breeze off the sea. A double-cornet of homemade ice cream with clotted cream dolloped on top and speared with a chocolate flake. A double 99. Doctor Feelgood. Holly's spirits rose higher with each lick.

The good feeling had started on the drive down in

Jenny's Range Rover, listening to Enya as they cruised through the New Forest, sunlight strobing the emerald canopy. Now the stroll along the promenade as the sun went down. She wasn't sure what she was getting into, but it felt right. She adapted Steely Dan, and sang, 'This is the day of the expanding woman . . .' New directions, and still moving. Leaving London. Just a day or two. Summer in the city was getting dirty, pretty, pretty dirty. Su-ming . . .

No. Not that now, it won't do any good. She forced herself to clear her mind. Centred herself on the here and now.

They were strolling by an ornate Victorian shelter. A public telephone hung in one corner. They walked on hand in hand. Licking. The perfect summer evening by the seaside. But guilt is a devious monkey. It creeps in and stabs even the most peaceful of hearts. Holly watched the seagulls dive for a holiday-maker's bread and knew she was behaving badly, hurting a good friend who was probably worried rotten.

'Just a minute, Jenny,' she said. 'Got to use the phone.'

'Can't it wait till we get home?' said Jenny. 'I'm shattered and it's still a good half-hour drive. Besides, you can try your new toy.'

Poor Jenny did look utterly exhausted. But so beautiful, standing against the iron balustrade. She was wearing a Ralph Lauren outfit, loose-fitting but perfectly cut. Silk shirt and pants in a magical shade of lilac.

Holly hesitated. Etching the scene onto her memory.

A moment to keep for ever. Behind her friend, the English Channel was dotted with sailboats and wind surfers, the sun breaking like an egg on the purple horizon to dribble gold across the water. Then Holly amazed herself – she ran back and awkwardly kissed Jenny's cheek.

'Just two ticks,' she said. 'Have to.'

She got through to the wine bar, but was told by Charley the bartender that Marika had gone out, expected back after ten o'clock.

'Tell her I called. I'm out of town for a day or two. It's work. Something important. Tell her I'll try and call tonight before bedtime. 'Bye, Charley, and say hi to everyone for me.'

''Bye, Holly-Jean. Take care.'

All the boys at the wine bar loved Holly. She knew it was because they thought her exotic, her mixed race, her aikido, her fascinating job – 'Hunting for pirates across the seven seas,' they called it. But Marika's Swedish wine bar in Islington was Holly-Jean's second home, and she couldn't help but feel she was betraying them all.

She replaced the phone, resolutely shrugged off the feeling and rejoined Jenny. They linked arms and walked back to the Range Rover.

They reached Jenny's lovely home in the last twilight, turning through a crumbling ivy-coated stone gateway into a half-mile curving drive through trees which revealed an Elizabethan house with purple wisteria and passionflower climbing between the beams and the ancient brickwork. Holly was enchanted. She stood for a moment, awed by the sounds of the forest all around.

And it was as though she'd become a child again. The city-wise woman, the tiger-Holly had gone someplace to rest awhile, leaving a little girl in her stead. 'It's magical, Jenny. I love it already.'

Jenny put her arm round Holly's shoulder and firmly dragged her indoors, saying, 'If we weren't so tired I'd take you to see the deer. There's a pond beyond the orchard where they like to come for an evening drink. But that's for another day.' She kissed Holly's earlobe and whispered, 'Remember, I'm the boss, I'm paying your wages, and I say now for a decent drink, some food and bed.'

'Sounds perfect, boss,' said Holly. And it was.

'Don't they have to be in bed by lights out?' asked Holly, drinking a fresh strawberry milk shake under the parasol on Jenny's dry-stone verandah. Crisp breeze, blue sky above the dewy forest, warm sun dissipating the mist that lingered around the tree trunks. Holly could handle this.

'Only the young ones stay in residence,' explained Jenny. 'We've limited space. Most of the older students choose home stay or bed and breakfast. Some of the rich Japanese stay in five-star hotels for the whole course.'

'Tell me about English seaside home stay,' said Holly. 'Sounds like hell.'

'Nonsense. You get to live with a local family, speak only English. Learn our customs.'

Holly smiled. 'Soggy fried bread, sausage of the unknown life form, cholesterol OD breakfast.'

'Ha ha,' said Jenny, unamused.

But Holly was irrepressible this sublime morning. 'Field trips to the dole office. Learn to sign on, cash the giro, place a bet at the bookie's, get legless by tea time.'

'Neither funny nor fair. There's a rigorous selection

process for host families.' Jenny picked up a pair of gold-mirrored sunglasses and propped them on her crown. She was wearing yet another beautifully cut summer suit. This one was peach.

'Not Ralph Lauren again?' interrupted Holly.

'Arabella Pollen,' replied Jenny, smiling.

'You've got some lovely stuff,' said Holly, trying to keep a stray sour grape out of her voice.

'Dressing for the trappings,' said Jenny. 'Trapping for the dresses.'

'Lucky sod.'

'Dear, dear, Holly-Jean, ever the uncut diamond,' said Jenny.

'Hey, call me pure, unrefined, any damn thing, but don't ever patronise,' said Holly.

'Uh-oh. Sorree.' Jenny reached out a placating hand. 'We're still learning, right?'

'Yep,' said Holly, smiling. 'No-go areas.'

'Anyway,' said Jenny, all business again, 'we do try to place our students with sound host families. Local teachers, community activists, that sort of thing. Actually, some of the students come back every year and insist on the same home-stay families. Become real friends. Even arrange for them to visit their own countries.'

'You're right,' said Holly. 'How can I be cynical on such a beautiful morning.'

'Quite,' said Jenny, observing Holly through narrowed eyes. 'Talking of beautiful mornings, you were up and about bright and early, weren't you?'

'I saw you spying on me from the bedroom window.'

'Doing your judo exercises.'

'Aikido,' said Holly, though she'd moved on with her teacher into areas far more arcane, deadly.

'And what was that *thing*?'

'This?' she said, reaching into her bag.

'I hope you haven't killed the horse chestnut.'

Holly handed Jenny the sheathed Gerber Magnum throwing knife, grip first.

Jenny took the weapon gingerly, weighed it, made a face. 'Ghastly thing,' she shuddered, handing it back. 'I take it you do use it – where on earth did you learn how?'

'Ah-so!' said Holly, rubbing a fleck of strawberry shake from her nose. 'Chinese girl have melly seclet.'

'Perhaps they'd better remain so,' said Jenny, lightly.

'Oh, don't worry your gorgeous head about it,' said Holly. 'After college I joined Whitelegg's Fair for a year doing the West Country. While you lot were off helping Mother Teresa in Calcutta or learning to scuba dive in Cebu, I thought I'd add something really useful to my CV.'

'So you learned to knife-throw.' Jenny was looking increasingly askance. 'Were you part of the act?'

'Only when Tiffany the Tattooed Lady got sick,' said Holly, laying it on. 'Comes in handy.'

Mrs Huxtable, the housekeeper, approached with a tray, and Holly stowed the knife away in her bag.

'Enjoy your breakfasts, m'dears?'

'Lovely, thanks,' said Holly, handing her her plate and glass. 'Isn't it a wonderful morning?'

''Tis that, my love.'

'I suppose you get to take it for granted. But believe me,' said Holly, smiling at the ruddy-cheeked country woman, 'I live in Camden Town, and this is paradise.'

'Mrs H lives in a cottage on the other side of Patchole,' said Jenny.

'Born and bred here all me life. Bliddy marvellous, 'tis. Never been to Camden, mind,' Mrs Huxtable said over her shoulder as she re-entered the kitchen.

'I'll need a car,' said Holly, done with the small talk and ready to go. 'A list of landladies. Copies of the victims' files. A map. All the casework.'

Jenny nodded. 'The school secretary, Eliza, will furnish you with everything. I've briefed her. She's fully available for help if you need her.'

'See you tonight then.'

'Doubtful, sorry.' Jenny consulted her electronic notebook. 'Something's just come up. Looks like I'll be staying over in Brighton.'

'Brighton? To do with the attacks?'

'No, actually not. I've been made an offer for the schools. Some City money wants in. I'll at least do them the courtesy of a listen. Frankly, I don't think I'm ready for pasture yet. Besides, the other stuff's entirely your affair from now on.' She looked at Holly with her clear intelligent eyes. 'I don't want to know. Do you mind?'

'Absolutely not.' In fact it suited her perfectly. Jenny wouldn't be around to get into her hair. The real luxury of Holly's life was that she got to work alone.

Jenny leant back in the wrought-iron chair and called to the housekeeper. 'Mrs H! Holly will be staying tonight. Can you rustle up some dinner? For say . . .' She looked at Holly.

'Late.'

'Nine o'clock, then,' announced Jenny.

'No worries, Miss Ravensdale,' called Mrs Huxtable from the open kitchen window. 'I've a 'andsome cauliflower cheese – 'er'll go in the oven with the timer set for nine o'clock. Do you all right, my love?' she addressed Holly.

'Cauliflower cheese?' said Holly, smiling. 'My favourite,' she lied.

It was late into the hazy afternoon when Holly reached Dilkhusa House, St Brannock's Park Road, one of the last on her list of home stays. Variegated ivy clung to the Edwardian pile set on a wooded hillside, surrounded by monkey-puzzle and towering cypress-trees.

Sweating, she negotiated the almost vertical zig-zag up from the road. The Fiesta's steering all baking day long had been about as easy as giving medicine to a cat. Grunting, she managed to edge in next to a battered Alfa Romeo with rusted-out sills and last year's road tax. She consulted the pile of files on the passenger seat, checked her face in the mirror, ruffled her hair and stepped out. *Wo-de tyan*! My God! Champagne air from a sudden delicious sea squall. She inhaled it deeply and used her right thumb and alternate index and fourth finger as plugs. *Chi kung*. Ancient stuff. English Channel in her right nostril. Camden out the left. She felt the energy enter her veins.

The patchy tarmac was squelchy with rotten rhododendron blossoms. A mouldy statue of Venus wore a red charity fun nose. The stained-glass paned door was wide open. Smells of roast cooking wafted.

'Anyone home?' she called.

'In the kitchen!'

She followed her nose down a tiled corridor, entered the kitchen and found a very round woman, glasses perched on her nose, cigarette dangling, warming her backside against an enormous Rayburn with a wine glass of something red in one hand, *The Times* crossword in the other.

'Mrs Vinnicombe?' asked Holly.

'Do sit down, my dear, and have a glass of wine. Be with you in just a mo'.' Muttering, the woman lifted the telephone from the wall beside her, punched a number, mouthed 'My son' at Holly, then said, 'What the hell is fourteen across, Frank?'

There was a short reply.

'Beelzebub?' shrieked Mrs Vinnicombe. Then fractionally muted exclaimed, 'Oh, the devils! How do they come up with it? Listen to this,' she said to Holly. ' "Honeymaker initially leaves the zoo for pal infernal." ' She resumed speaking into the mouthpiece. 'Ye-es . . . Bee. L. Z. Well, of course, I can see it now you've told me . . . But what about the "bub" bit?'

Holly took a seat at the massive oak table.

A wooden clothes line suspended from the ceiling by a pulley was hung with sheets. An empty wine rack dangled from the wall. On the floor were cases labelled 'House Red' and 'White'. Various good wines were standing here and there. Next to the Rayburn, a wicker dog basket was filled with a bewhiskered Labrador bitch whose row of enormous teats flapped over the side as she snored. Dog hairs and filled ashtrays were everywhere.

A vase of riotous garden blooms sat in the middle of the table, evidently just picked and arranged. The scent of the flowers melded with the roast, the dog, the wine, the cigarettes, the steaming sheets. Parfum D'Mickey Finn.

'Slang for friend?' bellowed Mrs Vinnicombe. 'Never heard of it. Oh well, must rush. 'Bye now.' She put the phone down. 'My son, Frank, in London,' she explained. 'Principal trombone at Covent Garden. Takes about ten minutes to do *The Times*. I don't seem to be able to get it at all and I've been trying for forty odd years.'

'So when you get stuck, you call him,' said Holly, warmly. 'That's handy.'

'Yes, it is, isn't it?' said the woman, examining Holly through her glasses as though seeing her for the first time. 'And what brings you to Dilkhusa – Indian word, Raj, beauteous bower – and where's your wine?'

'Thanks, I will,' said Holly. 'I've just had a hectic day visiting the good ladies of Bournemouth and I'm out of my head on Earl Grey.'

She sipped a soothing glass of Montrachet and they chatted for twenty-five seconds about the weather, the summer season, the state of the economy.

'Out with it, my love,' said Mrs Vinnicombe. By now Holly was getting used to the terms of endearment. Everyone she'd met in Bournemouth seemed amazingly friendly. So far.

'Just a few moments of your time,' said Holly. 'It's about the student from Taiwan, Chen Ba-tsun.'

'I had a feeling it might be,' said Mrs Vinnicombe, looking away. 'Poor, dear Chen.'

'I'm helping Jenny Ravensdale, the owner of the Language School.' Holly handed over her business card.

'I know Jenny well, we're in the Operatic Society Chorus. Wintertime, of course,' said Mrs Vinnicombe as she sank down onto the wooden chair, stubbed out her cigarette. 'To hell with the bloody scum,' she said suddenly, gulping her wine. 'Chen's been coming here since she was sixteen. Every summer for four years. Absolute tragedy. A lovely girl. Says she'll be back next year, but somehow I doubt it. Her eyes had changed, you know. After . . .' She lit a fresh cigarette. A Du Maurier from the Deco box. Holly hadn't seen one in a long time. Flashed memory of her father. 'Whoever could do that to such a sweet, darling girl? If I ever get my hands on them, I'll wring their bloody necks!' She exhaled a plume of smoke, examined Holly's card. 'Software Property Rights?' She looked at Holly. 'Isn't that computers? Bit out of your depth, aren't you?'

'You're absolutely right,' said Holly. 'But Jenny's an old friend. She thought since I've got some investigative experience – computers, yes, people, not much. In fact, this is the first time I've ever done something like this.'

Mrs Vinnicombe finished her wine, poured another glass and stared at Holly. She tapped her wine glass with a chipped red-varnished talon, her examination unwavering. There was a long awkward silence, broken finally when the dog farted and the room filled with noxious fumes.

Holly said, 'If you'd rather not dig it all up, I quite understand. It's just that I think every woman has a duty in situations like this.'

'Bloody right!' exclaimed Mrs Vinnicombe. 'Oh, don't you worry. I'd do anything to help catch the cowardly little vermin who hurt Chen. Actually, I've got something to show you that just might help. Something the police didn't care to bother with. No,' she hesitated, 'it's . . . it's something else altogether. I'm just wondering whether you could help me in a personal matter. You being the investigator type.' She paused again. 'You're Chinese, aren't you?'

Holly nodded, smiled. 'Half and half.'

Mrs Vinnicombe took Holly's hand and patted it. 'My daughter, Tracy. She's a dancer. Royal Ballet School, but couldn't keep the weight off. Like mother, like daughter.' She drank wine and slapped her meaty stomach. 'Ended up in variety. Totally respectable, mind. Good living, too. Travels the world, Dubai, Hong Kong, and then three months ago she got a contract to work in Taipei. Haven't heard a word since. The thing is, Tracy always writes. Never misses a week. Something her father, God bless the none too sober memory, taught her. Every Sunday, letter-writing day. I've tried the police, the theatrical agency in London, the Foreign Office. Nobody wants to know. Mention the word dancer, and they get snooty, imply she's some sort of whore or something.' Her voice tailed off. 'Other side of the bloody globe . . .' she muttered. She finished her wine, poured more, sloshed some in Holly's glass. Mrs Vinnicombe's eyes gave her away. The mother was drowning in fear for her brood.

Ai-yai-yai, thought Holly, availing herself of the Montrachet. Synchronicity is just a matter of being in the wrong place at the wrong time.

She reached forward and said, 'Now, there's no sense in worrying yet. First we have to get in contact with someone we can trust in Taipei. No easy feat, that, I'm afraid. Next, I assume you asked Chen Ba-tsun to check when she got back to Taipei.'

'Yes, I asked Chen to contact Tracy's forwarding address when she got home – you know, when she felt better, poor love,' said Mrs Vinnicombe.

'Any luck?'

'She called on the phone two nights ago. Nobody at that address had seen or heard of a troupe of foreign dancers.'

'How old's Tracy?' asked Holly.

'Twenty-two, this April. Don't get me wrong. Tracy's got a sensible head on her shoulders. She's been doing this kind of work for a few years now. Still, you can imagine I'm ever so anxious to hear from her. Is there anything . . . My dear, I'd willingly pay.'

Holly shushed her, said they'd deal with that way down the line.

'The worst thing is,' said Mrs V, 'nobody seems to know anything about Taiwan – apart from the bloody running shoes.' Her fingers shook as she puffed on the Du Maurier. 'The Foreign Office palmed me off with some ruddy nonsense called the Department of Treaties and Principalities or some such.'

'Unfortunately,' Holly explained, 'Taiwan doesn't have diplomatic links with Britain. Big China doesn't allow it.' She thought for a moment. 'Here's what we'll do. I'll lean on Tracy's agent in London. He's bound to be smart enough to have covered his rear with all sorts of cop-out clauses written into her contract. However, the prospect of litigation might get a response. If not, there's always Chinatown.' She winked, and touched her nose conspiratorially. Theatrical bravado she didn't feel an ounce of, but already Mrs V's face was lightening up. 'We also deal with some lawyers in Taipei. They might possibly be of some use.'

'I can't tell you what a comfort you are. Fancy that, you walking in like this. You must be Tracy's guardian angel.'

'Hardly. I'm strictly tenderfoot. So don't go getting your hopes up too high,' warned Holly.

'Any news would be good, my love. Thanks ever so much. I've been dreadfully worried . . .' Her voice cracked as she clasped Holly's hand in her warm floury fingers.

'Now, then,' said Holly. 'How about this something or other you said the police weren't interested in?'

Holly's last landlady of the day was in Poole harbour, and she finished there at seven in the evening. Cauliflower cheese wasn't enough to inspire the long drive back to the New Forest; besides, she still had to do the rounds of the clubs, pubs and discos. So she opted for a crab sandwich and a pint of Dorchester real ale at a pub overlooking the harbour.

Pleasantly numb, she drove west out of town towards the ruins of Corfe Castle. The night life wouldn't get going for a few hours yet so she had a moment to regroup. She parked in the lee of a sand dune facing the evening sea, rolled down the windows, selected Mozart's 'Jupiter Symphony' from the pile in the glove compartment and ran through the files, making notes and collating a list of facts she'd netted in the day's trawl. A paltry catch, on the whole.

Except for a scrap of paper. A gem.

She stashed everything under the passenger seat and reclined hers. She drifted, thinking of Jenny Ravensdale. Remembered something that had bothered her that morning.

She pictured again Jenny standing on the gravel as Holly had been about to drive away, the beautiful face, the purple wisteria, the french windows reflecting the summer sky. Something watchful in Jenny's eyes had made Holly linger, foot on the clutch – sunlight and the world gone silent – then a last nod and she'd sent the gravel flying.

Now that intuitive thud returned as the seagulls yelled around an overflowing litter bin and made Mozart sound plain silly. She punched the machine silent. Stared at the gulls inside her head. Promised sadness. Wartime goodbye.

She shook her head to dispel the fancy. And the other unwanted stuff. Emotions, things. Holly-Jean's treading the ocean deep. Too many nasties in the dark below, with sharp teeth and no fear. Back to the shallows, my girl. Back off.

Face it, Hols, she thought as the sunset drowned the car in amber, you're *unaccustomed*.

She suddenly opened her eyes. Shit! Idiot! She jumped out of the car and used the new toy. '*Fitta flykta!*' That was about as bad as it got. Rough translation: cunt girl. 'Vhere are you, for God's sake? I've been so vorried!'

'Didn't you get my message from Charley?' said Holly, words rushing on a tide of guilt. 'It's work. I'm in Poole. You won't know it. On the South Coast. I'm standing on a sand dune. Glorious. Listen, Rika, I've got myself a new assignment,' she bubbled on, drowning out Marika's protestations. 'Very different. I can't say much, but it's infinitely more worthwhile than computers.'

'What's wrong with computers? I thought you loved your work.'

'I do, but . . . this is real world stuff.' Pride, instantly regretted, blurted out, 'Racist rape.'

There was a sharp intake of breath on the other end, followed by a moment's silence as the words were mentally translated. Then the predictable avalanche of Swedish followed by jumbled English.

'*Det vrar som saan*! Sonnuvabitch! Holly! Dangerous things you got yourself into! Please, please, darling *flykta*, drop it! Come home!' Marika's fear was tangible through the wires. Holly felt it enter her like a tiny seed.

'No, I'm exaggerating,' she backtracked. 'Really. Just peripheral involvement, a bit of checking – I doubt I'll even do more than end up phoning the police—'

'She doubts it! She cares so little for her friend's fears!' Marika's words pierced Holly's heart. Little needles, dipped in guilt. 'Sweetheart, come home. Please.'

Holly spent the next few minutes vainly trying to convince Marika she was in no danger. Which was difficult as she stubbornly refused to give her distraught friend any details of the case. That would only lead to awkward questions about Jenny Ravensdale which in turn would unleash Marika's instinctive antagonism towards anything and anyone connected to Margot Silverman. Not to mention the Rika-Jenny disaster-in-waiting.

'Should be home tomorrow or the next day, silly. Now stop worrying and wish me luck!'

Long silence. 'I vish you luck. There. See you when you get back to London.' Marika's voice was Nordic, cool, emotionally void as she broke the connection.

A chill breeze came off the English Channel.

Holly stood staring at the sea. Aware of the goose bumps – '*chi-pi*', chicken-skin, the Chinese call it. Aware they had begun before the breeze arrived.

4

A summer evening in the discos and pubs of an English seaside town, albeit Bournemouth, the once and future (global warming permitting) pearl of the south, was, Holly-Jean found, profoundly unedifying.

'One thirty a.m. Finisterre. Southwesterly. Gale force seven. One eighty and rising,' Holly intoned. 'Lids bared, gritting her eyeballs, she entered a decrepit building on the ramshackle pier.'

Last on her list of night spots frequented by the ELS students, D'Urberville's, had a ten-pound cover charge which got you a plastic glass of lager slops, perforated eardrums and a spray mist of bodily effluvia. Holly declined the free 'fruit punch'. She liked her ecstasy real.

Skirting the thrashing mass on the dance floor, the reverb from the giant bass woofers felt like blows to her diaphragm. From every angle of sound projection the rapper insisted over and over, 'Ziggedy-boom-boom-yeh-yeh!' Mouths dangling whistles and dummies, the ravers catapulted about like Masai *moran* on speed.

Holly's objective: the DJ's suspended shark-fin Cadillac.

She was stepping over a prone body when the music cut out and the place was pitched into darkness. An air-raid siren sound-mixed to mighty enhancement glissandoed up. At mind-numbing climax, strobo-scopes of dizzying wattage jacked the rave a notch further frenzied.

Holly-Jean hung in perceptual gridlock, her eyes on the dancers' stop-go flailings. Mesmeric. Infinitely fun.

Oh, to be young.

Oh, to be home in bed.

But irresistibly the energy entered her, whacking her back through the years to Earls Court, front of stage, reaching out a satinned glove to grab Bowie's magical leotard. A sixteen-year-old tiger on Vaseline – and six-inch oyster-green platforms.

Holly found herself shrieking along with everyone else. Hey, thanks for the memory.

A half-naked body beneath her feet began to float and bob. Her lager went flying. The lights came up.

She moved on, reached the jammed rungs to the DJ's station and joined the wedge of supplicants, feeling the ebb, feeling her age in the vast domed mayhem.

Here, according to *The Historic Guide to Bourne-mouth and Poole* supplied by Eliza, the school secretary, the Gaiety Players had triumphed in the days of English seaside glory, when the ladies of kaisers and kings had gone down to the sea in horse-drawn bathing boxes to dip into a segregated sea, and dashing blades fancied an ankle and muttered entreaties on the promenade that night. Until the sixties when cheap flights to real sun killed the seaside. And the other flight, from art to electronics, killed live performance and seaside theatre. Not that Holly minded the displacement of learned skills. Creation for all, right? At the touch of a digit. Yo Caruso Hip-Hop! Dame Nellie raps!

She moved up a few steps and checked her watch. Two a.m. The place was just warming up. 'Really gets going after three,' the bouncers had told her.

D'Urberville's was one of two discos which Chen Ba-tsun had positively identified, prior to her memory blank-out. It was 'considered highly probable', by the investigating officer in charge, that D'Urbeville's was the location of the perpetrator(s)' first approach to the victim. This was what the police report stated. Eliza, the school secretary, had copied it. Quite illegally. And Holly now had it in her possession. Very illegally.

Holly had discovered by asking around that D'Urberville's was this summer's 'happ-un-ing loca-tion'. Her original plan had been to question the bar-tenders, but they were rushed. Off their feet. Off their heads. Besides, standing at the bar had been unpleasant for someone of her stature, race and age. Though not gender. For once. The females at D'Urberville's were quite as feral as the males.

At last she gained admittance to the Cadillac, a wonder-ful casket of gadgetry, glistening and winking above the auditorium. A sign read 'The Mad Hatter's Hat'.

'The holiest of holies,' she declared.

'Count yourself privileged,' replied the DJ, a tattooed white boy with a patrician accent and a baseball cap back to front on a teetering pile of red curls. 'You the detective?'

'Is it that obvious?'

The boy gave a wry look. 'Jimmy the security manager told me about you and it so happens, sister,' he leant into the microphone, 'Got-Red the Guide, yours true-lee, is on your side!'

The floor below erupted.

'Got-Red?' said Holly.

'The hair,' he pointed.

Holly nodded. 'Nice. Hair. Name.'

Smiling, he slid two knobs and segued into the next track seamlessly.

'We nice tribe,' he said, turning to Holly. 'Contrary to how the media would have it, raving – old word, partying is how we now refer to it – is a fairly harmless pastime. These are just ordinary kids who want to go wild, and why not? And you know something, sister? No barriers. No barriers. None. Everyone's in. What's it all about? Just say it's the pursuit of colour in days of darkness.'

Holly smiled and watched as a bubble machine spewed froth over the multitudes below.

'Anyway, violence against women is not part of it, and never will be. *Sisters unto the dawn!*' He screamed into the microphone.

Down below, hundreds of rainbow-glistening arms rose up.

He yelled again, 'One nation under one groove, one sex-u-al-i-tee, brothers, sisters! Un-un-un! Unto the dawn!'

Eyes lit high by the pandemonium he was causing below, he turned back to Holly, doing a nicely sepulchral Kenneth Clark, 'And there you have it, the dawn of

Dribbleisation.' He raised his eyebrows and yukked. 'Two forty-five at the front door. We'll have a word.'

'I'd rather stay and watch.'

'Be my guest.'

The scene below held Holly's fascination till two forty-five, time for the DJ shift change.

'Ever seen anything like this?' asked Holly as she and Got-Red sat in the Fiesta. She handed him a drawing. She had parked on the beach side of the promenade about a quarter of a mile from D'Urberville's.

'A West Ham posse,' said Got-Red matter-of-factly.

Holly felt a surge of elation. A piece down. 'A posse? What, cowboys and Indians stuff?'

'You don't know much, do you, sister? The term is derived from the rap scene. No self-respecting rapper performs without his posse, one to scratch the record, one to sound-mix the computer back-up, drums, orchestra, brass, whatever, a couple in the chorus, the rest to loon about as menacingly as possible.'

'So this lot are performers?'

'Depends what you mean by performance. Nah, posse's just a unit, like a gang. This lot?' He pulled down the sun visor and resculpted his Carmen Miranda. 'Could be five, ten or twenty of them. Varies. They come down about two weekends a month. This the Chinese girl's?'

'From her sketch pad. The police ignored it. Her landlady gave it to me.'

Got-Red handed the piece of paper back to Holly. 'It's tattooed on the inside of the wrist, across the pulse artery.'

'Sounds risky,' said Holly.

'Oh, very delicate work,' said Got-Red. 'One false prick and whoosh. Maximum machismo – in stunted minds.'

'What's the significance of the words, "The Treatment"?' asked Holly.

'It's the posse title. The hippocratic emblem is their subtle irony. They used to go to games at Upton Park in full surgeon's kit – mask, smock, skullcap and scalpels. Became too easy to spot by the police cameras, hence the tattoo. Worn under sweatbands. No one outside the posse would be caught dead wearing that tattoo,' said Got-Red. 'Literally.'

'I'm no soccer fan,' said Holly, 'but haven't I read somewhere that West Ham football supporters are recruited by the right?'

'Nazis? Could be.' Got-Red shrugged. 'They and Millwall are the fine young cro-magnons who post turds to Bangladeshis in Tower Hamlets. This sort of thing's right up their street.'

'The rape or the racism?' asked Holly.

'All the same, isn't it? The perfect ending to a seaside summer evening.' Got-Red gave Holly a look. 'Believe me, civilisation is circling the plug hole.'

'You said it.'

The promenade was lively with revellers. Groups, distinguished tribally by apparel, marched by chanting. A dozen or so shaven-headed girls linked arms and attempted to can-can drunkenly. They ended up in a shrieking pile in the middle of the road. A car stopped and hooted its horn. The girls jumped up and began cursing. Banging on the roof and rocking the car. The middle-aged driver reversed into a tyre-squealing three-point turn. Holly glimpsed his face, white with terror, as he roared away.

Got-Red chuckled. 'Contemporary rites. Harmless. Not like that sack of smegma.' He pointed to Chen's sketch. 'They're a whole different horror show. Hurting people's their kind of fun. Get the picture? Summer in the city. No soccer match. No rumble. No taste of blood for weeks. Bored out of their tiny minds. Let's do a seaside trip. Get gassed up on the choo-choo for the coast. Trawl the discos. Top out the evening pulling a train on a Nip language student. Oh, to be in England, now the twilight is there.'

'Pull a train?' said Holly. 'That the terminology?'

'One of them,' said Got-Red. 'Look, I'll level with you.' He paused as a gang of shirtless ravers came running past the car and vaulted down the steps to the beach, chased, a few moments later, by a swearing group of smart young men in polo shirts. 'I'd like to help. Really,' he said. 'If that tattoo's anything to go by, I think I can ID some mug shots, but that's as far as it goes. I'd never testify in open court. That'd be suicide.'

Holly looked at him.

'Serious,' he said.

Down on the beach in the glow of the promenade's fairy lights, a battle was taking place. The night air filled with the gleeful shouts of loathing.

'I earn my living from that lot,' said Got-Red, opening the car door.

'Thanks. You've been a great help,' said Holly sincerely.

'I might well take you up on that offer. How can I reach you?'

'Either at the club or on this number.' He gave her a book of matches from D'Urberville's with a phone number inscribed on the inside.

'You came prepared,' said Holly.

'Always do,' replied Got-Red, fanning a little pack of matchbooks in his palm. 'For the ladies, you understand.'

'Goodnight, Got-Red.'

'Nighty night.'

The New Forest was a haven after Bournemouth's rowdy night life. The empty house creaked with age and the whittled energy of past lives. A glass of Mumm from the fridge, then back outside, the canopy of stars aglitter, the scent of dewy honeysuckle. And no hurt feelings.

Holly carried the bowl of cauliflower cheese out with her as she walked the edge of Jenny's back lawns and peered into the rustling darkness. 'Here, deers,' she said, as she flung the contents of the bowl into the bushes.

She slept like a log and caught the mid-morning train back to town.

She called Mick Coulson outside Victoria Station, first finding a discreet spot behind a newspaper seller's hut under the station awning, not wishing to flaunt the toy. She asked for an update. Nothing so far, he said. She arranged a meet for early evening. London was drizzling. The air, steamed dirt.

'Usual place?'

'Five thirty.'

The usual was the Nag's Head, Gerrard Street. About the only pub in England where you'd see mahjong played by old men holding straight-glass pints and rolling their own. Speaking Cantonese.

She called Minty. After the first ring, she cut the connection and called again. Let it ring twice. Cut the connection. And so on. Till five rings. Troublesome, but the only way in heaven or hell to get him to pick up the phone when a canvas was going.

'A minute.' The phone was put down. Bombay Bollywood music blared. The bird-like females and the orgasmic males put her in mind of curry. 'Is it you, Holly?'

'Yep,' she said. 'How's GiGi?'

Long pause. Bhuna ghost. Butter nans. 'Oh, fine. I think.'

'You did feed him, right?'

Longer pause. Prawn tikka masala. Sag dhal. 'I'll just go and check.'

'That would be nice, Minty.'

Aloo Ghobi. Fish tandoori. Chicken vindaloo. Masala dosai.

'You back in town?'

'Yep.'

'I'll just open a tin then.'

'Do that,' said Holly, swallowing a mouthful of saliva. She'd be in Soho, after all. And as a rule, feeding Minty was a good idea. He tended to overlook such irrelevances. 'Fancy an Indian? I'll be home by eight. Put some plates in the oven. Clear some space.'

'Right-oh.'
'And Minty.'
'Yo.'
'Feed the cat.'

Holly took a taxi to Gower Street, had a coffee and a bite of a Stilton-pickle crusty in the Student's Union. London University, an amorphous entity spread out in colleges, ex-polys renamed universities, hospitals and institutes all over the metropolis, has its central core here on the edge of Bloomsbury.

As usual, on her way out of the canteen Holly stopped at the bulletin board to check for any odd bargains. Like a second-hand Morgan going for three hundred quid. No such luck.

She used the toy – hell, it was useful – to call the N.C.C.L.

A woman answered. 'N.C.C.L.'

'Can you help?' said Holly, 'I'm a private investigator looking for information on a gang of soccer-nazis known as The Treatment, apparently affiliated with the Far Right.'

The Civil Libertarian hesitated. 'Naturally, at the outset, we'd need to be clear from what, um, standpoint you're asking.'

'You mean, do I want to join 'em, or castrate 'em?' asked Holly.

'Right, I think we can help you,' the woman said drily. 'Just a mo'.'

She came back on a few moments later. 'The Treatment, a bunch of little charmers, so-called because they used to wear surgeon's masks, smocks and carry scalpels until TV surveillance cameras were installed at soccer grounds. They've existed for more than twenty years as a loose-knit gang of hard-core Millwall and West Ham supporters. Since the early days of the National Front and other far-right lunacy, they've been available as a serious rent-a-mob of very unpleasant steel toe-capped yobbery. Currently they're flavour of the month with the Britannia Party.'

'The Britannia Party?' said Holly. 'Never heard of that one.'

'Seriously deluded Empire loyalists. The sun never sets bit. Anti-Europe, anti-foreign anything, in fact.'

'Jokers, right?'

'Actually, no. They're taken a little bit seriously here because of rumoured backing by the League of St George.'

'What's the League of St George?' asked Holly-Jean.

'Been around since the start of the Cold War. A freemason-Establishment network of ex-Service ranking officers, police grandees, High Tory politicos and other heavy right-wing players. Very well connected, very well established. Pots of money to play with.'

'Can you get me a number for this Britannia Party?'

'I'd urge extreme caution,' said the woman.

'Heard that,' said Holly. 'Anyway I've got to reach them. In person.'

'Okay,' said the woman. 'But take very good care. Got a pen? This is the most recent number we have. Their Public Relations Officer. Brigadier Pennycate.'

Pertinent skinny duly noted, Holly punched in the

number. Using the cover-story she'd concocted on the train up from Bournemouth, she was able to secure a meeting for twelve noon the next day with Brigadier Pennycate.

Holly walked over to the School of Oriental and African Studies, had a pee in their squat-hole toilets for old time's sake, then used her reader's card to get past security into the SOAS library. She asked for Janet Rae-Smith Senior Lecturer in Economics, Asian Faculty. Head of Department, Newly Industrialised Countries Trade Relations, aka Nickers.

Janet was a gangly Scot, a six-foot genius in Holly's estimation, whom she'd met a few years before when Janet spoke at a Heathrow hotel conference on the Pacific rim electronics challenge. At the time, Deirdre H. Jones was getting shafted at work and she had attended the conference in a listless, migraine-infested condition she later recognised as severe depression. She was expecting to hear the same old sentimental whine: superior British invention being underfunded at home and stolen by the yellow peril. Then Janet Rae-Smith stood up and said that the invention was all happening over there by then and to all intents and purposes the British electronics industry was dead. That the best we could hope for would be Japanese and Taiwanese investment in any surviving local talent unless, Janet had stated, the government intervened massively. This was the reality in Asia where whole countries operated as one big joint venture of business and government.

Holly and Janet had bumped elbows at the hotel bar and on the strength of immediate rapport and a shared appreciation of fruity white wine had emptied the bar of Alsace varietals.

Janet Rae-Smith won few friends for her intervention-ist views and soon found herself shunted out of her government think-tank back into academe. She gave Holly the serious stuff as she needed it, and in return Holly fed Janet the latest scams, rip-offs and scandals of the industry. It was a two-way trade that had blossomed into good friendship.

Janet strode up to the counter reading Holly's card. ''Snae bad name, Holly-Jean Ho,' she said in mock Glaswegian. ''Sgot morruva rung tee it than wee Deirdre H. Jones, that's fer sure.'

'Kung Dz, he say, little Chinee girl better have damn good name, she wanna make it in big wide world.'

'Confucious was a sexist dickhead, Toots.'

'Amongst redeeming qualities, Stretch.'

'Name one.'

'Later. First I need all you've got on these.'

Janet took the paper and read aloud, her voice descending gloomily. 'One, right-wing exploitation of racism in football. Area of interest: West Ham United and Millwall. Special reference: affiliation known as "The Treatment". Two, entertainment industry law in Taiwan. Special reference: legal rights and protection of foreign contractees.' Janet gave Holly a wry look. 'You never want much, do you? Number one, wrong person. I know zip about soccer.'

'No harm in trying. Anyway I've made some progress on that one. How about the second item?' said Holly, observing with some shock her friend's unhealthy pallor and twin sets of luggage under the eyes.

'Number two's all in my head. Get me out of here, Holly-Jean.' Janet pulled on a summer Burberry. 'Don't you have an umbrella? Here, take one of these.' She selected one from the stand. 'Someone had mine away last week,' she explained as they walked in the rain to a wine bar on Southampton Row. Sipping a cold Gewurztraminer, Holly filled Janet in on Tracy Vinnicombe's disappearance.

Janet looked gloomy. 'Taipei is about the last place I'd send a daughter.' She went on to explain that, for the first time ever, following a great deal of pressure from the West coupled with Taiwan's desperate push to join GATT, the General Agreement on Tariffs and Trade, regulations governing foreign labour had finally just been enacted in Taipei. 'Which in reality means sweet FA. Rule of law is not a priority in the bastion Republic of Mammon. Genuine legal protection? Extremely doubtful. In fact until recently it was purely a question of taking your chances on making good money or ending up in a white slave trade. Shanghaied.'

'Worse,' said Holly. 'Taipeied.'

'But at least nowadays the law's in place,' said Janet. 'So, there's the theoretical possibility of legal redress.'

'Which, as you just said, means frock-all in Taiwan. God, what am I going to tell Mrs Vinnicombe? Poor woman. She's worried out of her mind.'

'So she bloody well should be,' said Janet, finishing her third glass to Holly's one.

'How about your *guanchi* with local officialdom?' asked Holly. 'All my contacts are in electronics. We both

76

know the British Trade and Culture Office is about as useful as the proverbial chocolate teapot.'

'Fancy new name. Bugger all use.'

'Come on, give us some *guanchi*; I'll owe you.'

'I've got a couple of names tucked away somewhere. I'll fish them out for you later.'

Janet's Taipei *guanchi* was legendary. She'd made many trips, first as a trade official, then as a visiting academic, and sometimes just to visit friends. Her Mandarin was near fluent and she was careful never to voice her real opinions of the island in public. Her working knowledge of the arcane Pacific rim was second to none.

'Thanks a lot. I need all the help I can get.' Holly went on to mention Su-ming and Janet looked sad.

'That's a hard one, girl,' she said. She looked at her watch. 'Look, I've got a lecture at five. Fax you tonight about ten.'

'You're a brick, Rae-Smith.'

'Order another bottle. I'll need it to face my under-grad class. All those earnest young minds about to enter a world gone terminal and me without the heart to tell them.'

'Since when did you become so cynical?' said Holly, deciding to broach the subject. 'Jan, anything wrong? You've looked better, and you're belting this stuff away like you know something the rest of us don't.'

Janet laughed. 'When you've been an alcoholic for the past five years and get hepatitis on holiday in Marra-kech, it's considered advisable for your liver's sake to give up the vino. Unfortunately, I haven't quite got the hang of it.' She paused, looked Holly in the eye. 'The giving up bit.'

Holly sighed. '*Ai-yai-yai.*'

'Aye, awfy raddled auld plonky, me,' she said, attempting a smile.

Holly said nothing. The silence grew.

Janet reached for her glass, held it up and said, 'Slange!' Gulped it down. 'To tell the truth, dear Holly-Jean, I've never been happier. Merely upped my intake to keep abreast of world events. Matter of balance, is all.'

'Horseshit.' Holly got up and walked to the phone near the ladies' cloakroom. She rang directory enquiries, then dialled again. She spoke to someone and called Janet over. 'For you. Bloomsbury branch of AA. Make an appointment.'

'Fer a wee Chinky, lass, ye've a helluva nerve,' said Janet.

'So I've been told,' replied Holly, handing her friend the phone and standing over her while she made an appointment.

As Holly walked into the Nag's Head, Mick Coulson's eyes lit up, the years dropped away and the schoolboy was revealed. For a second. As always. She'd probably have been disappointed if they hadn't.

'First things first,' she said. 'What news of Su-ming?' She signalled the bartender for her usual, Perrier. She never drank with Mick and the boys. Too near the Street. She had a reputation to protect.

'*Mei-you,*' said Mick, shaking his head.

Amazing, thought Holly, he's finally learnt how to say 'no' in Mandarin, except everyone on the Street speaks Cantonese, a different language altogether, with nine tones to Mandarin's four.

'Sorry, Holly-Jean. Nothing so far, but we're continuing with every effort. She's officially Missing Persons responsibility now, but the lads have all agreed to keep at it. How about you?'

'Busy, busy,' said Holly. 'Look, Mick. I need another favour.'

'Uh-oh. What this time?'

'Ever heard of a group of West Ham soccer thugs calling themselves the Treatment?'

'Who hasn't?' said Mick, tilting back the brown suds of his straight-glass pint of Wethered's. 'Legendary. Nazis in full OR surgeon's dress. Got shares in stitching thread. If, that is, they still exist. Thought they'd been run off the parks by closed circuit ID.'

'Apparently not. Refined the uniform down to a single tattoo, and business as usual.'

'Sailing away from software piracy, are we?' said Mick shrewdly.

'Just a one off. A favour for a friend.' Holly gave Mick a swift rundown of the brutal attacks on Jenny's students.

'Serial?' he asked. 'Connected?'

'My friend hopes not. Me, I'm only guessing so far, but my gut'd concur.'

'Feminine intuition,' laughed Mick. 'I ought to write a masculinist book.' He accepted a full pint from the bartender, quaffed and mused, 'Entitled *The Disadvantaged*

Male and the Seventh Sense Denied.'

'Get serious, Coulson,' said Holly sharply. 'The victims are always young, Asian, female, English language students. From Brighton to Torquay. Enough for even your P.C. Plod brain to connect.'

Mick looked hurt, gulped half his beer, the big baby. 'Go on,' he said.

'The fact is, I've only been able to see the police reports of the Bournemouth cases.'

'Don't tell me how, I don't want to know,' said Mick.

She handed him the scrap of paper. 'From the sketch pad of the latest victim.'

Mick looked at the finely drawn fist, bunched and rearing up from a sinewy forearm like a cobra on the attack. 'You made the connection but the police didn't?'

'Or didn't want to,' said Holly. 'After all, you can't miss the tattoo. Focal point of the whole drawing. The landlady swears she begged them to take it, even pointed out the words.'

'Yeah, well, local constabulary, not wanting to muddy the waters,' said Mick, shrugging. 'Places like Bournemouth are run like private clubs. I'd say the tourist industry'd be pretty friendly with the Police Committee, the magistrates, the Lord Lieutenant, the Chief Constable. Bunch of Masons wanking in a circle. If news like that got out it would ruin the English language industry, which I gather is the biggest tourist sector.'

Holly was impressed. Reminded herself not to underestimate Mick. 'Pretty much on the nail apart from the Chief Constable; he's *sympatico*, I hear.' Holly told Mick the red-haired DJ's story of the posse. 'Said he's prepared to ID mug shots. Couldn't you at least find out if anyone's gone down that line of enquiry? I mean, face it, Mick, if this turned out to be true, you'd have a major case on your hands. "Lowly Chinatown policeman smashes neo-Nazi conspiracy." '

'You're paranoid.'

' "Courageous Cop Coulson saves the day for vital UK trade interests on the Pacific rim"?'

'That I could handle.'

Mick pretended to think about it while he supped his beer but Holly already knew from the smug line of foam on his upper lip what was coming next. A favour granted is a favour owed.

'In return for the big one, Ms Ho, I will put my ear to the ground.'

'A very discreet ear, understand?' ordered Holly.

'Natch,' replied Mick, grinning the face off a Cheshire, as usual, happy to be bossed. By Holly.

Holly shrugged. What the heck, it was hardly her fault that he chose to be madly in love with her. 'And the big one?' she asked warily.

'There's a shipment of MDMA – Ecstasy to you – out of Rotterdam, due in Chinatown for distribution on the summer raves circuit. Trouble is, it's a botched job. Someone fucked up in the lab. Result: bad gear. Dutch KriPo have already logged related deaths and at least one permanent loss of sight. I'll dig around for your posse if you'll walk the shadowed side of Gerrard Street.'

Holly looked at Mick. Her temper was having difficulties. 'You're joking, of course.'

'Nope,' said Mick, grin wiped. 'Deadly serious. This stuff's lethal, unstable.' He put down his beer and looked at her. 'Holly, only someone with your connections in Chinatown, more specifically with the triads, can help prevent a major disaster.'

Triads. Frocking comic-book Coulson. Holly lowered her voice. 'You're way out of line, friend.' She looked across the pub at the old men in their dusty Shanghai fedoras slapping mahjong tiles on the beer-stained table. 'The Street's not just a load of stones, bricks and mortar,' she hissed. 'It's a living entity, a tribe. And I'm in that tribe, at least, halfway. You're asking me to betray my own.'

'Hey, don't be so melodramatic,' protested Mick. 'Just a bit of gossip's all I need, and maybe you might negotiate on our behalf – if what I've got turns out to be true.'

Holly slammed down her glass, exasperated, her face flushed. 'You fool! Don't you realise if even a hint of a whisper got out that I was informing, I could never walk the Street again? That's assuming I got out with my legs intact and could walk any street.'

'Yeah, well, think of it this way, Ms Compassionate,' said Mick, equally flushed. 'They'd be kids about Su-ming's age. Their whole lives ahead of them, just like her. During the rave, a friend passes along a cap, swallowed with a cup of grapefruit juice, and bingo, catatonia, or worse. Some kid in Roosendaal pulled her eyes out. Told the KriPo officer they were itching. A couple of others are playing squash in the rubber cells – without racquet or balls.' He paused, then sneered, 'Or is it only Chinese kids you feel sorry for?'

There was a frigid silence.

Mick broke in. 'Look, Holly, that was wrong of me. I'm sorry. Don't know what made me say it. Sorry, okay?' He hesitated. 'I had to watch a Drug Squad slide show this morning.' He looked down into his pint. 'What happens to those poor kids . . .'

'Okay. You've made your point. Don't overdo it.'

He looked up and fluttered his eyelashes. 'You know I'd never ask anything of you that I thought was really endangering.'

That did it. That unleashed the tiger.

'You simple-minded dickhead,' she enunciated without raising her voice. 'You haven't got a clue, have you? Look at you, propping up the bar, day in, day out. You've managed to learn one Mandarin phrase in all the years I've known you, the whole Street treats you as a joke and you presume to tell me what is and isn't dangerous in Chinatown. If you weren't so pathetic, I'd ram your offer right back . . .' She broke off, breathed deeply thrice. She stared out of the window at the fruit stalls doing a roaring homebound trade.

She could never be sure, looking back, whether it was his calculated goading that steamy summer evening in the Soho pub or some other impulse – fate, destiny, Tao – which altered her life. And others'. For ever.

'As it is,' she said, watching through the window, still now, calm, 'after consideration of the threat to young lives imposed by this unstable chemical, and on condition of my having absolute control of every aspect of the operation,' Mick nodded eagerly, the lying fuck, 'I'll see what I can do.'

'Attagirl, Holls,' said Mick, his boyish smile back in place. 'Don't worry, I'll follow up your West Ham posse.'

'You'd better,' said Holly.

'Anyone ever told you, when you get really angry, you're rea—'

'Piss off!' snarled Holly, slamming the pub door on her way out.

Wang Ts-ting was busy dispensing *swan la tang* from her counter. Holly, devoid of appetite, ordered a bowl of the hot and sour, tofu and duck-blood soup. In Chinatown, you sat, you made a purchase. She was dismayed to see Wang Ma-ma was using unrecyclable throwaway styrofoam bowls instead of the traditional colourful china.

The woman looked up on hearing Holly's Mandarin order. 'Ho *Shao-jye*! Tell me you bring news of Su-ming.'

'*Bauchyan*, Ma-ma. I'm truly sorry. Nothing, so far. But I can tell you that every authority is working on it.' She ran off the list of great powers, using her fingers, her face full of optimism, hoping to encourage the woman, give her something to cling to. And under the false smile knowing that with every hour that Su-ming spent on the streets of London, hope diminished. She pictured the face in the photograph; too much Oriental grace, too much virginal allure to survive the predators.

The hint of disdain on Wang Ma-ma's face signalled her failure to convince.

An unshaven man in undershirt and pyjama bottoms

shuffled in from the rear of the dark shop. Wang Ma-ma hissed at him and he took over the counter, handling the orders with eyes lowered. Wiping her hands on her apron, Wang Ma-ma joined Holly at her table.

'See how he looks?' she said, jerking a thumb at her husband. 'I've told him that if anything happens to Su-ming, my brothers will kill him. Right now, all his relatives and friends, as well as mine, are out searching the streets. Word has gone out in the little Middle Kingdoms. Manchester, Liverpool, Scotland. But you know as well as I do, Ho *Shao-jye*, that isn't where to look. Inside our little Chinas, Su-ming would be safe. For everyone knows my family has *guanchi* with the *Ju Lyan Bang*.' For a fleeting moment, Wang Ma-ma's worn face looked positively sinister.

Holly raised her eyebrows. Logged and filed. She, for one, hadn't known that Wang Ma-ma was connected to the Bamboo Union. Holly's *guanchi* only extended as far as the tidemark of the most powerful and feared secret society, its driftwood and flotsam.

'It's out there we have to look,' Wang Ma-ma said, gesturing bleakly to the world beyond Gerrard Street. 'And out there we Chinese have eyes but can't see. It is not illuminated for us.'

Holly protested, mentioning again the impressive organisations currently searching for Su-ming. But she could see from Wang Ma-ma's eyes that her faith had shifted away.

'We Han people have been over here for many, many generations, but this is not our country.' Wang Ma-ma shook her head. She pulled from her neck a jade medallion and touched it briefly to her lowered forehead.

Holly had to lean forward to catch her words.

'Yesterday I went to the Taoist temple,' Wang Ma-ma said. 'I prayed to Kuan Yin the Merciful Goddess. I vowed to her that I would lick the temple floor spotless with my tongue once a week for the rest of my life if she brings my daughter home.'

What could you say to that? The great divide.

Before leaving, Holly asked Wang Ma-ma to introduce her humble unworthy self to one of the esteemed relatives Wang Ma-ma had previously mentioned who had a position in the *Ju Lyan Bang*. There were two reasons for her request, the second of which she kept to herself: to coordinate the search for Su-ming, and Mick Coulson's MDMA shipment. *Guanchi*.

An aftertaste of hot and sour guilt on her tongue, Holly walked across Shaftesbury Avenue, noting as she passed by the fourth-floor address of Tracy Vinni-combe's agent. A sign in a window said 'The Augustus Talent Agency'. She looked at her watch; they'd be closed by now. Tomorrow.

She strolled up Greek Street as the evening punters embarked on their quests for jollies. The Soho sky was a plastic orange mackerel.

Holly-Jean's thoughts traced the patterns of entered knowledge as she made her way slowly over to Red Fort and the takeaway. These were the days of uncharted seas. This much and all she knew. Even the most peripheral contact with the Bamboo Union, the *Ju Lyan Bang*, was considered by those who understood these things to be hazardous to the health. In the extreme. And Holly-Jean Ho understood these things only too well.

Shortly after she'd brought her first complaint against a Taiwanese copy pirate a young Chinese businessman, with a Wharton MBA and a business card embossed with gold leaf, had paid her a visit and with impeccable courtesy had explained things to her. Janet Rae-Smith had filled in the rest of the details. Thereafter, when facsimiles originating from certain sources known to Holly hit the market, she advised clients against seeking full redress in the international courts. In her verbal explanatory reports she gave her reasons. First, that Taiwan, as a pariah of international diplomacy, wouldn't, in any case, be likely to respect the court's decisions. And secondly, and this she conveyed to her clients by subtle hint or, failing that, graphic illustration, that further action might prove extremely perilous to the continuing health and well-being of the client and family.

'The Chinese have, how to put it, a different outlook on death,' she would say. A moment later the words would sink in, the client's face would blanch, and all the hitherto frothing righteous indignation would be swallowed in a gulp. She advised them instead to discontinue the product line, redesign and start again.

She entered Red Fort and placed her order with attempted restraint. She decided to go for the prawn tikka masala, bhuna ghost, masala dosais and buttered nans. Weakening, she added sag dhal spinach and chana chickpeas. The latter extra spicy, please. She forced herself not to over-order, as she usually did.

Not that GiGi objected to the week-long feasts of crusty oil-smeared silver-foil cartons.

The maitre d' informed her that the order would take twenty-five minutes, so she stepped out and continued her evening stroll. She found herself once more in the gardens where she and Jenny had cavorted – when? Really only the night before last?

Mind-clock distortions. Holly felt a moment's panic that events were piling up too quickly, becoming top heavy and threatening to topple out of control. She centred herself under the giant plane trees and let the exhilaration of her new life overcome the fear. Prefer to go back to Micronet, Deirdre? Not on your nelly. She shunted it all off elsewhere and recalled instead the snowy Hogmanay night in Inverary where she'd been held spellbound in front of a flickering log fire by Janet Rae-Smith's lilting burr.

Tales of China, of Big-Eared Tu, boss of bosses, architect with Madame Chiang's brother Soong of Chiang Kai-shek's secret arrogation of the Central Bank of China as his personal piggy bank. Of the *Ju Lyan Bang*'s brilliant logistical organisation, on the orders of Chiang as he perceived the war against Mao was lost, of the systematic looting of China's treasures. The amazing feat of transporting the priceless trove, five thousand years of art, from every corner of the vast country to the east coast and the little boats to exile on Taiwan.

Holly had sat cross-legged on a Kungming silk carpet, sipping aged malt while her friend wove the tapestry of her ancestors. Learning.

She learnt that the secret society now known as the

Bamboo Union had been founded in the eighteenth century by Chinese nationalists dedicated to the over-throw of the hated Manchurian Ching Dynasty. How later the society worked with Dr Sun Yat-sen and the Kuomingtang, finally securing the end of Ching rule and the foundation in 1911 of the Republic of China.

By then, Janet declared, a glass of 25-year-old Macallan in her hand and one foot kicking the embers into place, the *Bang*'s activities were mostly criminal. Today, the Bamboo Union, Janet stated matter-of-factly, was within the top three most powerful crime organisations in the world. From its headquarters in Taiwan and major bases in San Francisco and New York, its web had spread throughout the world-embracing Chinese diaspora. Wherever there were Chinatowns, there also lurked the virus known as the Bamboo Union.

Twin fronts. Criminal: drugs, prostitution, gambling, bonded labour, illegal migration, and extortion from the miasma of Chinese commerce. Legit: brand-name mar-ket leaders in insurance, entertainment, hotels, shipping and manufacture. Not all bad, either. The society funded hospitals, orphanages, cultural activities, charities. Cur-rently they were being paid court by Beijing, naturally anxious to have them on their side in the countdown to 1997 Hong Kong. While for their part, the Bamboo Union leaders had no intention of letting the new economic powerhouse referred to as Greater China – Hong Kong, Taiwan, and the southern provinces of the mainland – fall into anyone's hands but their own.

Holly had also learned what so many China watchers failed to grasp: that the secret societies espoused a central tenet, their own dialectic of history. Namely, that through the twin strategies of economic power and the simple force of demographic numbers, the Han people would come to dominate the world, as was writ in their five-thousand-year history. And rightly so. For as all Chinese knew, they were racially and culturally superior. Naturally, the societies would control that domination.

Holly comprehended one thing more. That the Bamboo Union's methods were cruel beyond reason. Their lean soldiers were fanatically loyal, irrational sociopaths who made the Cosa Nostra look about as lethal as the Vatican Swiss Guard, the Colombian cartels just so much fat Latino jelly roll.

The wind rustled the plane trees above her. And Holly felt again the shiver of *chi-pi*, goose pimples.

Premonition of death? A distant thunder roll groaned above the wind. Spots of rain. Nah. More like anticipation of curry to come.

She looked at her watch. Time to collect the takeaway. And follow her Tao.

5

GiGi was on hand, marauwling for all he was worth, at the top of the iron stairs to the studio as the taxi deposited her at Camden Lock. Holly scooped him up and nuzzled his dribbly face, burbling on, 'GiGi, the man in my life, aren't you? Yes, you are, my sweety, my handsome boy . . .'

Holly-Jean Ho, defence systems down. Just for a sec. That's all you get.

'Minty!' she yelled, banging on his door, newly sprayed with the words 'The Glass Asulum'.

She cocked her head, shrugged, yelled, 'Grub up!'

There were calls to make as Minty emerged, paint-spattered, and set about serving up the takeaway.

Marika first. Relieved and forgiving, she wanted Holly to come straight over to the wine bar and tell all. Holly, equally relieved to be forgiven, gently fobbed her off with the genuine excuse that she had a pile of work to get through and at least an hour's worth of phoning. She did promise, however, to go round later on tonight if she had the energy.

Next, she tried the New Forest but only got the

answer-machine. She left a brief message to call Camden Lock – with love, added shyly, as an afterthought, feeling ridiculous.

By now, Minty had the food laid out and the delicious smells proved irresistible. She left the phone off the hook and joined him and GiGi at the wooden kitchen table.

'What are we drinking?' asked Holly.

'I've got some Grolsch in my fridge,' offered Minty.

'A valid suggestion, certainly,' said Holly, inspecting her fridge door. 'However, there's a flinty Cook's Bay Sauvignon Blanc here. Would you consider a Kiwi white appropriate for sub-continental spice?'

Minty, used to Holly's oenological waggery, responded in kind. 'Since the sustenance is originating from the same hemisphere, namely, the southern, I could hardly object, but my immediate and overriding concern is to slake my thirst and therefore to my mind the ice-cold Grolsch will suffice. In fact,' he jumped up from his chair, 'since the dosai's currently blow-torching my gullet, allow me to return to the Glass Asulum forthwith and retrieve a couple of frosteds! Aarrgghh!' He raced for the door and returned a few moments later bearing two dark green bottles, one already up-ended and dribbling foam from his lips.

But now that the feast was set, Holly's appetite again deserted her. She could only manage a nibble of nan. Her mind was on other things, she supposed.

Not so her guests'. GiGi scoffed all he was offered, regardless of chili content.

'That cat's got an amazing constitution,' remarked

Minty, awed by GiGi's ability to eat the incendiary dosais.

'Actually,' Holly explained, 'it's my belief that following castration, his Yin, the female shadow, which is associated in Chinese medicine with the "cool elements", has overpowered his male Yang principle, which is considered "hot" elementally. Thus, missing his private parts, he craves all things hot and spiceful.'

'Great balls of fire!' said Minty. 'Come and see me painting.'

'Finished it?'

'Yep,' said Minty, beaming.

'Lay on, MacDuff!'

'And damned be him who first cries, "Grolsch, enough!" '

'Glass Asulum? No "y"?'

'No whys, no wherefores, just break open the cabin boy!'

And so it sometimes went. A spontaneous outpouring of yelled nonsense that cleared the cobwebs from the brain and made their friendship, love – sort of. Inside Minty's studio, the painting, one entire wall, stilled their babble.

A huge dreamscape. Bright whirls and daubs on a canary-yellow background drew the eye towards a central hermaphroditic figure in satanic red, lying back ambiguously to receive in copulation or give birth to a prancing white hart. Coiled serpents in harsh black, indigo and gold leaf seemed to witness the rite. At the top and bottom of the canvas were scribbled phrases, 'In the Night of Time the Demons sleep', 'All we have to fear is ourselves'. Two small figures, schoolgirls in uniform, watched hand in hand, heads on shoulders.

'It's brilliant, Minty,' said Holly, when she'd got her breath back. 'Wish I could afford it.'

'Maybe I'll give it to you,' said Minty.

'You always say that,' replied Holly, her eyes now arrested by the two miniature schoolgirls.

'Adolescent secrets, best friend crushes, the formulation of the dream life,' said Minty, following her eye. Holly swore and struck her forehead.

'*Ai-yo*! I've been sloppy!' She dashed back inside her studio and called Wang Ma-ma. 'What about Su-ming's schoolmates?' she asked when she'd got through. 'Did she have any special friends?'

Wang Ma-ma didn't recall any. She pointed out, snottily, that like most of the mothers on Gerrard Street, she'd encouraged only Su-ming's Chinatown friends and of course they'd all been grilled extensively. She did give Holly the name of the school, Old Street Comprehensive, and that of the headmaster, a Mr Peter Regan.

With the painting finished, Holly confirmed Minty was now back on the payroll.

'Get hold of the headmaster, would you?' she said, giving Minty the name.

'What, right now?' asked Minty looking at the wall clock. 'It's nine o'clock.'

'Yep, try the school, summer hols don't start till next week. And there's bound to be Evening Institute classes. A janitor or someone'll be on duty.'

While Minty went off to use his phone, Holly called Mick Coulson. He was at home, off duty.

'The best friend.'

'Best friend?' He groaned with stagey exhaustion.

'Su-ming,' explained Holly, patiently. 'Schoolgirls, right? Best friends, secrets.'

'Not that I heard of. Look, I'll check in the morning. The lads are going out again tonight, doing the rounds of the shelters. I'm bushed. My turn to kip.'

'Okay,' Holly said. 'How about the West Ham boys?'

'As far as I could find out, the Met's not involved. Local constabularies only.'

'They haven't made the connection?' said Holly, incredulous.

'Or don't want to,' said Mick, yawning loudly. 'Goodnight, Holly.'

'Call me tomorrow,' said Holly, aware the yawn was faked. He probably had a girl in bed.

Next, Mother. And that was another strange conversation.

'You're seriously considering what? A trip to Taipei? Mother, I don't need this right now. I'm extremely busy—'

'*Fang-pi*! Fart to you! I'm booked already, and it's not for a trip, Little Orchid, I'm going back home, to stay.'

Holly said goodnight and disengaged. She would deal with that one later.

She re-ran her answer tape. Margot Silverman wanted to know the 'state of play', as she put it. Marika, no less than four times, calling to know where she was. Holly wistfully recalled her father's dictum, 'If rarity defines worth, then loyalty is the most precious thing in life.'

She resolved to be a better friend. If she could find the time.

Next came Beth Lawton at the colour lab. She confirmed the print jobs. One and the same. Sammy Yeh.

Minty popped his head round the door. 'Got Regan leaving a PTA meeting. Says the Student Counsellor will see me Monday morning.'

'Too late. Got a name, an address?'

'Wrote it down, let's see . . . Shirley Greenbaum. No address.'

'Check the directory.'

Minty returned five minutes later. 'Struck lucky. Only one Greenbaum with an S. Knows about your girl. The Missing Persons officer had called her. Says she has a handful of runaways at any given time, but agreed that Su-ming, being from the sheltered life of Chinatown, was a bit special. Couldn't think of any really best friends, but after I used my irresistible charm, she reluctantly gave me a name. A Sharon Watkins. No phone. Tower block.'

'Where?'

'Kern Street. I know it, off Roman Road, round the corner from my old studio.'

'Can you go tomorrow?'

'Definitely. My agent's coming to view. I'm always scarce on judgement days. Anyway, I haven't been out of the house for a week.'

'Great, Minty.' She looked at the table. 'Shall I keep the leftovers or will you?'

'You. Haven't had your fair share yet.' He turned to

go. 'I asked her if she was related to Norman. She wasn't.'

Holly looked blank.

Minty burst into song. ' "Spirit in the Sky . . . da-dum-dum when I die . . ." No?'

Nope. Holly was busy contemplating asking Minty to join her in doing the midnight rounds for Su-ming. It might be a bit much so soon after finishing a canvas.

But then he announced, 'Reckon I'll wander over to Kentish Town.'

'Pykey the photographer's?'

'Yeah, play some pool and drink some draught Guinness.'

'Have a nice one, Minty.' He needed the R&R.

'Will do.'

The phone rang as he closed the door.

'Just got in, got your message. Darling! Why aren't you here? I was really looking forward to seeing you, drove like a maniac all the way home.'

'Hi, Jenny,' Holly said – that shy feeling again, thinking, am I ridiculous? 'Had to get back to town. Loads to do. May have to go to Brighton . . .'

'Miss me?'

Holly swallowed hard and launched into a progress report.

Jenny was impressed. 'I'm wonderfully happy. Aren't you?'

Holly mumbled a confirmation.

Jenny didn't like the sound of the West Ham posse. 'Positively terrifying. But why me? Why pick on my schools out of all the hundreds along the coast?'

Holly had a thought. 'How was Brighton, the City money?'

'Tempting, darling. Ever so. But I think not. Not for the time being, at any rate.'

'I'll need to know who's behind the offer. Can't discount the possibility that the attacks are just a negotiating ploy.'

'Bit farfetched, darling. Scaring away the Orientals makes no sense. They bring in the big money. Besides, I hardly see Wendell Securities indulging in skulduggery. Very Eton and Oxford.' Jenny paused, 'Also, a very well-connected little bird whispered in my ear that Wendell represented Oxford ELSI.'

'Who're they?'

'Oxbridge ELSI, my dear, are only our biggest competitor on the South Coast and by far the most successful language school chain in the rest of the UK. I'm sure you'd agree that they'd hardly want to scare off the Yellow Peril either.'

'How about the properties,' said Holly undaunted. 'Could they just want the land for development?'

'These days? You must be joking. ELS is the *only* business on the coast. Apart from the old folks industry. No, can't see it,' said Jenny. 'Smart money knows that union with Europe leaves UK real estate about forty per cent overvalued in single market terms. Has to level down in the end.'

Holly said she was probably right, but she'd check anyway.

'God, listen to us!' said Jenny, huskily. 'Talking real estate drear while I yearn for romance. I miss you,

98

Holly. Just thinking about you is making me weak at the knees. And other places . . . Shall I tell you where?'

Holly laughed. Jenny Ravensdale took some getting used to. Then the laughter stilled in her throat. Cut by a whispered insistence, secret words in her ear that spoke only to her body, erasing all thought, making her cling to the telephone with sweating grip, eyes closed, while her other hand busied.

When Holly-Jean ever felt things got, as she put it, 'too weirdly weird', there was only one thing to do. She phoned the gym in Highgate. Luckily, Tommy Chen hadn't gone home. He said he'd wait.

A couple of Hendon Country Club types, freshly showered and Aramised, Nike sports bags in hand, were chatting with Teacher Chen as Holly emerged from the ladies' changing room, tying her belts and savouring the comforting sweet-sour scent of tatami imbued with the effusions of battle.

'So, basically what you're saying is, like, to achieve this *satori*, sortofing, works out about ten years daily reps of the four-point exercise, I got that right?'

Tommy Chen smiled politely at the young men. 'That is correct.'

'Bloody 'ellfire.'

'*Lao-shr hau!*' Holly bowed her head formally as she greeted her teacher.

'*Hau, sye-sye, swesheng,*' the Aikido master responded to his student, returning her bow, and inviting her with a simple gesture of his hand to step onto the tatami mats.

99

Any thoughts they might have entertained of going home were instantly forgotten by the two young men as they watched the steely ballet unfold. Nike bags dropped quietly to the floor, mouths gaped.

The tatami room was transformed now. Insulated from the outside by a deep and utter stillness, it became a silent other world, broken only by explosive breaths and sudden perfect motion.

The two men stood without moving, awed by their aspirations.

It was gone eleven when Holly came out of the ladies for the second time. Feeling a lot better.

'You were on pernicious form tonight, Holly-Jean.'

'Thanks, I needed that, Tommy,' said Holly. Formality went, once off the mats.

'You remembered the cardinal rule of our ancient arts: to succeed, one has to forget all and literally put one's heart into the moment.'

'And did I?'

'Tonight your heart was in it, yes,' said Tommy Chen. 'Controlled viciousness, just. I wonder what bee's flown into your bonnet?' Tommy was third generation Brit-Chink and liked to emphasise his Englishness with elbow-patched tweed and quaint expressions.

'You wouldn't want to know,' said Holly, but as had happened before on frayed nights, Tommy became her confessor, and she his. She withheld the details, of course but, as usual, there was seepage. Not that it mattered. Apart from the slant to his eyes, Tommy Chen was about as far away as you could get from Gerrard Street.

'Fancy a livener at Marika's?' asked Holly when she'd

heard all about his difficulties with the sport's governing body and his job on the bitchy England selection board. And once again she declined to be considered for a place on the national team. 'Too much on my plate as it is. I'd only let you down.'

Since he lived over in Highbury Fields, Tommy accepted a ride on the back of the Yamaha as far as the wine bar. He had his mind changed for him on the pavement by an ebullient Marika and came in for just one glass of syrupy frozen aquavit served from a bottle embedded in a huge round block of ice.

Holly stayed till closing. Then she went upstairs for a fraught conversation with Marika, fending off her dear friend's probes with glib lies and one truth: that her professional activities must for the time being take precedence over her personal life. Well, half-truth, anyway.

'Okay, so you von't tell me about your damn racist rape, then just answer me this. And tell me the truth, if our friendship means anything at all: are you putting yourself in danger?'

'I honestly can't say, Marika. I suppose, theoretically, it's possible I might come up against these thugs. But you know I'm smart and quick enough to take care of myself.'

'Well, I just hope you're not kidding yourself,' said Marika.

Me too, thought Holly.

She went home, judging herself to be too exhausted to be of any use driving round the homeless shelters this night. Marika's searching eyes, full of silent accusation, stayed with her as she drove past the working girls at King's Cross and raced the traffic lights up Camden High Street.

6

Holly-Jean woke with a perfectly clear head and, despite the pool of dribble GiGi had deposited on her collarbone during the night, in an excellent mood. Singing a snatch of Gaucho, 'Bodacious cowboys . . . will never be welcome here,' she flung open the window to let GiGi out, blinking in the early sunlight.

Had she finally discovered the precise measure of aquavit to ensure blissful slumber rather than stinking hangover? She'd have to call the wine bar and see if anyone had bothered to tally her tab. Or was it that last night was the first time she'd correctly executed *fan tyau szr-chu*, the backward kick at your opponent's private parts, one of the secret, ancient, lethal and hence illegal Chinese leg manoeuvres that Tommy Chen had been discreetly teaching her for the last few years, ever since she had attained black belt and outgrew aikido, turning instead to the pure aggression of *Wing Tsun* kung fu?

Who gave a flying frock? It was a new day: a Saturday to be precise, 6.45 a.m. and the Jap teen tourists were already milling around Camden Lock, looking in vain for

103

action – seems nobody had told them the vendors would still be in bed.

Reality set in as she brushed her teeth in the mirror. Who was she kidding? Her agenda of non-accomplishment was perfect. No sign of Su-ming. Time must now be running out. The Treatment posse was little more than a figment of imagination, a theoretical entity, lamehead Coulson notwithstanding. Tracy Vinnicombe languished somewhere east of Katmandu.

Holly dabbed off her cleanser and took one last look at the face in the mirror. A face that was looking decidedly older but no wiser.

Holly-Jean Ho, she said, if you want to be more than just a theoretical entity, you'd better pull your finger out.

She showered, dressed and coffeed. Left new instructions on her answer-machine tape. Walked over to her work station where she'd spent the late hours before bed. Janet Rae-Smith's fax, a still-of-the-night mover – her friend obviously kept strange hours – was waiting for her, and she tore it off with a loud zip. She read it while she began to hit the keys, accessed, composed, checked for an E-mail port, found none, printed, faxed Taipei.

A creative dawn. Holly loved all the modern magic. Today she ordered it to yield.

By eight forty-five Holly was sitting in the Plum Blossom Tea House, watching Chinatown from her fifth-floor window table.

As usual at this time of day, the huge room was half full; the bleary-eyed on their way home, others, spruce like Holly, just starting the day. The twenty-four-hour air in the tea house always stayed the same, a combination of XO and nicotine. Essential oil of trade. Essence of China.

'Morning, Ho *Shau-jye*.'

A flotsam.

'*Dzau, Ah-fu*,' replied Holly, smiling at the dark-skinned Yunnan southerner. 'How's the world this morning?'

'Hear you've got an important guest.'

'Did you now?'

'Later.' He scuttled away.

Holly's meeting with Wang Ma-ma's second cousin thrice removed went succinctly. Few wasted words with this handsome dark suit. He listened impassively while Holly told him candidly that she'd been asked by ALCO with great respect to beg an intercession to prevent the contaminated MDMA from reaching the young people of the rave/party circuit. She emphasised the inherent catastrophe, the potential for permanent disability, blindness, even death that might result and humbly craved kind indulgence for so impertinent a request.

He merely nodded and said, 'I understand you are helping in the search for Wang Su-ming.'

'I am,' said Holly.

'That is commendable,' said the man and left. Two other dark suits rose from a nearby table and followed him out. Six white socks.

Nice. Unobtrusive. Very Harry Lime, thought Holly, sensing the whir as every hooded eyeball in the place swivelled in her direction. Sod it, Chinatown, you couldn't break wind without the whole Street knowing. She stood, picked up her receipt and made her way across the now hushed room to the cash register lady, about as incognito as radiant Di gliding up St Paul's on old boy Spencer's arm.

The flotsam bobbed by and was told to scram.

On the Street, she called Mick Coulson. She didn't mention the Plum Blossom meeting.

'My pal in Special Branch says the Treatment are all fat and thirty now,' said the policeman.

'How about a revival with the kids on the terraces today? The reports estimate the attackers would all be around twenty-one.'

'Mentioned it. He was cagey.'

'How about ties to the Nazis?'

'That too. Very cagey.' Mick knew more.

'You're telling me Special Branch don't want to know about possible orchestrated hate. What if I call my journalist friends – shades of burning Turks in Germany.'

'For fuck's sake, don't even think about it!' blurted Mick. 'That's precisely why they're all so sphinctered up. They don't want the slightest hint of this sort of thing in the public domain.'

'Too late, pal. I am the public domain.'

'Hold your horses, Holly-Jean. DIC Brighton and Hove is an old Hendon College mate. I'm calling him later this morning. See if there are any similarities, the tattoos, suchlike. I'll mention your posse theory and this disc jockey in Bournemouth who says he's prepared to ID.'

Snow job. Pathetic. Predictable. 'I wonder how many Special Branch officers are women,' mused Holly. 'Because if there were some, and they knew about the possibility of organised gang rape, I reckon there'd be some bloody quick action. Well, let me put it this way, Mick.'

'What?'

'Balance your sheet or I call my networks.'

'Holly-Jean,' he pretended outrage, 'are you threatening me?'

'Nope, because I don't expect you to let me down. But just in case; consider me when you contemplate life and weekly wage from the Nag's Head bar.'

'You can trust me, Holly-Jean. We go back a long way. Right? I mean, *I* trust *you*.'

'Of course you do, Mick, I'm your only hope.' She cut the connection, looking through the Plexiglas at a group of young Chinese boys hanging out in front of the Empire Ballroom. Looked at them looking at her.

'Tracy Vinnicombe.'

'Tracy . . . Oh yes, lovely girl. Marvellous *danseuse*. Let me see . . . Oh dear, oh dear: Taipei. Sleazopolis.' John Augustus stabbed the keys of a slimline notebook computer on his Italian chrome and suedette desk, slid the screen round to show Holly a full colour close-up of a pretty face, blonde, blue-eyed. He stabbed some more and now the display was full length, in pink body stocking, elevations merging: front, side, back and, last, bent double, rear-facing. Holly got the picture. On the left of the screen a grid showed Tracy's specifications.

'Inclined to put it on a bit, terrible shame,' said the agent, a ringer for Danny La Rue at forty. 'But I suppose we all suffer from that problem. Well, maybe not all,' he said, perusing Holly's perfectly slim frame. 'I suppose some of us fortunate few, with the right genes . . .'

'Mr Augustus, have you heard from any of the dancers you sent to Taipei?'

'Taipei . . . You see,' he read from her card, 'Ms Ho, how to put it? You earns your money, you takes your chances, know what I mean?'

'I understand you're a licensed agency,' pointed out Holly. 'Equity has an excellent investigative mechanism in place for the purposes of scrutinising the talent industry. I just happen to know the person who heads their review committee.'

'Oh, it's all in the fine print, lovey,' said the agent. He stood up, and paced. 'Look, angel heart, I'm not your evil couch-caster cliché. I love my girls, simply adore them, and my boys, too, for that matter.' He stopped, smiled coquettishly. 'My dear, I'm quite the mother hen. Ask anybody.'

'Cut the shit. Tracy's gone missing, her mother's had nothing but brush-offs, and I'm in your face till I get some action. Understand?'

John Augustus sighed and contemplated Holly for a moment. Then with little finger cocked, in one unbroken swoop he fished a coffee-coloured oval cigarette from a mahogany box, slid it into an ivory holder, lit it from a stainless steel Art Deco lighter in the form of a cloche-hatted flapper and billowed clouds of fragrant Latakia. Or something.

'Nice routine.' Holly hadn't seen one as good since the summer she hung out at the Mangrove and watched the Rastas wield their chillums.

'Thank you,' said the agent and bowed.

'You were about to get cooperative,' reminded Holly.

'When it comes to certain places,' he said, taking his seat, 'Abu Dhabi, Seoul, oh, anywhere in East Asia, and particularly Taipei, I tell them the risks. I make it very plain. Crystal clear, in fact.'

'What risks, exactly?' asked Holly, though she could quite well imagine. She knew just how much face any Oriental, but especially a Chinese man, would gain from having a blonde, blue-eyed Westerner. Of either sex. Not to mention the Chinese's additional sublime satisfaction in scoring one up in the eternal vendetta against the hated English.

'Well, the more obvious ones,' said Augustus.

'Go on.'

'Let's see.' He counted them off on his podgy fingers. 'That there's a very high likelihood of them having their passports held hostage. That a large proportion of pay will probably be kept back as a "bonus" to be paid on contract completion. And, of course, the inevitable: that their extra-curricular duties will be extended somewhat.' He doubled his chin and leant his head to a shoulder, palms up.

'Okay,' said Holly. 'Let's agree she's a big girl, understands the nature of the game. That still doesn't explain why she's apparently disappeared.'

'No, it doesn't, does it?' said Augustus, looking worried.

'How many were there in the troupe and what was the act?'

'Six in the group, two boys, four girls, the usual stuff that appeals over there: blonde wigs, black latex, studs and chains, techno-dance music.'

'And nobody's heard from any of them?'

He punched keys. 'Seems not, judging by the number of concerned enquiries.' He punched some more. 'Now that you've so kindly brought it to my attention, I have to admit it is a bit worrying.'

'Worrying's not good enough. What are you going to do now?'

'Actually, there's really little one can do. I don't know how familiar you are with Taipei . . .'

Holly nodded. 'Very.'

'Then you know we have no representation there and I'm afraid I can't go hopping on a plane every time one of my kids goes missing. I'd never be home.'

'That bad?'

'Seems to go in cycles,' he said glumly. 'Right now, very.'

'So what do we do next?'

'We?'

'Don't worry, I'll be around.'

'Had a nasty feeling you might be. Well, let's see.' He poked the notebook keys again. 'Here we have it. Ding Hao Entertainments. First-time booking for the Augustus Talent Agency – that doesn't help matters. I've not dealt with them before.'

'How do you vet the bookers?'

'You don't, darling.'

'So it's about as safe as a blind date.'

'Very apt, lovey. But don't despair. I have a regional rep based in Hong Kong. I'll give him a call.'

'You'll be hearing from me.' She stood up and gave him one of her looks. The one that always worked.

'No doubt,' muttered John Augustus, eructing noisily and mangling his cigarette stub in the silver swan-shaped ashtray.

'Vicious, vicious,' said Holly.

From Shaftesbury Avenue to Roman Road took the Yamaha less than fifteen minutes. It was ten forty-five.

'Bang on time,' said Minty, detaching himself from a concrete bollard. There was a tattered patch of green, a broken playground and behind, looking like giant gravestones, the tower blocks of the spitefully named Exmoor Estate. 'Sharon Watkins lives in Withypool, eighteenth floor.'

They entered the concrete hutch and Minty held open the once-orange swing door to the staircase.

'Sorry, but we'll avoid the elevator. It's on the blink, and not a place you'd want to spend time in.'

Silver graffiti read, 'Gloo means No-Harm'.

'Watch where you put your feet,' added Minty unnecessarily as they picked their way up.

Eighteen floors was a cinch for someone in Holly's condition. Not so poor Minty. They made it with a number of wheeze stops in the wells that were less strewn with detritus – discarded Tuolene bags, broken bottles, stubbed-out joints, torn cardboard roaches and spilled grains of tobacco, the occasional blood-flecked syringe. And, always, the pervasive stench of wino urine, vomit and excrement.

'Along here,' said Minty, gasping, finally, in the whistling wind. 'Number one hundred and eighty-eight.'

They knocked a couple of times. There was no sound from beyond the grey door, indistinguishable from the other grey doors of the narrow corridor, high up above East London. The view out towards Tilbury was on a par Mordor-wise with Katowice, Timosoara and Debrecen.

Minty banged again.

Eventually muffled noises came from within and a tousle-haired girl of about fifteen opened the door on the chain. 'Wha'?' She'd obviously just woken. There were suppurating scabs around her nose and lips. A dirty yellow Rupert Bear nightdress hung down just below her pants.

'Sharon?' said Holly, gently.

'Herpes or glue,' muttered Minty under his breath, receiving a sharp dig from Holly's elbow in the abdomen.

'Wotovit?'

'Sharon, we're not the police, okay?' said Holly.

The girl yawned, and rubbed her eyes. Rank breath soured on something chemical.

'I'm just looking for your friend, Su-ming. I'm a family friend. See, half-Chinese.' Holly smiled till her cheeks ached.

The girl scratched her belly. Eyes vacant.

Holly persevered, feeling her way, speaking language she hoped would reach Sharon. 'I know Su-ming's a good mate of yours, right? And I know all about the

112

trouble she's had at home. Bloody pig of a father, it's a terrible shame. Thing is, her mum's ever so worried. She would be, wouldn't she?' Holly held out her hands palms up. 'We just want to know if you've seen Su-ming since she left for school last Monday.'

'That cow Greenbaum put you onner me?' demanded the girl.

'Everybody's really worried, Sharon,' explained Holly. 'See, Su-ming's so young, and the Chinatown girls, you know, they're different, right? They're not allowed out like you other girls. They don't know about things out on the street, in the real world. That's why we're so worried . . .'

There was a long silence. Metal music could be heard from a flat along the corridor. A flock of seagulls winged in from the river, screaming around the big steel rubbish tubs down below.

'Fing is,' Sharon suddenly said, 'wot 'er dad did to 'er is, like, really awful, knowotImean? Like, if my dad did summink like 'at ter me, I'd fuckin' kill 'im, knowot-Imean? Anyway, my dad don't live wiv us no more. Just my mum an' me. And . . . she's my mate, right?'

'I bet you're a good mate, too, Sharon,' said Holly.

Sharon sniffed, licked the sores around her lips. 'Monday, it woz,' she said, finally. 'Sue, I calls her Sue, like, she's cryin' like, in the bog at school, so I sez to 'er, I sez, iss awright, you come over my place, like, stay wiv me an' mum, mitch off school.'

Holly and Minty exchanged glances.

'She here now?' asked Holly, feeling the weight start to lift.

'Maybe she is. Wotovit?' said Sharon.

Adrenaline flooded Holly's system. 'Okay, look, Sharon,' she said, thinking fast. 'We don't want to bother her now. But can we perhaps see her, just for a second? She doesn't have to talk, just come to the door where we can see her. Then I can call her mum and tell her she's safe. Because her mum's been ever so worried.'

Sharon yawned, scratched herself. Turned back inside. 'Sue?' she yelled. ''Ere-aminnit!'

Holly watched through the few inches of chained door as a young girl, black hair tied in twin ponytails, olive skin showing below T-shirt and pants, emerged from the dark inside the flat. Holly confirmed the match to the photo in her hand. An exquisite, adolescent, Oriental angel, Wang Su-ming.

'Hi, Su-ming,' said Holly in the gentlest of tones through the chained doorway. 'I'm Ho *Shau-jye*. Miss Ho. *Ni-dr Ma-ma-dr peng-you*. Your mum's friend. I'm so happy you're all right. Everyone's been looking for you, everyone's been so worried.'

'I don't speak Chinese,' said Su-ming sullenly, keeping well into the shadows of the room.

'That's all right, I only speak a bit myself,' said Holly softly. 'Look, is it all right if I call your mum and tell her you're okay? Even better if you'd just pick up the phone and give her a call yourself.'

'I'm never going back there.'

'Nobody's asking you to. Just a call, okay?'

Sharon said, 'She's been dying to get out of the place for ages.'

'Yeah,' said Su-ming. 'After what my dad did, I ain't going back home. Never.'

Holly, who was totally inexperienced at dealing with runaway girls, ad-libbed desperately. 'Su-ming, look, I expect the school people will want you to go back to school, but I don't see why you can't stay with Sharon for a while.'

'Yeah, stay wiv us, Sue, as long as you like,' said Sharon.

Holly said, 'And if you feel like it, you can discuss everything with Miss Greenbaum.' Uh-oh. Mistake.

'That fuckin' cow!' spat Sharon. 'No way.'

'All right, all right, no problem,' said Holly, back-pedalling fast. 'I'll just call your mum and then I'll leave it up to you.'

'You'll go an' call the law now, I betcha,' said Sharon.

'I promise I won't, really. I swear,' said Holly. 'Look,' she added reasonably, 'why would I call the police? It's much better for Sue to be here, Sharon, with you and your mum to take care of her, right? I know she doesn't want to go home and she'd be far worse out on the street. I mean here she's safe, and you're her friend, so of course I don't want her running away from here. That's obvious, isn't it?'

'Maybe,' said Sharon reluctantly, turning to mumble something inaudible to Su-ming. Then she turned back to Holly, one finger pointing through the doorway, 'Awright, but I'm tellin yer, one little sniff of the Old Bill round ere, and Sue's outtavere, knowotImean?'

'It's a deal,' said Holly. 'Thanks, Sharon, you're a good friend to Su-ming. And you, Su-ming, take care.

People love you, remember that. Here, take this, Sharon, for emergencies.' She didn't feel the three twenties leave the palm of her hand. They were *gone*. The door slammed.

On the way back down the eighteen flights of stairs, Minty asked, 'Reckon she'll stay or do another runner? It's illegal not to report her whereabouts. After all, she's underage. We'd be harbouring a runaway, or something. Contributing to the moral delinquency of a minor. Could be setting yourself up for a prosecution.'

'We'll hack it,' said Holly. 'The important thing is we found her, safe and sound. In fact, it was too damn easy, if you think about it. Why didn't the authorities check out Sharon? Today's Saturday, she's been gone since Monday. What about this Greenbaum woman?'

'I don't think you can blame her,' answered Minty as they descended the rank stairs. 'She sounded on the brink of breakdown, completely out of her depth in terms of the truancy numbers. It's the nineties jungle, every kid for himself, 'cos no one else is looking out for them.'

'Well, at least Su-ming's not in immediate danger.'

'I don't know about that,' Minty said gloomily. 'Judging by those cold sores, you've got a bad case of solvent abuse there.'

'Look, nobody said it was a perfect world,' declared Holly, jumping the last steps and leaping through the swing doors into the open air.

'You don't say.'

'I don't, but just to be on the safe side, are you free for the rest of the day?'

'Don't worry, I came prepared. Figured it would turn out to be a long one. Besides, I don't want to know my agent's reaction to the picture. Not just yet.'

'You brought the mucoid monster?' Referring to Minty's rusting, obscene-green Saab.

'Sure did. And I've got a hip flask, a book on Chaos Theory and a couple of sandwiches I bought from a Greek at Highbury Corner on my way over.'

'Right. You keep your eye on them, I've got places to go. Call this thing if you need me.' She held out the toy.

Back at the Yamaha, Holly called Wang Ma-ma whose first reaction was hysterical thanks and wailing until Holly told her Su-ming wouldn't be coming home. That brought a sharp intake of breath and rapid demands for an explanation. When Holly refused to tell her Su-ming's whereabouts, Wang Ma-ma began to turn nasty. Mentioned her family connections – as if Holly needed reminding.

Too bad. There went years of nurtured *guanchi*. Uncharted seas, all right, she thought.

As gently as she could, Holly told Wang Ma-ma that was the way it was, at least for the time being, and cut the connection. It was time to call her own mother.

But there again things were still strange. Mother was still insisting that she was heading home to Taipei, and why hadn't Holly been round to help her sort out the house, adding that she had found herself a very nice estate agent. What Holly thought had been a slightly senile whim was turning into a very worrying reality. Just what she needed.

'Mother, stop right there!' ordered Holly. 'Tomorrow's

Sunday, I'll be over for tea, around four. We'll discuss everything then. You're not to do another thing till then, understand?'

Mother grumbled in Hakka till Holly told her she'd be bringing a friend. That perked her up.

'A nice young man, is he?'

'No, Mother, he isn't,' said Holly drily. 'See you tomorrow.'

Using the *A to Z*, she found Pulteney Street, a cul-de-sac off Bethnal Green High Road, not far away.

Holly buzzed the Yamaha across the city like Mercury on a vibrator. She parked on the cobbled street just as it was starting to spit rain. She looked up at the Union Jack and Cross of St George hanging limply from twin poles set in the crumbling brickwork of an old warehouse. This was going to be interesting.

'Ms Ho to see Brigadier Pennycate, appointment for twelve noon,' she announced to the skinhead manning the door, handing over her card.

The skin took the card and spoke into a desk phone. He was wearing pressed black Levi 501s, black braces, and a plain white T-shirt. On his left hand only he wore a black soft-leather glove – Michael Jackson or a professional snooker player. Which was a pity as it obscured Holly's view of the pulse artery.

She followed the skin up a central ascending marble staircase. Pretty fancy for a former warehouse, or was it a remodelling job? Holly wondered, pausing at the top to check the carved, gilded coat of arms. That was definitely fake – rampant lions, black curlicues suggestive of the SS, Totenkopf twin lightning flashes and the motto below, *Britannia Eternum Est* – got the gender wrong, you berks, thought Holly, who'd got a Grade 1 in Latin 'O' Level.

She followed her guide along a second-floor corridor to a door marked 'Britannia Front, Public Relations Office'. Knocked, entered to a shouted 'Come!'

'Miss Ho, appointment for twelve noon, sah!' The skin clicked his steel-toed DMs.

'Good afternoon, Miss Ho, just,' said the brigadier, checking his watch.

Holly ignored the proffered hand, busied herself with her bag and sat. The skinhead left. On the desk was a brass plaque engraved 'Brigadier Johnny Pennycate, Royal Corps of Transport (Retd.)'.

'Good of you to see me at such short notice, Brigadier. Your timing was appropriate, the location, however, not so,' said Holly sternly, sailing straight into the attack. She had decided on the formula earlier – aggressive bluff to blur her many disadvantages: female, half-breed, short of stature, youngish. 'I had expected to have the meeting at the Belgravia HQ, but your people insisted I first pass through this PR office. My superiors back home were not wholly impressed by this slight. The giving of face is of the essence when dealing with the Oriental mind-set. By contrast, sir, the taking of face is a perilous activity.'

The brigadier, a florid man, wattle-nosed, shiny-domed with black sideburns, a rugby club tie, standard civvy brown and beige checked shirt, cavalry twill trews and a green tweed jacket, harrumphed and fiddled with his tiepin, a regimental field gun.

'Yes, well, of course,' he spluttered, reddening further to a crimson hue and desperately trying to regain his composure. 'What you have to understand, Miss Ho, is that these days one can never be too careful. What with all the gutter press johnnies poking about, ready to sell their country short for a not so few pieces of silver, we have to vet anyone cold-calling, as it were. Though in your case, since you represent, ah, shall we say, similarly inclined interests in the Far East, we were only too happy to make contact. As I said on the phone, if I might just see your references, then we can quickly establish high-level communications channels.'

'I concede your point,' said Holly magnanimously. 'The need for absolute security is of the utmost import.'

She handed over a file of clippings, the letterheads of which bore addresses in Tokyo, Kyoto, Taipei, Kaohsiung, Hong Kong and Singapore. Some of them were doctored versions of genuine correspondence, others were simply the fruit of her imagination and her reference bookshelves, the harvest of her dawn creativity. The thick cardboard file confirmed her current position as clandestine Press Officer/PR rep. for various extreme right-wing cliques among the many which fester in East Asia, and attested to her long and loyal affiliation with them.

'Of course, these will have to be scrutinised by a more expert eye than mine own,' the brigadier grinned, flashing Holly the blatant eye.

Uh-oh, thought Holly without expression, we've got ourselves a Gay Hussar here, or rather, a Dashing White What-not.

Upon eliciting absolutely no response to his charm, two things happened simultaneously. An unsightly temple vein began to throb alarmingly, and the man's face displayed a look of defeat so poignant, and so obviously habitual, that Holly had to feel sorry for the pathetic toy soldier.

Pennycate harrumphed, got serious, stood and began pacing. 'At first glance, however, it all looks well in order, and might I say how fortunate this meeting of like minds must surely be. These are grave days, Miss Ho. We of the pure races who abhor miscegenation, the dilution of the breeding stock –' He stood still, eyed Holly beadily, as if detecting a hint of mint, a not-quite-yellowness about her Chinkery?

Harrumph. Stride. Hands clasped behind his back. 'As I was saying, we of the pure races must forge new alliances, work together doubly strong, doubly true! To *riiise*,' here he waved his hands in the air like a just-shriven penitent, '– above the anarchic global village to re-create the historical vision of an earlier, brilliant, never-to-be forgotten generation! In short, we must hew from the zeal of our mutual faiths a *new axis order*!' The brigadier's voice had crescendoed to a rather tremulous, reedy tenor, beads of sweat appeared on his temples where the nasty vein throbbed and pulsed.

Dickhead, thought Holly.

The conversation went along these lines for as long as Holly could stomach it, then she broke in with the suggestion that, to save time, the brigadier might want to call collect one of the numbers, a certain law firm practising on Minsheng East Road, Taipei. 'It's about eight in the evening there,' said Holly breezily, 'but don't worry, our chaps work late.'

The brigadier complied, dialled, connected, and enjoyed a short but obviously rewarding conversation with the party at the Taipei end, which party owed Holly a few favours and had been primed by her late last night.

'Spoke damn good English, that wallah. Seems to be expecting great things of our new-found friendship. Still, as for the rest . . .' He tapped the file with a nasty smile.

'Be my guest,' said Holly, smiling confidently. Who cared if he found it was all thin air. She'd be long gone. Her intention had never been to legitimise any potential relationship; all she wanted to do was to upset the barrel of dead cats and see what scum floated to the surface. And that she was now ready to do.

She got up to leave, and at the door turned to say, 'Oh, by the way, there is just one thing. We, that is my superiors in the *Orient*,' she emphasised the word, hoping to conjure up wordly import in the tiny mind opposite, 'would greatly appreciate it if your organisation might be of assistance, as a gesture of good will, you understand, in a certain extremely unfortunate matter.'

'Of course, of course, just say the word,' said the brigadier urbanely.

Holly gave him her look and said in hard cadence, 'There is a problem of serious, sexual and violent harassment of our East Asian nationals studying English in British seaside resorts. It has come to the notice of our intelligence services that certain youthful cadres, not far distant from this organisation, are involved. Sort that out, would you, Brigadier.'

She left him with mouth agape, a look of dementia, and the temple vein throbbing madly.

It was lashing rain from black clouds when she got outside. Thunder growled to the east and there were strobes of lightning. In the strange darkened noontime, the street took on the eerie 3-D technicolour artifice of the movies.

Her bike had been moved. She spotted its rear number plate poking out of a narrow alley at the closed end of the cul-de-sac some fifty metres away. They'd probably moved it for security reasons, she thought as she hurried through the rain, down the cobbled lane and entered the dark, ill-lit alley.

There were three of them. They quickly moved back into the gloom but she'd seen enough. They were much younger than the type she'd seen inside the building, but wearing similar garb, though their hair was not shaved, rather it was short, neat and ordinary. Just like the police descriptions at Bournemouth and Poole.

She tensed, swung her bag to the ground – she figured she wouldn't be needing the Gerber or the mace for this lot – and automatically moved into the wide-spread stance of the tatami mats. Waiting for them, marshalling her thoughts, controlling her wayward anger, focusing it down to a single bright beam.

A weapon.

Her *chi* was gathered now in the howling wind of the steep-walled alley as the rain blew like needles against her face.

Time.

Stepping with delicate precision, she moved swiftly forward. Purchase on the sodden cobbles was difficult. She trod lightly, feet wide apart, moving like a sailor on a rolling deck, a cat avoiding water, as Chen *Lau-shr* had taught her.

'Come and get it, yellow fuck-meat!' sang a taunting voice from the soaking gloom.

Oh dear. He shouldn't have said that.

Holly lunged, spinning on her left foot, launching into the epicentre of the disembodied words. Mid-air she discerned her targets through the driving rain. She delivered a vicious liver kite which felled the one to the left, moved in with rapid throat strikes aimed at the larynx of the middle youth. Despite the deluge, she connected and he went down, a gurgling, gagging sound evidence of a ruptured windpipe. The last one was moving now, and Holly whirled, caught the glint of metal – the monkey had a gun!

She ducked, there was a deafening detonation, she felt the whizz of rent air. Lightning-fast she reached out, grabbed the wrist holding the gun, and with her other hand snapped the young man's little finger, disarming him. Two rapid punches at the base of the neck, carefully avoiding the Adam's apple – she wanted this one – rendered him unconscious. She made sure, with deft skill, that the other two would eventually waken to not too little agony.

All wore the single leather glove. She tore one off.

Sure enough, the Hippocratic emblem and the words 'The Treatment' tattooed across the pulse artery.

She opened the Yamaha and extracted the twine

124

fastener she kept there for emergencies, and the spare helmet. She straightened her clothes, pulled on her helmet, picked up her bag. Happy she hadn't needed it. Then she remembered the gun. She found it in an oily puddle, a semi-automatic – she knew that much from her scant knowledge. She hated the damn things. She pondered a moment then stashed it in the bike trunk.

Poking her head into Pulteney Street, she first made sure no one was hanging around in the ferocious downpour, wondering whether the report of the weapon had been heard. A pointless exercise. You could hardly hear yourself think in this monsoon.

Satisfied, she hefted the thug onto the back of her Yamaha and fastened the spare helmet on his lolling head. She grabbed the young Nazi's arms and pulled them either side of her waist, used the plastic twine fastener to secure the wrists as tight as a belt, then turned the key in the Yamaha and pressed the start button.

He woke up somewhere after Walthamstow, groaning and fidgeting as she was about to enter Epping Forest in the unremitting deluge.

After a few miles, Holly found a quiet glade down one of the muddy tracks. There was little traffic about today due to the heavy rain, but still she was careful to make sure no one had spotted them. It was Saturday, after all. There might be the odd horse rider or hardy recreationist.

She stopped the bike when it could go no further in the boggy soil and parked it behind a thick, dark clump of rhododendron. She got down with some difficulty and much ugly obscenities from her travelling companion. Intentionally using unnecessary force to cause maximum suffering and mental anguish, she dragged him behind her, still secured round her waist, into a dark thicket of the woods.

It didn't take long. It was distasteful. It wasn't pleasurable. It was necessary.

Any squeamish thoughts that strayed into her consciousness were quickly banished by the memory of the police files and the ferocity of the rape which Chen Ba-tsun had endured. If that wasn't enough, the unforgettable sound of the bullet's passing – the first time she'd been fired upon in her life – kept her mind on the job.

She thought that the Cockerel at Half-Moon manoeuvre was probably the one that broke his resistance, but just to make sure, she knelt down and very precisely, using the ball of her left thumb on the meridian pressure point of the aortic artery, brought the unfortunate young man to the brink of ultimate trauma. By a process of apply-release, she extracted in terse sentences, spoken into her mini tape recorder, all she needed to know.

The last words on the tape were: 'This is a true and voluntary statement made without duress to a personal acquaintance, Ms Holly-Jean Ho, by myself, Dexter Danny Alderman, this day, July 29th 199—' and he slumped into a faint.

She untied his wrists and rubbed vigorously to ensure the arteries were pumping normally. Then she pulled him, semi-conscious now, a bag of rubbery bones, to his feet and re-secured him, only this time the trunk of a towering silver birch served where her waist had before.

She walked back through the forest, scuffing the summer growth, the rain hushing the world with its watery breath, making an orchestra of the descending leaves. Sweating from her exertions, automatically practising her habitual *chi-kung* breathing, calming, centring, Holly-Jean tried to erase the memory of the last twenty minutes of her life.

She couldn't.

She was awed rather than repulsed by her actions. She felt giddy with power. Wearer of ten-league boots. Scary stuff under the dripping leaves. Where would this great thudding stride in her evolution lead? The Teachings of her discipline said that only when all other paths have failed to bring an end to violence might violence be used, and then only till calm has been re-established and not a step further. Had she overstepped the line back there?

Days of uncharted seas, most definitely.

She found the bike and rode up through the soggy mulch to the main road. At the entrance to the muddy path there was a warning sign depicting a horse rider, and across the road a gravel driveway with an elaborate wooden Private Road post. She called an outraged Mick Coulson on the mobile phone and told him where to collect his felon, describing the horse rider and Private Road signs and the distance to the silver birch.

'You'll be facing charges on this one, Holly,' he spluttered angrily, 'and there'll be sod all I can do about it. You've gone too far this time!'

He calmed down a bit when she told him about the tape. 'Okay, okay. I'll call the local nick, they'll collect and hold the kid overnight, let him sweat a little. But you'd better not be shitting me, Holly. Without that tape as solid evidence to present to a magistrate we'll only be able to hold him for twenty-four hours, not to mention the fact that your backside will then come into hunting season.'

Holly agreed to let him have the tape on Sunday morning. She'd need the time to make copies. They negotiated a mutual meeting place. He lived in Shepherds Bush but had business on Sunday morning at the maximum security police HQ at Paddington Green. They finally settled on Paddington railway station for the tape handover. Sunday noon, south entrance, on the one-way system.

'Hey, Mick, you'd better hurry up and get someone to fetch your little thuggee before he catches pneumonia!'

It was three forty-five. She had plenty of time to get home to Camden Lock, negotiate the Saturday afternoon madness, change her clothes and prepare for the big night ahead. Her friend was coming to town.

7

Because of the bucketing rain, the Lock wasn't too insanely mobbed when she eventually arrived back there just before four.

First thing she did was to use her spare key to open Minty's studio and nail the gun to a piece of hardboard she found lying among the working debris. She picked up a spray can from a pile, sprayed the thing purple, then wrote in a spherical line round the dripping, glistening tool of death, 'If it inspires, use it; if not, trash it. Either way, don't give it back to me or the curse of the Snake-Women will DOOM thee!'

Holly fed GiGi from the cold curry selection.

She received a call from Mick confirming the retrieval of the tethered suspect, babbling nervously that her activities would come to the notice of certain highly placed persons. 'The brass. The big boys,' was how he put it. Big deal.

Holly dropped her clothes, put on her current favourite CD – Arrested Development's *Tennessee* – and bopped around the studio naked to 'People Everyday' till the weirdness of the afternoon had gone away.

Jenny was due to arrive any time after five, so she had time to nip downstairs and buy a big bunch of freshly cut garden blooms from the spacy lady in the granny specs and massive straw sunhat, a Camden Lock market regular who drove up from her Chilterns cottage each weekend.

They'd go out to dinner, so she didn't need to buy food. Breakfast? She went to the deli and bought newly baked croissants and some home-roasted Blue Mountain.

The place was looking fairly respectable by the time Jenny showed up, complaining about the rain, the traffic, finding a parking space for the Range Rover, and London in general.

'How can you stand the crowds?' she asked, dropping her bags, kissing both Holly's cheeks.

'I usually go down to the country at weekends,' said Holly in mock aristo tones. 'Hey, why so much baggage? You off somewhere?'

''Fraid so,' sighed Jenny. 'I have to be in Barcelona on Monday morning for a conference of language educationalists. My flight's at eight on Sunday night from Gatwick.'

'Oh,' said Holly, her crest plummeting. It showed and she was annoyed with herself. Jenny, standing by the table, came over and placed her soft hands gently either side of Holly's face.

'Hey, hey. Don't be like that. I'll be back Wednesday night, time to stay over. You'd better get used to it, my girl. I'm a busy, busy woman. Right now I've got calls to make.'

'Oh, don't worry about me,' said Holly. 'I'm just a bit bonkers right now.' And she went on to relate the day's

130

events while Jenny made three quick business calls, punctuating Holly's saga with distracted noises of shock and sympathy.

Until Holly told her about the three young Nazis, the tattoos, and Epping Forest.

Jenny threw the phone down and grabbed her by the hands. 'Why, you're absolutely brilliant, Holly! You've solved the case already! And you've got it on tape for evidence. So who is behind the attacks, who wants to put me out of—'

'Wait, wait, wait a minute,' said Holly. 'I've done nothing of the sort. All we have so far is one alleged rapist, being held overnight. And only overnight. A taped confession, which I understand will not be admitted in court as evidence. As for who's been orchestrating the attacks, I've yet to discover anything other than that whoever it is uses an intermediary.'

Jenny shook her head, her smile glowing. 'You're too modest. You've done absolute wonders. In just a couple of days.'

Holly smiled for the hell of it. But inside she knew her score card was filled with blanks.

Jenny, suddenly bleak, said, 'I just curse myself for not getting you earlier this year when the attacks started. Just think. We might have saved so many of the girls. What a bloody stupid fool I am.'

'Cut that out,' said Holly sharply. 'History. And as my dear old dad used to say, self-pity is the one luxury you can't afford.' She sat down at the table. 'Get real,' she said. 'There's been serious orchestrated intent directed against your operations. What I've done will amount to nothing more than a gnat's bite. A minor setback. All we can realistically hope for is there'll be a respite, a lull in the attacks, at least for the time being.'

'I suppose you're right,' said Jenny. 'Still, you're the most impossibly modest person I've ever met.'

'I try.'

While Jenny finished off her calls, Holly announced that after dinner they'd be spending the latter part of the evening on vigil at the Green Gate public house, Bethnal Green High Road.

'You might be, darling,' said Jenny nonchalantly, 'but I've got other plans. Which, I might add, include you. Margot's got tickets for the opera. *Tosca*. Covent Garden. Early start. In fact, we'd better get our skates on. I promised we'd be at the crush bar for champagne at six fifteen. It's after five now.'

'Say *what*?' Holly was incredulous. 'What about our quiet dinner for two at Champers? I told my old friend Simon Pearson to fix us something special.'

'I know, I know,' said Jenny placatingly. Apparently Margot Silverman had just come by some fabulous Royal Circle box seats, out of the blue, could hardly refuse, and after all, Holly was included in the invitation.

'Well, you can count me out,' said Holly, peeved. 'I've got work to do tonight, after our *intended* dinner. According to my hard-won information, which if you'd care to listen is on the tape over there, the posse's seaside diversions have nothing to do with the Britannia Front or any other right-wing nastiness.'

'Bang goes the conspiracy theory,' said Jenny. 'So what, who, why?'

'If you'd just shut up and listen a moment, I'll tell you.'

Jenny pouted. Holly guessed she was unused to being spoken to in that tone of voice. She softened.

'It seems, dear friend, that the gang are being paid, and handsomely so, by a private individual to attack your East Asians. An intermediary comes to their pub every other Saturday night, hands over instructions and an envelope containing two thousand in crisp fifties. A city gent in a black BMW was all the description I could extract. Except for one stroke of luck.'

'That is?'

'He's due there tonight, and I'm going to be there waiting for him.' She stood with hands on hips, unsmiling.

'Well, let's work this out. What time is he expected?' asked Jenny, stripping off her clothes and stepping into the bathroom.

'According to the miserable little wretch, this agent usually comes around ten when it's packed so he won't look too conspicuous in the Saturday night mob.'

'So, no problem,' said Jenny, turning on the shower. 'We'll be out of the Opera House by nine-ish. If you really want, I'll accompany you to the depths of, where was it, Bethnal Green?' she called from inside the shower, mollifying the bristles, a bit. 'Sounds awfully exotic. Never actually been to the East End.'

They might just be able to do it, thought Holly, trying hard to be reasonable. After all, Jenny had told her from the start she didn't want to be involved in the investigation. In fact, she'd said unequivocally that she didn't want to know the details of her efforts at detection. And here she was getting all uptight because Jenny had other social plans that didn't involve spending Saturday night hanging around some lowlife East End thugs' hang-out.

Or was it really something else? Was it, in fact, that pervasive *éminence grise*, Margot Silverman, that so irritated her olfactory organ?

'Does this mean we have to get dressed up?' asked Holly.

Jenny mumbled something from inside the shower.

Holly sat down at the table and toyed with GiGi. What to make of Jenny Ravensdale? The woman exerted a magnetic attraction over her, a literal weak-at-the-knees physical reaction. Yet at times the jet-setting dilettant-ism, the fin de millennium decadence, real or posed, was just a bit too rich for her to stomach. Jenny and Margot's lot were so damn smart, intelligent, informed, confident. Complete opposites of Holly-Jean who was certain only of uncertainties, contradictions. What was it Janet Rae-Smith had once called her? A jangling bag of unstoppables and immovables.

Margot's crowd said things like, 'As the millennium approaches, do our thoughts turn to death or rebirth?' Cringe, cringe. Yet underneath, Holly knew that Jenny was a gentle, warm, dear soul. Fronts. We all have them. Ways of dealing with the world. So they were the odd couple, sure. But it was working, so far. And Holly knew that it was all down to Jenny. Her delicate, intelligent handling of her total inexperience. Like the fact, thank God, that Jenny never alluded to the L-word. She kept the levels serene, as they used to say.

'So, GiGi,' Holly said to the cat. 'What to wear for a night at the opera?'

The cat climbed stiffly to his three feet, yawned cavernously and curry-rank, stretched his single front paw and stuck his bum in Holly's face. She stroked his arched back, and he shivered with pleasure, tail erect.

Now *he* Holly could love. Which didn't have the slightest bearing on the matter in hand – what to wear? Did she have anything to match up with the Margot mob?

Of course she did. A dark navy slip with a charcoal print motif of Sanskrit from Monsoon. It was short, above the knee, but with Holly's perfect trim it showed off her long legs to perfection. That and a single string of pearls that had belonged to her paternal grandmother, and her best occasion black Italian medium-heel pumps. After all, Holly-Jean Ho had never experienced the privilege of a box at the opera. It would be churlish to dampen the sense of occasion, wouldn't it?

But Holly was nothing if not a stubborn Tiger-born. She walked to the bathroom door and yelled, 'Do I have to get *really* dressed up? Make-up and all?' It was not her forte.

'Of course, darling,' called Jenny from inside. 'Togging up for the opera's one of the last opportunities one has of getting decently dressed without feeling guilty or, for that matter, being spat on in the streets. Don't worry, darling, if you'll allow me, I'll lend a hand.'

'I think I can manage, thank you.'

She took out the Monsoon dress from her sliding walled-in wardrobe, shook it, sniffed. Stale-ish. She laid it on the bed. 'I'd better call Simon,' she said to herself. He'd be really upset.

He was. She offered to pay. He wouldn't hear of it. She promised to bring all her customers to his wine bar in future. He told her to have a good *Tosca*.

'You know the trouble with you, Holly-Jean,' said Jenny, dabbing perfume on her wrists and pulling on a silk body-clinging black dress, elegant and simple.

'What's that?'

'This? Donna Karan.'

'No, I mean what's the trouble with me?'

'Not only too modest, which can get dreadfully boring, but I detect a streak of the puritan in that mish-mash of a personality.' She finished off her make-up, turned and smiled.

Holly's angry retort never made it. Jenny looked exquisite.

'You need to make room for indulgence in your life. All that martial arts at dawn stuff. Too darned disciplined for my liking. Let's face it, darling,' she said, turning back to the mirror, 'a little narcissism never hurt anyone.'

Their eyes met in the mirror. Holly couldn't help it, she was mad about the girl.

Tosca.

Wo-de tyan! It made her cry.

Do yourself a favour, once in your life, go and see it live, done by a world-class opera house – Holly decided this would be her new dictum for the gang at Marika's.

The gang? Ex-gang, more like it.

She shook her head and swam back to the glorious, fabulous spectacle unfolding before her eyes. The view from the box was undeniably superb. Holly was held spellbound, transported by the magic of the Opera House's production into another world. Till the last cry of encore faded.

Afterwards she had the satisfaction, admittedly childish, of once again putting Margot's nose out of joint by whisking Jenny away as she stood with a small group of designer-dressed women under umbrellas on the pavement by Bow Street Police Station, debating where to go.

'You see the damnably awful shame of it is,' Holly said aloud to herself as she drove up in the Range Rover she'd retrieved from underground parking on Long Acre, 'designer fashion is just *soh* utterly, utterly un-nineties.' She was still giggling when she pulled up alongside the group.

'Sorry, Margot, business,' she called.

Jenny shrugged at the others, looked bemused, pecked the proffered cheeks, and climbed aboard with the words, 'Just followin' orders, ma'ams.'

Holly drove out to Bethnal Green in high spirits, elated still by the opera. On Bethnal Green High Road they parked opposite the Green Gate pub. With some difficulty and no interior light – they did not want to attract attention in such a hard place – they changed into jeans and T-shirts.

'You're sure you want to go through with this?' asked Holly, opening the car door.

Outside was rain-splashed Bethnal Green. Chill,

uninviting. The darkened streets of the East End were forbidding and pitted with shadowy black holes like some Fassbinder film in black and white.

'The Harsh Halluces of Holly-Jean Ho.' She chuckled to herself.

Jenny looked at her oddly. 'Halluces?'

'Look it up.'

A sudden raucous blare reached them as the door of the pub opened and consumed a gang of toughs. The bright lights of the Green Gate, sparkling in the drab graveyard of tower blocks, seemed menacing, not comforting.

Now that they were here, Holly knew it had been a mistake dragging Jenny along. 'Perhaps you'd better wait in the car, it's raining cats and dogs out there.' This really wasn't any place for her. Besides, she might prove a liability in the event of violence. Holly had already tasted these boys' affection for the steel-toed boot.

But Jenny was having none of that. 'You've got to be joking, darling. You haul me all the way out here when I could be enjoying pastime and good company, then expect me to miss out on all the fun of a hard-core East End pub. I'm on my way.'

Inside the Green Gate, the pub proved to be impossibly crowded, deafeningly noisy, smoky and dominantly male, drunken and grabby. There was some kind of rock band playing on a tiny stage at one end. At the tables, the women, painted up for Saturday night, were getting pissed. In a huge drunken swathe round the circular bar the men were getting smashed.

'This is ridiculous,' pointed out Jenny after they had

struggled through from end to end, twice. 'We'll never be able to spot our man in this mob.'

She was right. The trouble was they didn't really know what to look for. An awful lot of the men were wearing very nicely tailored suits.

'Gangsters,' observed Jenny. 'Fascinating.'

Then Holly noticed one who really did stick out. A handsome straight-backed type, but nervous, edgy, constantly fingering his collar, brushing his blond forelock back as he talked. The shoes gave it away. Spit 'n' polished Lobbs, hand-stitched to measure. Eton, Oxford, the Guards, the City. Escalator for the right-born. What's more, the group of lads he was talking to resembled in apparel and style her afternoon acquaintances.

She sidled by, ears flapping. Picked up a few 'Yahs', 'Quites', and 'Oh rathers'. Distinctly un-Bow Bells. Very Honkers and Shaggers Banking Corporation.

When she got back to Jenny, the look on her friend's face signalled she'd reached tolerance breakpoint. 'This is utterly diverting, darling,' she said. 'I have to hand it to you, Holly-Jean, you certainly know how to give a girl an absolutely original Saturday night out.'

'Okay, enough of the sarcasm already. Let's go and find the black BMW.'

Unfortunately there were three black BMWs among the luxury cars parked within walking distance of the pub.

'Lawd, someone's surviving the recession.'

'Get a load of the Mercs. Obviously the hard boys' favourite.'

'How about this one?' said Jenny, peering into one

of the black BMWs. 'It's got a car phone and it's immaculately polished and clean.'

'So's this one,' called Holly. She wrote down the numbers of all three. It was still drizzling and there was only the odd street light left unvandalised. Jenny muttered something. Then yelped.

A rat the size of a cat unhurriedly crossed the pavement in front of her, stood on the brink of the kerb, nose whiskers twitching, sniffing the air, before climbing down and waddling off into a sewer gate.

'I think I'll wait in the car, if you don't mind,' she said.

'Go ahead,' said Holly. 'I'll hang for a while.' She moved into the shadows under the eaves of the pub.

A gaggle of young Bangladeshi kids appeared from nowhere. One was carrying a massive blaster-box thundering out *Bangra*, the Asian immigrant sound, a proud dance-mixed blend of subcontinental diatonics, hip-hop, rap and Midlands reggae.

Holly loved it. The way it suddenly filled the cold, dark night with heat and colour.

The boys passed cheerfully without comment till they reached the door of the pub, where one of them kicked the door open.

'Nazi wankers!' they yelled before tearing off helterskelter into the night, taunting the spill of toughs on the pub pavement.

'Fuckin' Pakis.'

It was over in seconds and the pub door closed once again. A cold wind blew in from the east, a North sea cut to it. Holly shivered.

The fat rat appeared again. Whiskers and nose first,

twitching, sniffing. It hitched itself up onto the pavement and went its nocturnal way inches from Holly's shoes. Utterly indifferent to her stamped *shoo*!

That's it, thought Holly. When a rat treats me with contempt, it's time to quit.

She trotted through the rain back to the Range Rover. 'Stupid to wait any longer,' she told Jenny who had semi-reclined her seat and was listening to the stereo. 'I've got enough for the police to get a handle on, and they've got our young Nazi in custody.'

But then something made her turn, the light spilling from the pub as the door opened, and she spotted the odd one out leaving the pub. She wound down the window and waited.

Bingo! He climbed into one of the BMWs and drove off with a loud wheel spin.

Holly underlined the number in her notepad. 'Home,' she said.

'Back to town,' said Jenny. 'The night is yet young.'

The only sound during the drive to Southampton Row came from the car speakers. Four Non-Blondes, 'What's going on?'

They parked on the silent, dark, east side of Southampton Row and walked into the fairground ambience of Covent Garden. Jenny wondered where the others might have gone.

'Who cares?' said Holly. 'Right now, I'd settle for a quiet glass of wine.'

'Let's just try Joe Allen's,' said Jenny. Holly relented, she'd asked enough of Jenny for one night and they walked over hand in hand.

No sign of Margot, thank God.

Rather than waste the last of the evening, they took stools at Joe Allen's bar, drank Muscat d'Alsace, ate Caesar Salad, and had a ball. Shared laughter. Obliterating any lingering Bethnal gloom. Times like these, thought Holly, the two of them, without the intense edgy competition that Margot's crowd thrived on, were very special. It just needed the right set of circumstances. Here and now was right.

Jenny laid her head on Holly's shoulder as they drove back to Camden Lock, the eerie romanticism of the 'Last Tango in Paris Suite' on the car stereo. It seemed the rightness didn't want to lie down and die, it wanted to blossom.

And it did. As they soaped each other's naked bodies in the shower. Giggling in the confines at first, then quieter, more intent, as their skins slickly entwined, slipped and slid in exquisite friction.

From the shower to the table and a glass of ice-cold white port, to the rug in front of the telly, to the bed and the late-night movies, and on into the bewitching hours.

The second to last thing Holly remembered before finally dropping headlong into exhausted sleep was when Jenny changed channels by remote and they caught someone on the *Late Show* saying, just as the credits came up, 'The Ironic will triumph over the Literal.'

'Yeah?' said Jenny. 'Meaning the hell what?'

'Search me,' said Holly sleepily. And she did.

That was the last thing.

8

In the morning they lolled with the Sunday papers. Till Minty emerged from his studio looking hungover.

He thanked Holly drily for her contribution to art, the purple gun. Then, jerking his head, got Holly to follow him out into the corridor.

'Bad news.'

'Tell me.'

'I stayed to watch the Watkins flat all afternoon. At five they came out and I followed Sharon and Su-ming to another of the tower blocks. This one was at the back of the estate where the really derelict towers are being left to crumble and rot. It backs onto a disused railway embankment which is obviously well used as an escape route for anyone trying to get off the estate in a hurry. Anyway, the girls entered one semi-inhabited block. Bloody state of it! The entire fifth floor consisted of boarded-up squats. Which was where the girls got out of the elevator.'

'Oh shit, don't tell me. Not a glue-sniffing den.'

'No such luck. Far, far worse. I watched from the stairwell as they knocked and were admitted into one of the squats. The one with a sheet-steel reinforced door. The one with a video surveillance camera and sliding hatchways. You know what that means, don't you?' said Minty, looking grim. 'Crack house.'

Holly slammed the wall. 'Not crack, dear God.' She felt it in the pit of her stomach. 'You're positive, Minty? Please don't tell me crack.'

'Yep. I asked a couple of kids hanging around the stairs where I could score. They showed me. So I had a try. The operators wouldn't let me in without a vetting. Told me through the sliding hatch I'd have to get clearance. How was I to get that? Easy. Get a friend. Only way I could get in there was on the arm of one of theirs. At which point I was told to get fucked, the barrel of something gun-like was pointed at my eyeball and then the hatch slammed shut. Extremely efficient operation, by the look of things. People coming and going all day.'

'How about the girls?'

'The girls came out about forty minutes later. That's about two hits for kids their age. Probably used the money you gave them yesterday.'

Point taken.

Minty looked at her, absently picked up GiGi and stroked his single front leg. Old pals. 'You understand this is a frigging disaster,' he continued. 'Crack is instantly addictive. *Instantly*. We've got to get Su-ming out of there. And I mean by yesterday.'

'You don't have to tell me,' said Holly. Her mind was blank. She tried to think. She'd recently seen a documentary about the soda-purified rock cocaine, the smoking of which gave an instant mental orgasm, endorphins flooding the brain, laying waste the chromosomes, the most intensely pleasurable drug-induced altered state so far devised by humankind. Unfortunately it was followed about twenty minutes later by a mental comedown of skull-cracking depression, hence one version of the name's origin. To Heaven. To Hell. Crack. Crack.

'Oh, sod the world,' she sighed. 'At least we now know the worst. Thanks to you, Minty.'

He knew she meant it.

'Right, what to do?' she said, forcing herself into action. 'You'll be needing some running cash.' She walked back into the flat, apologised to Jenny. 'Other stuff, Jen, nothing you'd want to know about.' Then she walked down to the futon end of the studio and lifted up a large potted palm, removed a cork floor tile, and dialled the combination of the tiny floor safe.

'D'you want your pay now also?' she said when she was back in the corridor.

'No way,' replied Minty. 'Not until Su-ming's safe.'

'Look, the way you tell it,' said Holly, handing him an envelope, watching while he counted out three hundred pounds in twenties, 'nothing short of armed siege is going to shut the place down. And besides, that's not our business,' she pointed out. 'Our sole priority is to make sure Su-ming doesn't OD, or start to steal or prostitute herself to get the stuff and risk exposure to HIV.'

'Right.'

'So slip them some of that if you get the chance. I know, I know,' she warded off his predictable response, 'they'll blow it straight into a water pipe. I know the ethics are shaky but right now I just want to keep the girls from doing anything drastic, keep them from desperation. Also, don't forget the cash should help you win their confidence.'

Minty finally nodded, 'Okay. You're the boss. Though I want it on the record that I think we should bring in the law now.'

'Not just yet,' pleaded Holly. 'What we've got to do is give it one more try to get Su-ming either to reconcile with her family and go home of her own accord, which if I know Wang Ma-ma will not be easy. Or else voluntarily enter foster care or something condoned by the social services. I . . . I just don't know enough about this stuff. I do know we can't force her to go home against her will.'

'You mean because she'll just run away again. I'd have thought Wang Ma-ma capable of keeping her secure.'

'Oh yes. No problem there,' said Holly, drily. 'That's after they've thrashed her to within an inch of her life and chained her to her bed. But one day, some day, the very next opportunity, she'll be gone and gone for ever. We'd never find her, and even if we did, she wouldn't listen to us because we'd have broken our promise and lost her trust. Look, Minty,' she said, 'there's nothing more you can do today. You look bloody awful. So I'm calling it off for now. Time to regroup. You'll be needing all your energy for the coming days.'

'No way.' He was adamant. 'I'm heading back there right now. I'm not letting those kids out of my sight. Daren't, for God's sake! *This is crack.*'

'All right then, call the toy on the hour.'

146

Minty stuffed the enveloped into his pocket and left.

'I love that Minty,' said Holly closing the flat door.

Jenny, who'd been sitting quietly on the sofa through-out, agreed. 'A good man. So, what about us?' she said. 'I couldn't help but overhear. Poor Su-ming. Oughtn't we to be doing something?'

Holly knew she was being decent. It was endearing. But no. She thought not. Jenny Ravensdale would blend into the Exmoor Estate about as naturally as the Pope in a termination clinic waiting room.

'Minty can handle it. Too many strangers, too con-spicuous. We'd set off alarm bells at the crack house, which might endanger the girls if the connection was made between them and us. Minty's going to keep calling in. Besides,' she looked at her watch, 'we're due to meet Mick Coulson at eleven forty-five to hand over the taped evidence for your case. We'll figure out what to do after that.'

The phone rang. She thought of leaving it for the answer-machine, changed her mind and picked it up.

'The consignment of goods you referred to has already entered the market and is therefore beyond our influ-ence. However, you may wish to know where the transaction is to take place.'

Holly listened and logged.

'By the way,' said Jenny as they hurried down the iron staircase. 'I can't believe you just did that.'

'Did what?' asked Holly defensively. When Jenny took that tone of voice, Holly knew some kind of veiled criticism was in the offing.

'Took money from that safe. You actually keep cash

around the place. You must be mad.'

'Jenny,' said Holly impatiently, 'in my line of work I need cash.'

'Nonsense. I'm a businesswoman. Even plastic's on its way out. In a few years we'll be doing everything, including paying bills, by something electronic strapped to our wrists.'

'Well, I won't,' said Holly as they negotiated the Sunday market throng. 'Don't get me wrong, Jenny, I love all the modern gadgetry. It's my work, after all. But when it comes to the filthy spons, I like cash.'

'Spons?'

'Sponduliks, gelt, the folding stuff.'

'Oh.'

'With me, if it's money, it's cash. You know where you are. No hidden charges. After all, I'm half-Chinese.'

'Really? I hadn't noticed.'

'What's that supposed to mean?'

'Nothing, darling.'

Suddenly they found themselves jostled by a group of the inevitable purple-mohicaned Japanese punk tourists ten years after. Holly pushed her way through the black-leather, chained and zippered scrummage, leading Jenny by the hand. She overheard one comment, *'Tamada ni! Chau ni-dr yin-di!'* Which was Mandarin for fuck you, and fuck your pussy.

Holly spun round.

The group was aligned in classic Hong Kong movie hoodlum poses, one rubbing his leather crotch lewdly.

'Ni she-ma la, shao-jye?' sang one of them jeeringly. What's your problem, miss?

Japanese tourists? Definitely not. Chinatown. What they call *shyau lyoumang*, baby gangsters. Lowest level toughs.

Holly had been expecting some response to her meddling, but not as quickly as this. Nor was such public display normal practice. Who the hell was she up against this time?

'*Gang ying nimen-dr ba-ba pi-gu!*' she shouted, hurrying Jenny away.

'Whatever did that mean?' said Jenny, looking back. 'Because I don't think it entirely pleased them. In fact, they're coming after us!'

'Penetrate your fathers' rear orifices,' replied Holly, grabbing Jenny's hand and dodging the traffic across Chalk Farm Road to the Range Rover.

'Charming.'

Mick Coulson was waiting in an unmarked police car at the south side loading bay at Paddington Station to accept the tape.

Holly and Jenny climbed inside.

'What've you got for me, ladies?'

Holly handed over a cassette, the copy she'd made of the original confession. He pocketed it. Then she relayed the terse phone message from Chinatown. 'Now you can do something else for me.'

'Here we go again,' groaned Mick. He turned to Jenny, sitting in the back seat. 'This is one slick little lady operator.'

'Tell me who these cars belong to,' said Holly. 'Three Beamers. This one in particular – Series Seven, I think.'

She read out the car numbers of all three of the BMWs that had been parked outside the Green Gate, just to be on the safe side. After all, there was no way of knowing whether the man they'd spotted was in fact the intermediary.

'We think the owner of the Series Seven one might be a blond-haired city gent. About six foot tall or just under. He'd be in fairly good shape, I'd guess at a glance; say about eleven and a half stone. Very well spoken, nicely tailored suit. Lobbs' hand-stitched shoes.'

'I don't suppose you'd like to tell me why you're interested in this bloke?'

'You suppose right.'

He looked at her and slowly shook his head, 'If it were anyone else but you, Holly-Jean, I'd tell 'em to go fly their frigging kite.' He shrugged and sighed. 'Ah well, here goes Mick's crucifixion. What were those numbers again?' Using an electronic pen, he entered her information into a tiny pocket-sized notebook PC. 'My new digital assistant,' he said proudly. 'The Met has just issued them to certain designated officers, including yours truly. Neat, isn't it? I can even pay my bills with this smart little bugger.'

'See what I mean?' crowed Jenny.

'Jenny, you don't have to tell me, computers are my game.'

Mick said, 'I'll do what little I can with your description, Holly. As for the Beamers, just watch this!' He plugged the notebook computer into a port of entry on the side of his console-mounted police radio and punched in a command.

150

They waited.

'Takes a second or two.'

Nothing happened. Mick looked flustered. Punched the command again. This time a little whirring could be heard and he looked up happily.

'Right now,' he explained, as enthusiastic as any kid with a new gadget, 'I'm accessing Central Registry at Transport Police HQ which is re-routed through GCHQ at Cheltenham, Big Brother of Brothers.'

The notebook thrummed and buzzed softly.

'This one's my little Brother.'

But neither Holly nor Jenny found that particularly funny.

'Bloody sinister, if you ask me,' said Holly. 'What else have you got in there infringing the civil liberties of the citizenry?'

'Everything you ever needed to know about anyone, anytime, anywhere in the UK,' said Mick with a sly grin. 'If he's in the system.'

'The "system" – nice word. I hope I'm not in there,' said Holly.

'Pay your taxes?'

'Of course I do.'

'Then, sweetheart, I've got you under my skin,' he crooned. 'In fact, unless you've never signed your name to a single official form within the last ten years, you'll be right here in the palm of my hand.'

'Bloody cheek,' observed Jenny.

Mick turned to her. 'I take it you have occasion to use the local library?'

'I do.'

'There you are then,' he gloated.

'You're jesting, of course.'

'Noooo,' he shook his head. 'Ah-ha! Here we go!' The first name came up. 'Andi Stephanopoulos, 33 Mildmay Park, Stoke Newington. Contender?'

'Scratch him,' said Holly. 'This was no Greek bearing gifts.'

Next was a Martin Kray. Kray? That was too much. Jenny giggled.

'Gotta be kidding,' said Holly. 'Where's he live?'

'Upon Lane, Forest Gate, London E7.'

'E7. Is that gentrification territory?'

'Definitely not. That's hardest East London.'

Which left the third BMW, the one she'd underlined the night before.

'Company car,' said Mick. 'Pity. That makes the chances of identifying your man considerably harder. In fact, very slim, Holls.'

'Not necessarily,' said Holly, with a gleam in her eye. 'Here, give me that thing.'

He handed her the notebook.

Triumphantly Holly read the name of the company under which the third BMW had been registered. 'Wendell Securities.'

'The bastards!' swore Jenny.

Mick was highly intrigued to hear Wendell had been negotiating to buy the Ravensdale ELS chain. He logged it all down and said he'd get the information to his friend DIC Brighton and Hove.

Then on impulse or from some premonition, Holly heard herself blurt out the Su-ming situation. She'd

152

wanted to wait for one more chance to get the girl home voluntarily. But Minty was right. They had to get her off the streets, and if that meant the law, then so be it.

'Good work,' said Mick when he'd logged it all down. 'But you really should have told me when you first traced her to the Watkins place. I hope for your sake nothing's happened to her or you could be finding yourself in deep shit.'

'What happens next?' asked Jenny.

'Because of the father-rape angle, the social services will have jurisdiction. Trouble is, the care regimes can be a bit harsh, especially for an innocent like Su-ming. But if your friend Minty is right, anything's better than one second's further exposure to crack. Something like a ward of court order with an involuntary, secured place-ment in care is probably going to be the outcome. I'll do my best to see she gets a sympathetic case worker but the trouble is the relationship between the police and the SS lot is a bit them and us.'

Now that it was too late, Holly felt a sudden change of heart. Poor Su-ming. Secured placement in the bankrupt state sector social services of the nineties would be a bewildering nightmare for an adolescent Chinatown girl. Some of those farmed-out, privately run residential centres were no better than the workhouses of Dickens's day. Not only that, Wang Ma-ma would throw an absolute fit, and as for Holly's Chinatown *guanchi*, it was totally compromised.

But Crack was involved. That realigned all perspec-tive. Drastic measures were called for. And anyway, who was she kidding? She was a software property-rights investigator floundering way out of her depth in the stinking bog of gang rape, lethal addictions and runaway kids. She had no right to circumvent the law. No right at all.

Trouble was, her guts just wouldn't shut up.

'Can you wait till Monday, at least?' she bargained, praying she wouldn't live to regret it. 'Minty and I might be able to persuade her home. I'll work on Wang Ma-ma. If her reaction is to punish Su-ming, I'll try one of the Wang clan relatives that I know is a softy.'

'Too late now,' said Mick, tapping the plastic note-book. 'The system should already be kicking in. Besides, I told you already, it's out of my jurisdiction. In fact, I never was involved officially.'

Holly looked stricken, and Mick, softening, said, 'At any given time there are literally thousands of other Su-mings on the lists. If you get your skates on, you've probably got time to reach her before the plods.'

Holly nodded.

'I'll keep my ears open,' added Mick. 'If I hear of anything heavy about to go down, I'll try to let you know beforehand. Best I can do.'

'What about the crack house?'

Mick let out a long bitter sigh and swore under his breath. 'Any fool can see we're losing the war. There's at least one crack house on every housing estate in Britain, let alone London. Until the police are fully armed and protected, there's never going to be any serious attempt to shut them down and put those bastards out of business. In fact, if you ask me, and this one you definitely don't quote me on, the POA are content to let the drug situation continue to slide until there's just so much violent drug-related crime the British public will finally overcome its traditional hatred of guns and agree to arm all police.' He amazed the two women by adding, 'The only sane, logical answer is to legalise all drugs, and supply the demand through a government monopoly which could then plough the money back into education.'

'Too right, but it'll never happen,' said Holly.

'Yeah, and meanwhile we'll go on getting shot at. So,' he announced breezily, shrugging off the gloomy conversation, 'how about me buying you lovely ladies a pint and a bite to eat? It's turned out to be a gorgeous day. Look at the blue sky.'

The women declined and drove off. They had intended to go to Hampstead Heath for lunch, but now the Su-ming scenario had changed and Holly wanted to reach Minty. Why hadn't he phoned in?

As she sent the Range Rover flying up Haverstock Hill, Jenny's nerves betrayed her and she spoke bitterly of the iniquities of Wendell.

'Those shits! To think I found that smarmy financial officer pleasant company. If I ever get to see him again, I'll spit in his face!'

'And I'll be right alongside you remodelling his sex life.'

But Jenny's livid bit hadn't run out, which Holly knew was just a surface sheen for guilt and fear. 'The cowardly animals! How could they? When I think of those poor girls . . .'

'Don't worry,' said Holly. 'We're going to get him and

whoever gives him his orders. I promise you that, my friend. You know what the real puzzle is? Why in the frock go to the extreme of organised violence against those particular girls? I just can't see it as a negotiating ploy. Okay, from what you say ELS is a good cash cow, but hardly worth this sort of terrorism. Nope. I think we'll find the motive is something quite different altogether.'

They drove past Jack Straw's Castle. The heath looked green and lush, the sky clearing, the Sunday lunch crowds spilling out into the fresh air. Holly braked by the pond to let a traffic snarl ease itself out.

Jenny looked at her. 'Are you holding something you know from me?'

'Instinct talking,' she shook her head. 'On the other hand, I think it's high time I had a really good look at Wendell. But since this is England and a Sunday, and since I'm neither the Prime Minister nor the Archbishop of Canterbury, I won't be able to reach a soul in the information industry. So let's put Wendell out of our minds for today and concentrate on Su-ming. I'm a little bit nervous as to why Minty hasn't called in. It's past one. Time for a very discreet look at the Exmoor Estate.'

There was nothing for them at the bleak estate. It looked even meaner in the brilliant sunlight. There was no sign of Minty or the girls. Holly left Jenny parked some distance away and tried Sharon's flat. No answer. Worried and depressed, she returned to the Range Rover. 'I daren't risk trying the crack house.' She looked at her watch, shook the mobile phone and checked to make sure it was working and ready to accept incoming calls. 'I'm seeing Mother for tea at four. It's not yet two. You got any suggestions?'

'Well, the heath did look rather inviting. How about a skinny-dip at the Ladies Pond?'

'While Su-ming might be losing her brain or worse? I couldn't face it.'

'Of course you could,' insisted Jenny. 'You need to recharge, I heard you tell Minty the exact same thing. Come on, do yourself a favour.'

Holly wavered, then relented. 'I suppose it'll put me in the right frame of mind for dealing with Mother. She's got some mad idea about going to Taipei I've got to try and talk her out of.'

They drove back to the heath, parked in Mill Lane, and entered the sunlit glade of the Ladies Pond.

The water was freezing and absolutely exhilarating. Jenny had been right. Holly felt much better. They dried off in the sun, enjoying the warmth, the camaraderie.

At four they drove to Kentish Town and tea with Mother.

That went surprisingly well, despite Ma's obvious disappointment that Holly had not brought a prospective son-in-law. Holly was amazed just how well she and Jenny got along, gossiping like old friends over cups of Oolong, Mother speaking in her best Kennish Tahn, with just a hint of lingering Chinese.

They discussed her trip to Taiwan. It seemed she really was serious. She had actually bought a ticket with a confirmed date for a fortnight's time.

Holly was dismayed. But Ma laid it all out for her daughter carefully. She had thought about going 'home' for a long time. Ever since Father died, in fact. She'd looked at her life here, weighed it all up, and finally had made her decision.

'Is this just some trick to get me to move back in?' demanded Holly.

Mother shook her head, spoke gently. 'Little Orchid, I just want to go back home to live out my last years. With my family. My own kind.'

Holly was unconvinced. The whole thing was a plot to get her to quit her job, sell the studio and return to Woodsome Road.

But then Ma said, in Hakkanese, 'Daughter, I see now that you have made the right decision to start your own business. I've made enquiries and they tell me that you're making a success of your new life. You've left the nest, grown up, an adult woman. You no longer need me, I'd be just a liability, getting older, starting to forget things. Not to mention the fact that I'd be getting damn bloody poorer, thanks to the pimping DHSS snakes.'

It sank in then. Ma really was going to leave her and Holly didn't like the thought of losing her one bit. She was all the family she had. She tried to argue her out of it, but Ma's mind was made up.

'I've never liked the winters here, too damn bitter cold. My bones have frozen to ice every year since your father brought me to England after he'd done his National Service in Hong Kong. Back home in Taipei, it's always nice and hot. Do my arthritis a power of good.'

'Too hot, too humid, too crowded, too expensive and too polluted,' muttered Holly-Jean, knowing full well that if Ma had decided, there would be no budging her. She had no choice, therefore, but to ensure that her mother got all the protection she needed with the estate agents and solicitors and the general hassle of property sales in a recession.

Ma took Holly's hand, ran her fingers through her daughter's spiky hair and stated, 'Half the money from the proceeds of the house sale go to you, daughter.' She shrugged. 'Half to me.'

Holly would sort that out later. It was time to go. Su-ming was still out there somewhere. And where in the hell was Minty?

''Bye, Ma. And don't let anyone try to sweet-talk you out of the house.'

On the way home, Jenny wondered, 'Why the big panic? Seems reasonable enough for her to want to go home to her family. What's with you and Taipei, anyhow?'

'Other than the fact that it's the Pacific hub for white slavery, drugs, gambling, prostitution, bonded labour? Leaving aside the fact that the Bamboo Union and numerous Taiwan-based triads have their base on the island, were you aware that the ROC has the world's highest foreign reserves, more even than Japan, at some eighty-five billion US dollars?'

'So, congratulations, already.'

Holly snorted. 'According to last week's *China Post*, a local English-language newspaper, domestic underground economic activity accounts for forty per cent of the national turnover. Total trade figures for the shadow economy hit forty trillion NT dollars last year. That's one trillion pounds, in very nasty money.'

'A thousand billion pounds – you're kidding.' Jenny looked disbelieving.

'Nope. A cool trillion a year. And basically all of it derived from illegal activities of some kind or another. Underground futures and stock trading are the cleanest it gets. Money games, the Chinese love 'em. Money games riding on the global inflow of crime cash. As for the rest, you wouldn't want to know how that cash is conjured up.'

Afterwards, when they were back at Camden Lock preparing for Jenny's departure to Spain, Jenny said she still thought Holly was being unreasonable. 'Surely now that your father's gone, it makes sense for your mother to go back to her ancestral home. She's Chinese, after all. And anyway, what's Kentish Town got in store for her twilight years?'

'Me, for one. Besides, from a selfish point of view, Ma's going will leave me stranded. No family,' said Holly. 'You don't know Taipei like I do. It's no place to send your ageing mother.'

'I thought you'd never been there.'

'I haven't, but I've accessed it and faxed it and talked to it so many times I feel I know the place like the back of my hand. Enough at any rate to know that it rates E for evil.'

'Well, if you ask me,' said Jenny, 'she has every right to go home, and you should encourage her.'

'Well, I didn't ask you.'

'Okay, okay, sorry I spoke.'

'Look, Jenny, she's all I've got. I need her.'

They looked at each other.

'Remember me at Camden? Weirdre Deirdre. Oh, I tried, God, I tried, but I didn't fit in. Not really fit in, did I? Be honest. That's why I was always leading those silly campaigns for this and that. Agit-prop we used to call it, remember? Games, friend. Desperate adolescent games. Of a very lonely mixed-up kid. Student politics was the only way I could feel a genuine part of it all. Let's face it, I'm a half-caste. Not quite white. Touch of the yellow brush in the wood pile.' She snorted and shrugged. Jenny was nodding with understanding.

'Parts of my brain even feel different,' Holly laughed. 'Really they do. As though there're two opposing logics nesting in the synapse. Gets to be a tug of war at times, with little old me in the middle. Sure, it doesn't matter so much these cosmopolitan global village days. But back then, oh heck, did I feel it. Colossal insecurity. The tough stance masks. But it's still there.' She bit her lip. 'That's why the thought of Ma leaving London frightens the living shit out of me. Can you understand?'

Jenny nodded, kissed Holly's cheeks, ruffled her hair. 'You're not alone, Holly. You've got me now.'

While Jenny showered, changed and packed for Gatwick, Holly kept herself busy and checked her faxes, E-mail, generally tidied up her backlog of software-related work. Got on with work she'd been neglecting these days, along with a few other elements in her life.

She thought of phoning Marika. Decided she couldn't

face her, nor the probable myriad messages on the machine – at least, not until she'd seen Jenny off.

'Bloody nuisance I couldn't get a Heathrow flight,' said Jenny when she was ready to go. 'But don't worry, I won't ask you to drive me on the M25 hellway. Just as far as Victoria Station.'

As they were about to leave, the phone rang. Holly raced over and grabbed it.

Minty. At last! Sounding desperate. 'Lost them! Swear they never came out of the place! Unless there's a back way.'

'Why didn't you call?'

'I've been bloody calling that effing toy of yours all day long. Couldn't get a connection. Check your answer-machine, I'm on there half a dozen times.'

'Shit.'

'What about the girls, what are we going to do?'

'Maybe they're still inside the crack house.' Holly felt her heart pounding.

'Can't be,' said Minty. 'The average stay is an hour. A rock'll cost you twenty. You need three an hour. Since I haven't given them any money yet, they couldn't afford to stay there.'

'When did they go in?'

'They were on their way over there when I arrived mid-morning,' said Minty. 'That's seven hours ago.'

'Look, I've already told the police all about it. If you want you can make an emergency call, say you think there's a runaway kid being held against her will at the crack house. That might just do something. Meanwhile, I've got to go to Victoria. Stick with it and I'll be over a.s.a.p. Give me about an hour and a half. We'll meet by that Greek corner shop.'

Jenny wanted to take a taxi after that, but Holly insisted she see her off. After all, it was Jenny's Range Rover she was driving.

The rain came hurtling back when Holly dropped Jenny off at Victoria with a kiss and wave. As her friend turned to step past the line of waiting black cabs, that strange premonitory feeling came again.

'Jenny!' she called out. Jenny came running back.

'What, darling? Time's short.'

'This,' said Holly. She gave Jenny one of the door keys to the studio. 'Use it whenever you want. But definitely this Wednesday night when you get back from Barcelona. I might not arrive till late, but be there, please.'

Jenny looked at the key in the palm of her hand, closed her fingers over it, nodded her head a couple of times, then impulsively leant into the Range Rover and kissed Holly's lips. ''Bye.'

Holly watched her enter the crowded concourse.

'Miss Ho. Holly-Jean Ho?'

'Uh, yes?' Holly was off guard.

The man, plain-clothes, showed her his badge through the driver's window. Holly's eye caught the words Serious Crimes Squad as another opened the passenger door, climbed in and deftly removed the keys from the ignition.

'Step outside, please, Miss Ho.'

Holly did so.

'This is not a formal charge, and I shall not be reading you your rights.'

'That's handy, since I haven't done anything,' said

Holly as the man took her arm and led her towards an unmarked grey Sierra which swished diagonally to a halt in front of the Range Rover.

She stood her ground. 'I'll need an explanation to which I'm entitled before I get in that car.'

The officer pursed his lips, looked around, murmured, 'Fucking armchair lawyers, every-fucking-where,' then in loud, bored tones, 'we'd like you to accompany us to the police station for voluntary questioning.'

'What if I don't volunteer?'

'It's flexible, miss. You get in that car with or without a broken arm.'

Holly thought she could take him. But a fracas in front of Victoria Station was pointless.

'How about my car?'

'My colleague will drive it.'

Holly climbed into the back of the Sierra and they screeched away, narrowly missing a family of harassed tourists pushing an overladen luggage trolley plastered with Australian flags.

9

Paddington Green Police Station, the multiple steel-reinforced concrete monolith on the north side of Marylebone where the Edgware Road snakes under the Westway flyover is North London's only purpose-built maximum security detention centre. It's where they put the IRA bomb suspects, the Libyan suicide squads, the serial killers and the criminally insane. And, of course, any unfortunate Lisson Grove denizen picked up on a misdemeanour.

It is reputed to be able to withstand attack from the air, including laser-guided missiles, and those modern toys of evil intent such as the Stinger, the Exocet, the Scud.

The Serious Crimes Squad officer was true to his word. Holly was neither formally cautioned nor charged. She was not allowed to make any phone calls, nor did she receive any satisfactory answers to her questions as she was frog-marched inside the building.

'I demand to make a phone call. I am entitled to make a phone call. Are you listening to me?'

The receiving officer merely turned his back and went back to his desk.

'This way. Hurry it up!' came a stern female voice. Holly turned to find two women officers close behind her.

'Look, there's been a mix-up. I demand my right to make a phone call,' she announced. 'Be reasonable. Please.'

If she had entertained any hopes that the women might be gender-biased in her favour, they were rapidly dashed. Her arms were firmly taken on both sides and she was escorted past a busy office area where she thought she glimpsed Minty sitting at a desk. She looked back but was wrenched firmly face forward and led at the double down a long corridor of what looked like holding cells. She repeated her request for a phone call, but no words were forthcoming from these two tough professionals.

'Look, I don't know what they've told you I've done, but I can assure you I'm entirely innocent of any crime. Could you please get a message to my lawyer?'

They stopped outside a cell, one of the women produced an electronic card key and the door buzzed open. Holly was led inside. One of the women now spoke for the first time. Her voice intoned the litany, 'Please remove the following: all your clothes and any bodily accessories, including watch, pagers, attached mobile phones, or electronic devices. All decorative artefacts such as jewellery, pierced or unpierced rings, studs. False teeth or teeth-adjustment braces, plates. All disability or impairment implements such as hearing aids, contact lenses or any other physical health-related object, including false limbs. All your belongings will be secured and signed for. Now begin to remove your clothes.'

Holly didn't budge. 'Look, I know my rights. I demand to make a phone call to my lawyer. I demand to know under what charges I am being held, and for what reasons I am being forced to undergo the humiliation of a forced strip search.'

'Just get on with it, there's a good girl,' said the other woman officer in kindly tones. 'We've been on duty for fourteen hours straight and we're not really in the mood for a chat. You just hurry up and we'll see about finding a nice cup of tea. How's that?'

Holly bandied Sergeant Mick Coulson's name.

'Never heard of him. Now just get your clothes off. I don't want to have to tell you again.' This was the first woman. It was the traditional Mutt and Jeff.

'He's with the Asian Liaison Crimes Office. Detective Sergeant Michael Coulson. He'll vouch for me, whatever it is I'm supposed to have done. Please. Woman to woman . . .'

'Forget it, love,' said the 'nice' one. 'Look, we know as much about why you're here as you do.'

'So do all of us a favour and get those effing clothes off, right now,' said the toughy. 'Or else we'll have to do the job for you. And that wouldn't be very dignified, now would it?'

'Call this dignified?' said Holly bitterly as she folded her clothes over the single chair. Then she froze, her eyes glued to the surgical gloves the 'nice' officer was tugging on.

'Sorry about this love, just doing our jobs.' The

woman officer ran her hands expertly over Holly's body. Fingered carefully between each of her toes, used a penlight to examine inside her mouth, her throat, her nostrils, her ears. 'Now then, I'm going to be gentle, so don't be afraid. But I must ask you to place your left hand on the chair. That's right.'

Holly complied. She said nothing, she knew what was coming. Felt rage, humiliation and fear churning up inside.

'Legs apart. Little bit further. That's right, love.'

Holly knew there was only one way for her to submit to this. Using the *chi-kung* breathing and mind-emptying technique, she placed herself apart from the proceedings, removed herself from the cold tiled room with its single chair.

'Now place your right hand on the floor in front of you. That's it, love, and now straighten the knees.'

Holly was bent double, her body open to the woman now behind her.

'It'll be over in just a moment,' spoken soothingly like a dentist. 'Don't tense up. Don't contract the muscles! That only makes it much more difficult for both of us.'

Holly reached the other side of altered consciousness, and her body relaxed. She had become apart from the proceedings. She felt nothing, neither sense-perception nor emotion, as both her anus and vagina were searched by the woman's gloved finger. Then it was over.

Her clothes were taken 'for further examination'. She was given back her knickers and was handed a freshly laundered green linen smock with elastic-waisted pants and a new pair of disposable paper slippers.

The chair was removed. The door closed.

Utter silence.

She glanced around quickly, took in the room. There was a polymer bed with folded grey blanket. A polymer seatless toilet was set into the wall with no visible means of flushing it. The bowl was fitted with a fine mesh.

For panning the river of the soul, thought Holly, feeling the distant ocean swell of panic begin its first lapping at the shores of her mind. She closed her eyes, shut it out, and began her breathing exercises. Only when she had totally centred, calmed, her pulse slowed some ten minutes later did she open her eyes.

There wasn't much to see. One lighted ceiling tile. No window. No graffiti on the smooth, white polymer-sheet walls. She was inside a bright, white silent cube. She estimated it was about eight thirty in the evening.

She began with her usual warm-up routine, counting as a means to keeping track of passing time. When she felt her body become fluid and primed, she moved on to the more energetic patterns.

It was two hours later when she finished off with *Sarvasana*, the Indian hatha yoga meditational relaxation pose, flat on the floor, legs spread, every inch of spine in full contact with the floor, arms limp. Thirty minutes of empty mind and she felt utterly at ease. No panic now, just a disinterested body and a level head.

Still no one came.

She slept. Woke disorientated. Tried to guess how long she'd been sleeping. The whole night? An hour or so?

She went into *Sirhasana*, headstand.

Which was how they found her when the two women police officers opened the door of the cell some twenty minutes or so afterwards and handed her a glass of water.

'What happened to the cup of tea?'

'You were sleeping, love, didn't want to wake you.'

One of them watched while she drank the water. The other checked the WC mesh for any passing gems. Seeing nothing, she spoke into a hand-held radio. 'Flush Number Eighty-eight.' The sound of water could be heard.

They handcuffed her arms behind her back. A blanket was hung round her shoulders and she was led silently to a lift, down to basement parking and into a waiting black Rover. The 'nice' officer joined her in the back, the other disappeared. The driver was a male. They raced up the ramp into the night. Drove east along Marylebone, the city streets quiet. Must be about four in the morning, thought Holly, judging by the lack of traffic. At Euston they turned left down Gower Street and swung, tyres squealing, down a ramp into another basement parking area. The driver and the woman officer led her by the arms into the building and along a corridor smelling of surgical spirit, disinfectant.

They entered a brightly lit room, air-conditioned to a chill frost. Rows of sheet-covered trolleys stood against one wall. Another wall held a bank of steel drawers. About the size of coffins.

Holly was standing in the middle of a morgue. Death's abode. The maw of the maker.

Her mind jangled like seven unanswered telephones.

It was bloody cold. The lighting was too harsh. Her head was pounding. She was afraid. And through all this mental hyper one diamond-bright message flashed in her mind: this room contains Jenny Ravensdale. She didn't know why she thought this. Maybe it was her Chinese fatalism. Expect the worst. Her stomach eructed, and her mouth filled with rusty saliva.

'And who do we have the pleasure of?' said a voice, making Holly jump. 'The meddlesome Ms Ho, if I'm not mistaken.' The man signalled to the two accompanying officers and her hands were uncuffed. He dismissed them with a nod. 'Come here,' he said to Holly.

She rubbed her wrists to get her circulation back. Tugging the blanket round her, she walked hesitantly over to where the man stood, between two of the covered trolleys.

Methodical as an altar boy, he lifted the sheets off each trolley and unzipped the plastic body bags.

Holly looked from one to the other. A moment's blurring. The faces came into focus.

'I think you can make the identifications, Ms Ho, correct?'

She couldn't speak.

'Cat got your tongue? In that case, allow me, if you will. Wang Su-ming, Sharon Watkins.' He began to intone, his voice remote: 'Bodies discovered in a builder's skip off the Caledonian Road. Evidence of rape, sodomy, extensive trauma to various internal organs, multiple lacerations, contusions, both skulls fractured in a number of places.' He paused, swaying beside her, his breathing audible. Holly remained mute, his words accepted as blows to the diaphragm.

'The unprettying process fairly complete, wouldn't you say?' The man went into asthmatic spasm, lungs whining. He pulled an inhaler from his jacket pocket and sucked junky breaths. He took a moment to recover, then spoke again, curiously distant in tone, as though she was not present and he was addressing himself. 'Moments like these make me want to retire from the Met and take up breeding chocolate-point, short-haired Siamese, but they never last long because I am usually too angry by then to remember having them in the first place.' He sucked once again on his inhaler. Came over and stuck his face close to hers. 'And right now I am very, very angry. So I look around for someone to lay it on, and there you are. The fucking unlicensed private detective, Ms Fucking Ho.' His arm swung back, and in the same instant Holly moved into a defensive posture. The policeman shrugged, lowered his arm, stifled his invective, aware that he'd lost control. He moved away but Holly still managed to pick up mumbled words like yellow and shit. The usual.

After a moment of pacing he resumed once again in formal tones. 'I understand that you delayed reporting the whereabouts of the missing person, Wang Su-ming, until Sunday noontime. Yesterday.'

Holly stared at him.

'Had the police been able to intervene when you first located the runaway child on Saturday, these young girls would still be alive. Take a good look, Ms Ho. I want you to remember these young faces. Look at them!'

He lost it then, grabbed Holly by the hair at the nape of the neck. She allowed it to happen, curious to observe this unravelling man. Her head was pulled down, first to one, then to the other of the mutilated, snuffed-out young lives.

'I want these faces in your dreams!' He spat the words. 'I want you to wake in the night and find them staring back at you, out of the dark.'

She could smell his breath. Chemically sour from the inhalant.

With that he marched away and stood by the wall of steel drawers, shoulders heaving, fists clenching, unclenching, the inhaler wavering.

Holly watched. He'd say he had an impossible job in impossible times. A policeman in the UK in the nineties. Holly would say he was a man racing the edge, knowing as an old friend the boundary with sanity.

She cleared her mind, as though to avoid contamination from this sick entity. She breathed deep and became lucid. She noticed his raincoat was a summer Burberry, like Jenny's.

He was speaking, his back to her still. 'But for the intervention of Sergeant Coulson of ALCO Squad, you'd be facing charges of criminal negligence, possible manslaughter. You'd be a delicacy at Dykoway.'

Another officer entered carrying a clear plastic sack. Holly recognised her clothes.

'Sign here,' he ordered, handing Holly a pen.

Reaction came at last. The darkling dazzle of the two young faces, destroyed. The clever disorientation the state had dished out over the last however long it was.

With all the *chi-kung* in the world, there was nothing she could do to stop the shock waves breaking on her, buckling her, making her body stagger and retch bile from her empty stomach.

An arm dragged her upright. 'Get on wivit!'

She signed the paper, her arm extended like a robot's. Then she straightened, suspended in perceptual neutral as she took back her possessions and wiped the dangling spittle from her chin.

'Get changed,' ordered the policeman. 'Over there!' He indicated a curtained screen. 'Move it!' he yelled in her ear. Holly flinched. Felt the flood of a new emotion: outrage, rage. It galvanised her into motion.

Behind the screen, she threw off the green cotton and put on her own clothes. Checked her things. The toy phone, keys. All seemed to be there.

'This way!'

Clutching the toy phone in her hand like a talisman, she followed the summer Burberry out of the morgue, down the long corridor, through twin steel doors back into the basement car park. Burberry stood by a black Daimler Jaguar. The door was open and Holly climbed in. Burberry followed. A word to the driver and the Jag surged forward and out of the basement. Up on the still pre-dawn black streets Holly glimpsed Goodge Street Tube as the Jag sped by. Passing Nelson now. Down Whitehall. Big Ben. All lit up. Frock Big Ben. Past Westminster Abbey, Victoria Street, down yet another ramp. New Scotland Yard. They slammed to a halt inches from a concrete wall. 'Out, out!'

Across the concrete floor at a hustle, into an elevator.

Up, up, fast, nonstop, till doors opened to a rush of wind and the deafening thrash of rotor blades. A helicopter was poised on the heli-pad.

'Get yer fuckin' head down unless you want your brain turned to spaghetti hoops!'

Running at a crouch, she followed Burberry to the waiting Westland and scrambled aboard. The helicopter took off with a stomach-heaving lurch and they were instantly up into the dark sky, looking down on the orange glow of London.

A man in black paramilitary garb handed Holly a safety harness. Staggering in the swaying motion, she strapped herself in. She looked around. There was no means of attaching the harness to the hammering dark bird. She searched for a hook, some kind of link-fastener. None. The helicopter lurched in an air pocket and she grabbed hold of something metal. There were no offers of help. Burberry had disappeared.

This was obviously not a passenger helicopter. The wide-open rear section and small swing-mounted crane and pulley indicated it was a heavy-duty air-sea rescue craft. Lights from electronic equipment blinked on the wall above her. In the gloom the rest of the cabin seemed utilitarian; it contained untidy coils of cable, metal boxes stacked and tethered with webbing. Like the back of an empty truck. As her eyes adjusted to the dark, she made out a second man, dressed in civvies. Both wore helmets and Holly understood why. It was deafening and freezing in the dark interior.

'Got a helmet for me?' she yelled.

Neither man bothered to answer. One mouthed

something to the other and they both threw back their heads and laughed.

Holly shrugged, spotted a strip of discarded newspaper and balled it into two earplugs. If she had to freeze to the bone, she'd do it without her eardrums coming apart.

The two men began talking, ignoring her as they discussed the disastrous cricket at the top of their voices. Holly noticed that the civilian was slung about with cameras. A Yard PR Photographer or press.

Holding onto a handrail, she looked out and down at the passing earth below. They were leaving orange London behind. She looked for landmarks. The striped layout of an airport came into view. Gatwick? Where was the golden circle of the M25?

There was no circle, but a golden snake, shooting out of the city. The M4. So that was Heathrow. She should have known from the sheer size of the swathes of glittering landing lights laid out like neon abstract art. There was Windsor. Eton College Chapel and the castle lit up like a fairy tale. There the fire-blackened scars.

They were moving out into the darkness of the countryside, following the M4 serpent, heading west towards Bristol. She had an inkling of their destination. An apprehension of very bad news. Her stomach tightened with fear.

She moved back inside and hunkered down against a stack of metal boxes. She was numb and freezing, and beyond exhaustion. She began to nod, head wrapped in her arms, knees hunched up to preserve her body warmth, hunched up against the insanity of this hard day's night.

Thirty minutes later she was kicked awake. Two men had come in from the front cabin. Burberry and another Yard type.

'This the self-appointed private clit?'

'Unlicensed, strickly armachur,' offered the press photographer.

'Been nosin' abaht, she has, Geoff.'

'So I heard. Intruding into the affairs of some upstanding British patriots.'

The picture was as she'd imagined. Pennycates will have their fun.

'Know the species: Camden lesbo lefty. Congenital shit-stirrers. Typical fuckin' female.'

'What you got against loyalty to the crown?'

Holly just stared back at them.

'She ain't true Brit, mate, is she? Half Chink, that's her problem.'

The press man nodded. 'They had the right idea in Nam with your uncooperative gook.'

Holly tried to keep calm.

'Yeah,' said one of them. 'If Victor Charley made trouble, withholding information and such, they took a couple for a chopper ride and slung one of 'em out. Soon made his pals loosen up.'

'This makes my day,' said Holly. 'I'm in a helicopter with wankers who rent Rambo videos.'

'Shut it, cunt.'

'Maybe we ought to give it a go,' said another. 'After all, she's a gook. Kind of.'

'Slabhead, mate. Impure and adulterated slabhead.'

'Ready?'

'Do it.'

There was a sudden movement behind her and Holly was hauled to her feet. Something was done to her harness and she was pushed to the open door of the helicopter and shoved out.

She pitched headlong into the darkness.

Her scream died to a choke as force-fed oxygen filled her lungs. She felt the cell phone drop, things falling from her pockets.

Hardly begun to live my life. Bloody shame. Jenny. Dear God, help me.

THWAP!

Her body violently jerked as downward flight suddenly halted and she was catapulted upwards. Now the helicopter appeared to drop out of the sky, its underbelly hurtling towards her. The faces of the men leapt into sight, laughing, gesticulating, as they leant out. She was about to smash into them when her body was flung back down again, plunged once more head first into the night.

Down, down, then oblivion was plucked away as she felt the harness suddenly jerk her back up into the night. She soared up through the wind to the laughing men, not quite as close this time, then down once more. She glimpsed the looping cord; understood.

Bungee. How amusing. Unfortunately her bladder had not shared the joke. She had wet herself in the process.

When gravity had had its fun, they hauled her back inside the Westland.

'Stay away from politics in future, darling. Next time we might forget the rubber band, har, har!'

'My guess is computers are a lot less accident-prone than poking your nose into the business of your superiors. Get the drift?'

Holly got the drift all right. She stared at them. Memorised the faces. They would get theirs. One day. That was a promise.

'Then again, you have been of some use,' said one. 'And we'd be derelict in our duties not to reward you.'

'Derelict. Nice one, Geoffo.'

'Not to have you along to partake of the glory.'

'So remember us with due affection and gratitude.'

'I'll remember you all right,' said Holly. 'You'll be wishing I didn't.'

'Say what, yellow fuck?'

'Fuck you very much,' said Holly, drowned out by the rotor blades.

Twenty minutes later the helicopter began a sharp descent, then they were coming in low over fields. Searchlights from the Westland illuminated the scene below and loudhailers opened up from speakers housed on the helicopter wall.

'Halt all movement immediately! Repeat. Halt all movement immediately, we are armed police officers! Repeat. We are armed and have authority to open fire unless you immediately comply! Cease all movement and raise your hands above your heads!'

Below, Holly could see the flashing blue lights of police vehicles, men in military fatigues, dogs barking. A few fields away were the lights of a motorway service station. A blue sign lit up: 'Eastern-in-Gordano Services'.

She'd guessed the destination correctly. But what was her role in this little drama?

The helicopter hovered one last moment then landed with a bump, and then men jumped out, automatics drawn. Holly followed, her limbs stiff from the long night and the cold, stumbling on the tussocks in the dark.

She watched the garishly lit scene from the shadows, keeping herself inconspicuous.

The car boots of four private passenger cars were open. A file of men, about a dozen in all, were being body-searched. Then they were handcuffed and, one by one, led into two waiting police vans. Among the group of swearing, struggling felons she noted without surprise two stony-faced Chinese. Instinctively she retreated further into the night shadows.

A TV camera operator with lighting and sound man now appeared. Running across the grass, they set up quickly in front of a reporter in duffel coat, hair flying in the night wind, speaking with dramatic gestures into his microphone. A suitcase full of neat stacks of fifty-pound notes was opened and brandished before the camera. Five metal airline cases were then displayed, their padded interiors nestling large flasks of liquid. One was lifted out carefully and held before the camera. A police officer struggled with two Alsatians straining at the leash, foaming at the mouth and barking madly at the metal suitcases. A senior officer in plain clothes shielded his face but said a few words before the lens.

From the darkness of the field, Holly watched silently.

The consignment of contaminated MDMA from Rotterdam had been busted thanks to her information from the Plum Blossom gentleman. She had been doing Coulson a favour. Now the double-cross, her payback. Thanks to whom? Pennycate's toy soldiers in the Met? Mr Plum Blossom? Or his Chinese *bang* rivals?

Just then the press photographer from the helicopter who'd been running around banging off film at every target, noticed her standing there. He stopped by the TV cameraman, spoke a few words and pointed in Holly's direction. She ducked and turned, ran straight into the clutches of two big officers who must have been lurking behind her.

A royal set-up. Snitch, informer, grass. What a fool she was! She'd let slip years of training to be caught from behind. And now it was too late for resistance.

The camera lights flashed over towards her. She tried to cover her face with her hands. The reporter struck his pose. His ham voice carried on the wind.

'And so thanks are due to the painstaking and highly dangerous work of, my sources have led me to under-stand, a female narcotics special agent. A young woman who must for obvious reasons protect her identity,' the camera zoomed in close as Holly hid her face, 'a young woman who bravely went undercover for months into the violent and mysterious underworld of the Chinese triad gangs. A netherworld where death comes as easily as a take-out chow mein. And so this night the police have scored one up in the never-ending battle against the scourge of drugs, in particular the narcotic Ecstasy which has found such fatal attraction among the youth of Britain today. This is Michael Lavington, for *Breakfast News*, in a field somewhere outside Bristol.'

It was over just as suddenly as it had begun. The police vans pulled away, the flashing blue lights faded into the night. The TV live news crew piled into their van and rushed off to the next breaking story, the civilian cars were driven away by police officers, and the Alsatians, muted at last, were shoved into the back of their handler's dog van.

Across the darkness, came the roar of the Westland's engines. Holly noticed Burberry climbing up into the helicopter and she hurried across the field for the ride back to London.

Suddenly the gloating press photographer appeared before her, his lenses confronting her, the flash blinding her tired eyes.

'Just a few full facials, sweetheart,' he yelled above the building thud of the rotor. 'Front page jobby, this one. Don't worry, they're holding the late edition. With the chopper ready and my electronics, you'll be on most of Britain's breakfast tables, so give us a smile.'

Holly lashed out at him, caught something metal. Drop-kicked his crotch, heard him scream. She ducked and weaved, raced through the thrashing turbulence of the accelerating rotor blades towards the Westland. The press man was hauled aboard just ahead of her. He turned, cursing, and began to snap her face as she reached up. She grasped the handrail with one hand as the helicopter lurched off the ground. Her shoulder socket wrenched as the great metal bird began to hover and sway.

'For God's sake, help me up!' she shouted as she strained to hang on. She looked up, desperately hefting her body weight. The faces of the men above her were laughing, and she felt her fingers pried off the handrail. Her hand tugged free and she dropped down to the muddy earth.

'Forget it, Suzy Wong, you can find your own way home.' The Westland lifted off and with a roaring swoop flew away into the night.

Holly-Jean lay on her back in the dark, silent field. For a moment, overcome, her eyes filled with tears of rage. She would get them, oh, one day she would get them.

Energised by anger-pumped adrenaline, she jumped up and stamped off across the field. Aloud, she furiously recited her schoolgirl Blake:

> Tyger! Tyger! burning bright
> In the forests of the night,
> What immortal hand or eye
> Could frame thy fearful symmetry?

It took her ten minutes to slog her way across the turf in the pre-dawn dark, heading towards the lights of the Easton-in-Gordano M5 service station.

There she found a pay phone. Fortuitously her wallet, tucked up inside her jeans, with credit cards, keys and cash, had not dropped out when she'd taken her involuntary bungee jump. Using Yellow Pages and after a few refusals, she finally found a mini-cab willing to drive out from Bristol, pick her up and take her to Bristol Temple Meads Station.

Dawn was streaking the eastern sky as she waited on the platform for what used to be called the milk train back to town. The grimy old diesel pulled in, she found a seat and passed into unconsciousness. She was woken by, 'This is London-ah Paddington-ah. All change-ah.'

Aching, stiff-limbed, she made her way to the door. She sniffed the city air, her city air, and felt instantly rejuvenated. The night receded. Back to work. Su-ming was history. Wendell now. And not forgetting Pennycate. No chance.

As she hustled through the commuter throng, she saw them and her heart missed: six white socks. She ducked, stopped, was barged from behind. She swallowed hard. To have been expected, after all, after this night's work. She walked on. There, below the clock; the taciturn gentleman from the Plum Blossom Tea House and his silent menagerie.

Holly-Jean, walk on, walk on, with your head held high, and you'll never walk alone . . . you'll n-e-e-ver walk again.

Unfortunately, she was smeared with mud, bruised, dishevelled, exhausted, and to top it all, still wearing soiled knickers which chafed the tops of the thighs. Her stride faltered, the pathetic smidgen of confidence she'd summoned wavered.

Sod it. Perhaps it'd be easier all round just to have them lop her head off right there and then. Save everyone a lot of bother. But, hey! This is Holly-Jean Ho

here. The Tiger-born, remember? *Noli mangare faecae.*
Right.

She went straight up to Mr Plum Blossom. Stood,
shrugged.

He nodded at her, and the two cohorts glided in beside
her. Without speaking they walked across the concourse
to the taxi pick-up where a gleaming black Lincoln
Continental stood breathing mutely. A uniformed chauf-
feur dropped his cigarette butt, ground it under his heel
and swung the rear door wide.

The *lao-ban*, as befitted a higher level officer of the
society, entered first. Holly was ushered in after him.
The two others climbed into the partitioned front.
Nobody spoke.

Holly sank back into the soft cushions. Felt what?
Curious. Awaited her fate as a neutral observer.

The silence flowed on as the black whale glided along
the city streets. How many car rides had she involuntarily taken in the last twenty-four hours? Must be worthy
of the *Guinness Book of Records*. Regent's Park now. In
the velvety nice-smelling void, she wasn't going to be the
first to break the silence. After this night, she'd had it
with men. Men in toto, any creed or colour, the species,
the genus: Homo Dickheadicus. As far as Holly was
concerned, they could all go and wave their willies in the
threshing machine.

The limo was cruising the Inner Circle now. Mr Plum
Blossom stirred. From a side compartment he held up
the early edition of the *Sun* with its screaming headline,
'Chinese Drug Terror Smashed!' and below in slightly
less lurid type, 'Your Sun Asks: Is This The New Chink

Opium War?' A dramatic photo showed Holly, partially shielding her face but clearly defined in the foreground, while behind her the drug dealers, cuffed, defiant, were being led into the police van.

'Ho *Shao-jye*, have you lost so completely your Chinese ancestry? Or did you simply forget we too read the papers?' asked Mr P.B. 'To show such ignorance of the Chinese insistence, above all other considerations, for complete anonymity, for utter discretion.' BBC phonemes, deep jet eyes that never left hers.

Holly shrugged. 'You know it was a set-up, pure and simple.'

He considered this. 'That maybe, but for we Chinese the forced spotlight is unforgivable. There is, additionally, the loss of face to consider.'

'Loss of face? Chinese? Surely some mistake,' Holly murmured.

'Not the moment for levity, Ho *Shao-jye*.' His eyes glinted. 'Loss of face, yes, and worse: this lying headline implies the British fought the Chinese against opium instead of for the right to trade it. The toilet-paper press never misses the chance to insult us. Chinese everywhere will feel *mei-you mien-tz*.' The worst: without face.

Frankly, Holly couldn't have cared less. She wanted bed and a shower. 'As I already said – set-up.'

'Tell me.'

She listed her adversaries. 'Well, there are these right-wing lunatics, the Britannia Front, with high-ranking pals in Scotland Yard.' She looked at him. 'Or maybe it was Chinatown *guanchi*. Though I wouldn't presume to inform you about that.'

He was quiet for a while. The car planed beneath the limes, past the Nash Terraces.

'This Britannia Front is of no consequence.' He looked at her. 'Though now perhaps it's time to tell the whole story from the beginning.'

'You wouldn't be interested.'

'Oh, but I would.'

He listened carefully, those intelligent, beautiful, hard-as-nails eyes never leaving hers as she chronicled selections from the incredible sequence of events that had begun with Margot Silverman's invitation to Kettner's. Selections pertinent to protect but yet to convince.

Editing requires a complete viewing. She heard those parts that were spoken, she listened to the rest inside her skull. The rapes of the ELS students, the Treatment, Wang Ma-ma and Su-ming, Sharon and the Exmoor Estate, the crack house, Tracy Vinnicombe's disappearance in Taipei, the Britannia mob and Pennycate, Epping Forest and a boy left in pain tied to a tree. The purple gun, the Green Gate pub and a suave city gent from Wendell Securities. The gang of Chinatown boys who'd jostled her at Camden Lock. The police, the cold white cell, the morgue and two dead girls. The helicopter ride and the muddy field outside Bristol.

In the end her voice trailed off. 'Fancied myself, didn't I? Now two kids are dead.' Her cheeks were wet. Anger and shame in salt solution.

The Bamboo Union officer looked away. Chinese loathing of public display. Embarrassment at such loss of face. 'Despite the unfortunate outcome, you were diligent to the best of your ability.' Pause. 'Ho *shao-jye*, your new career in investigation proceeds admirably well.'

Holly watched a V formation of mallards land water-skiing on the pond. 'I don't need your comments, but thanks for the twisted logic,' she said. 'Diligence is hardly the word I'd use. Besides, what would you know?'

'Ah, but I would,' he said, smug chops. 'Since Wang Ma-ma's first visit to your office you've been under our surveillance.'

'Then why didn't you do something to stop that?' She pointed at the newspaper.

The Bamboo Union officer inclined his head. 'The *Ju Lyan Bang* is without doubt the most powerful of the societies operating in the Chinese diaspora. However, in Britain, ever the Cantonese stronghold, we are under-represented. An alliance of two Hong Kong triads, the 14K and *Wo Shing Wo*, headquartered in Manchester, exert a greater control in UK, Amsterdam and Brussels.'

She'd guessed right – rival triads. Still something struck her as very odd. 'Okay, since, as you said, the Chinese value discretion above all else, why would any of the societies invite the spotlight?'

His response was typical bloody arcane Han and a glass of brandy. 'We are always working to undermine the alliance.' He opened the walnut veneer cabinet and poured two palm-sized snifters of Remy XO. Holly accepted one and waited for the correct etiquette.

'*Gan-bei!*' Dry glass! Chinese for bottoms up.

She shrugged, upended the lovingly matured amber liquid designed to be savoured at great leisure, and poured it straight down her throat. The Chinese way of brandy.

The distillation fired her belly like a blast furnace. She controlled the fumy thoracic spasm without so much as an audible hiss and set her lips rigid. He showed his appreciation with a bow of his perfumed, expertly shaved and finely coiffeured head.

'The society has thus acquired some debt from you.'

Ah, now I get it. 'Another snifter, please.' She held out her glass.

He poured and smiled. 'Owing to your success in locating my second cousin Wang Su-ming, which, despite the regrettable outcome, proved more successful than all the society's efforts on Wang Ma-ma's behalf, it has been perceived that you are more of an asset alive than dead.'

'Golly gosh, that's jolly dee of you.' She wiped her lips. 'Spare another slug?' Serene thoughts fumigated as the XO fired her veins and the trees of Regent's Park soothed her tired, pricking eyes.

'The truth is,' said Mr Plum Blossom switching to ornate Mandarin, 'you walk with agile steps in the English-speaking world. And that makes you of immense value to us.' He poured a fourth brandy for her. 'Penance will be forthcoming.'

Great, thought Holly, swilling it down, must I perambulate on my knees again?

'The society has now acquired your services for a discretionary period.'

She replied in Mandarin, the brandy stoking the eloquence of the necessary abasement. 'Surely lowly

189

knowledge as bumbling and insignificant as mine can be of no possible value where the monopoly of excellence is held by such an honourable and esteemed society as the *Ju Lyan Bang*.'

'We Chinese are addicted to many things, but above all to euphemism, Ho *Shyau-jye*,' said Mr Plum Blossom with a smile. 'Yourself, any time, any place, any activity.'

He dropped her off near Chalk Farm Tube. As the stretch limousine readied to pull into the traffic, the window slid down and he leaned out. 'Go carefully.'

Fabulous, thought Holly, reeling from the XO.

With a swish, the gleaming black boat lunged away, riding the surf of its massive pillowy radials. She staggered back to Camden Lock. GiGi would be starving.

He was.

He plainly disapproved of her staying out all night and coming home reeking of brandy at a severe list. He gave her the puckered greeting of his rear orifice as he hobbled stiffly inside ahead of her. She finally got her key in the lock.

Minty. Had it been him she'd glimpsed at Paddington Green? Or a blur in the brandied mind? She banged and hollered at his door. There was no response so she let herself in. No sign. The bed was unslept in. She careened back down the corridor. Inside her studio she hacked off the last of the chorizo for GiGi and inspected the fridge. The cold curry was all but gone; she dumped the remains in his dish and filled his drinking bowl with water. No milk.

She wanted sleep, the sleep of the dead. She bit her tongue and tried not to think any more. She left the phone off the hook, stripped off her soiled clothes, bunged them in the machine, and stepped into a scalding shower. Shampooed thrice, letting the suds wash down her aching body. In the teeth-grinding exhilaration of the brandy morning of no-sleep, she recalled shared lather and with soapy fingers found quick release.

She put on a crisp clean kimono, left the window ajar for GiGi, and fell onto the bed and instant oblivion.

10

Someone was nudging her awake. She opened her eye from under the covers. Minty.

'Whassatime?'

'Tea time. Five in the evening. You look bloody awful.'

'Thanks,' said Holly, half asleep, not ready to face the world. She missed Jenny. 'That you at the nick?'

'Yes.'

Holly looked at him now. 'Life's a bastard.'

He nodded, his eyes red-rimmed.

Holly thought about that. Not the world. Not yet. 'Set of keys on the table?'

He looked. 'Ah . . . yep,' he called.

'If you don't mind, get hold of Coulson, find out where they stashed Jenny's Range Rover. There's a receipt somewhere there.'

He rummaged on the table. 'Got it.'

He made the call while Holly buried her head under the pillows. 'Vine Street nick, underground car park. I'll retrieve it for you if you promise to be up and dressed when I get back.'

Muffled voice. From the world. She held her breath in the warm pitch. Go away, world. Just erase yourself.

'Hey,' he called out. 'I get nervous when I see the human dynamo in bed at five in the evening. Not self-pity, not from the great iceberg herself, that I don't believe.'

No reply from under the covers.

'Yeah, well, I feel sorry for me too.'

'Piss off!' she shouted angrily, but the door had already slammed and she heard her dear old dad's gentle admonition, 'Self-pity's the one luxury you can't afford.'

She forced herself up, put the phone back on the hook and took another long hot shower.

When she came out of the bathroom, a message was blinking. It was in Mandarin, a formal announcement of the Taoist mourning rites for Wang Su-ming, to be held at the Taoist temple in Gerrard Street, starting from tomorrow noon. It would last for five days.

The phone never stopped ringing after that. They'd all seen the papers. First to get through was Janet Rae-Smith: concerned, was there anything she could do? Holly got rid of her. Next was Marika. Holly did likewise. Then came Mother: likewise.

Enough. Off the hook.

She drank some Oolong. Talked to GiGi. Thought about Jenny. Tomorrow night. *Chi-pi*.

When she was good and ready, she called Mick Coulson for an update.

'Think you're so clever now?' was his immediate response. 'I'm history, Holly. You got me? You never heard of DS Coulson.'

194

'Maybe, maybe not,' replied Holly. 'But it was your pals at Scotland Yard who arranged my little night flight.'

'Night flight? What are you talking about?'

'Oh, didn't the papers say? I was a privileged guest on a Metropolitan Police helicopter direct from the roof of Scotland Yard, Victoria Street, Detective Sergeant.'

'You're not serious?' He sounded definitely worried.

'Never been more so. If I ever come across that particular bunch again they might be lighter by a dangling sphere or two.'

Mick spluttered nervously. 'The only ones who get to use the helipad would have to be at least commander level.'

'Or else their Masonic Lodgers.'

'My God, you've got to keep my name out of this, Holly. This could mean my career.'

'Your career, my life,' said Holly, bone-dry. 'Let me think: yes, well, it depends, doesn't it?'

'Depends on what?'

'Depends on you helping me nail the Treatment and the people who hired them for the job.'

'That's another thing I wanted to tell you: your lad's out on the street. Sorry.'

'The man say's he's sorry!' she sneered. 'Can't say I'm surprised, though. When applied to rape, the rule of law suddenly develops testicles.'

Mick ignored her comment. 'The magistrate listened to your tape in chambers and found it inadmissible.'

'Inadmissible my eye! It's a full and complete confession, including reference to the professional agent who hired the felon and his pals to systematically rape a series of young Oriental girls. What more do you men need?'

'I'm afraid it gets worse,' said Mick. 'The alleged rapist, Dexter Danny Alderman, very rapidly got himself represented by an expert brief. Charlesworth Cadwallader, QC.'

'Charley the Cad,' Holly said bitterly. 'Only one of the best criminal lawyers in the country. No prizes for guessing who paid his seven hundred quid an hour.'

'Yeah, well, Cadwallader came damn near to convincing the magistrate that he should be bringing charges against you. Luckily he'd just used the argument the tape was inadmissible, so the judge didn't want to know. But your name is dirt.'

'So the magistrate let Alderman off scot-free and he's out on the street.'

'Insufficient evidence.'

'It doesn't matter,' she muttered. 'I'm after the ones with manicured nails who pay the Dexter Dannys of this world to do their dirty work. I'll be needing your help.'

'Listen to me, just for once, Holly,' said Mick, his voice panicky. 'Give it up. You're out of your league. Go and stay in the country for the next six months, paint the mushrooms, smoke some pot, stand on your head and do yoga – I don't give a fig what you do. Just get the hell out of London and my patch. Those boys have to react. A lone, female private investigator? Gotta be jesting, karate, kung fu notwithstanding. At some point down the line they'll come for you, and they won't come alone. According to whispers I've heard, there's a score of steel-toed Doc Martens with your name on them.'

'So what's new?' said Holly. 'Half of Chinatown, most of the senior Met and a bunch of halfwits wearing Union Jack willy-warmers are after me.'

'Well, I tried,' sighed Mick. 'Just leave my name well out of it.'

'No way, pal. You're going to help me get Wendell or whoever is really behind this whole thing.'

'Forget it. Don't even bother calling because I won't be home.'

'In which case, expect to see your name featured in an in-depth investigative article which will cover at least two pages of one of the serious Sundays. A juicy scandal linking senior Met officers, a bunch of highly placed city financiers, right-wing extremists and the cover-up of a series of orchestrated rapes of Oriental ELS students.'

Mick pleaded, begged, cursed. To no avail. Holly figured she'd be needing his wrist-implement access to GCHQ's giant Crays at Cheltenham.

Before he rang off, he said something which disturbed her. Expressed with levity, he couldn't disguise a change in attitude towards her. 'By the way,' he said. 'I listened to that tape myself. With crossed legs. Holly-Jean, the kid sounded like that tortured airman paraded on Iraqi TV. What the hell did you do to him?'

'You'd rather not know.'

She left the phone off the hook and busied herself at her work station till Minty came back.

He was terse. He'd parked the Rover over on Harmood Street, the keys were on the table. Said he'd be going down to north Devon for a few days to see his three-year-old daughter Maisie and her mother Jane. He went to the cottage most fortnights for a few days but Holly got the feeling he wouldn't be back in a hurry this time.

She paid him off, handsomely and with genuine affection. His goodbye didn't meet her eyes. Holly-Jean, you frock-up.

Ah, well. Time to get to work.

She called the John Augustus Talent Agency. He had nothing much. A couple of the dancers in the original troupe had been located, they'd taken other gigs in East Asia. No sign of Tracy as yet. 'I'll keep at it, sweety.'

'Lest you forget to,' said Holly heavily, 'it's only a few paces from Chinatown to your office.'

'Are you threatening me, Ms Ho?' John Augustus's voice rose petulantly. 'I think you ought to know I tape all calls.'

'Make sure the tape's working and listen to this,' said Holly. 'The specialists of the Bamboo Union Society nowadays wear full scuba diving gear for their work. The threat of AIDS from even the smallest spot of spilt blood, you understand. They roll out the plastic sheeting, then start with the appendages – the toes, the nipples, the penis, whichever is the smallest . . .' She let the black humour sink in. 'Then they work their way up to the limbs. The resulting bundle is rolled up and collected by the daily slop run out to the Chinese-owned pig farms of Essex. Main source of pork for the restaurants of Chinatown. Very ecological, recycled Gussie. Organic. Sustainable. Doing your bit for the planet.'

'Yelp.'

'You said it.' She put the phone down. Caught sight of

herself in the mirror. What demon had possessed her? Was it just reaction to all the turbulence? The turbulence that had begun with Wang Ma-ma and Kettner's, or had violence entered her life to stay?

There were two ways to look at the problem. Western: armchair shrinkery. Freud, Jung, Skinner, R.D. Laing. Personally she preferred k. d. Chinese: Exorcism. Infinitely more practical. Routine cure for ghoulies, ghosties and things that go bump in the brain. Not your Max Von Sydow job. Just a couple of places to visit.

But first back to business. She called Mrs Vinnicombe in Poole. Dissembled and comforted. 'Some progress, I'm happy to report.'

'God bless you, my love. So where's Tracy?'

She sounded so expectant, it nearly broke Holly to have to say, 'Not quite yet, Mrs V. But I've spoken to the agent and he's getting his skates on. I've spoken to Taipei. I've got feelers out everywhere and everyone's working flat out, so do try and stop worrying. We're nearly there. I'll have Tracy on the phone by next week. That's a promise.'

'Oh. You haven't found her then.' Mrs Vinnicombe's voice had dropped. Holly heard Wang Ma-ma's cynical echo.

'I promise you I'll find her.'

'It's always the same,' the woman's voice broke. 'It's all talk. And I sit here like some damn old cow doing absolutely nothing. My God! Do you know how a mother feels? You've got to help me, please, please, I . . . I just don't know how long I can go on. The waiting and nothing, nothing. I have money, I'll take out a second mortgage, I'll go to Taipei myself if I have to. But I can't stand any more waiting! Tracy, my darling girl, where are you?' Mrs Vinnicombe sobbed noisily.

Holly tried to soothe her with a few words, but in the end all she could do was say, 'I'll try my best, that's a solemn promise. Goodbye Mrs Vinnicombe,' and gently lay down the receiver.

She did her breathing routine for a few minutes. Emptied the weight of others' emotions. Whoever said the PI's life was all twilit glamour and sunshades forgot to mention you have to leave your heart on hold.

She rode up to Highgate, to the gym for a solo work-out, avoiding Tommy Chen. She flailed the air till her body was heaving and spent. First place of exorcism. The second would have to wait till tomorrow.

Telling herself she had nothing better to do but actually feeling an unaccustomed pang of despair, she dropped by Marika's wine bar for a glass of kir and a chat with Charley and the gang, purposely choosing the busiest time of the evening when Marika would be rushed off her feet, socialising with her customers, dispensing the joyous charm which had made her wine bar famous. Thus they spoke only a few pleasantries while Holly savoured Charley's gossip – real lives, banal and comforting. Well before closing, Holly slipped out and home.

Tuesday she went for Wendell.

Jenny had left her the file. Posing as a journalist for the Taiwanese monthly, *Business in Taiwan*, she obtained from the Institute of Directors the names of the board, voting and non-voting members, and all senior company officers. Using her networking codes, she posed as a credit-rating agency to access Wendell's financial status. She needn't have bothered. They were extremely credit-worthy.

Wendell Securities was a Luxembourg-registered trading company, eighty per cent of whose shareholdings were owned by an entity called King Strong Corporation. Holly networked for an hour or so until she found someone who got her access to Luxembourg. Then she set about trawling for information concerning King Strong.

After hours of frustration dealing with a Luxembourgian miasma of electronic subterfuge, no hard information was forthcoming. This was only to be expected from that tight-lipped financial hub. Finally, by resorting to the threat of legal redress owing to loss of billions of yen in a convoluted foreign exchange deal unless a transaction was completed before the close of US markets today, a contact address was finally extracted. KSC was based at P.O. Box 1079, Turks and Caicos Islands.

Dead end. For now.

She looked at her watch. Nine in the evening. She had an appointment in Chinatown. The second place of exorcism.

She dressed in white and rode downtown. For the Chinese, white is the colour of death.

The Taoist temple was situated on the second floor of an old brick warehouse in one of the tiny alleys in the hidden warren behind Gerrard Street. The reception area was packed with Chinatown regulars paying their respects and signing their names on a silk bereavement sheet. Some handed over cash-stuffed *bai-baus* – white envelopes instead of the usual red. Others left white-wrapped gifts, XO brandy or costly high-mountain Oolong.

The Wang clan were distinguished by their head gear – peaked hoods roughly sewn from unrefined rice sacking. The professional mourners were wailing deafeningly into karaokes to the traditional live accompaniment of crude screeching reed pipes, crashing cymbals and banging gongs. The relentless din was to frighten away any restless evil spirits who might want to inhabit Su-ming's dead body.

The temple was thick with the smell of incense and cut flowers. All white, chrysanthemums or camellias, towering teardrop arrangements of solid blooms, set on bamboo stands and reaching to the ceiling. People moved with lowered heads. They would *ker-tou* to the deities on entering, head to the floor three times, before abasing themselves at the closed coffin and the motionless, bowed Wang family sitting in attendance on either side of the wooden box.

Holly laid her flowers on the lower steps with the lesser offerings. Keeping her head down, she approached the Wang family and bowed thrice as was custom. As she turned back, she confirmed an awareness that had been growing since she'd entered the temple, that other heads were turning away from her. Aversion to her. People she'd known all her life. They blamed her. Her meddling had cost Su-ming her life. She looked down. The thought struck with sadness that ached in her chest that the temple floor would remain unlicked, the prayer of a mother had gone unanswered.

Mother. There she was on the far side, sitting with her mates. Another thought: shunned by her own tribe, with Mother apparently set on leaving, not only was she to lose her childhood home, she had already lost her spiritual home in the Chinatown community.

The cymbals of the mourners clashed loudly. She met her Mother's eyes as she found herself a spot to kneel, and Ma nodded sadly. The funeral of a daughter. The Chinese were no different from the rest of the world. To lose a child is the greatest heartbreak. For the Han, it is the greatest calamity – even worse had it been a son. The Chinese family is revered, comes before all else; it is the reason for living and the focus of one's life of unremitting toil. The rationale behind all that insane reverence for money is the protection of the family's future.

And Holly knew that, like all Chinese mothers, hers was waiting for the day Holly gave birth. The piercingly sad look she had just sent Holly across the crowded temple was compounded by that lack of progeny. The reason for the return to Taipei was a signal that she was losing faith in her daughter.

Holly looked up at the serene womanly smile of Merciful Goddess, Kuan Yin. It had been a long while since she'd waved smouldering incense sticks, the act of *bai-bai*, and said her prayers. It was time she gave it a try.

She drifted a long drowsy while on the din of the mourners and the fumes of the incense. At some point she felt the smile smile. Nice goddess.

Stiff-kneed, she got up. Bowed once more the requisite three times, and walked out of there, blinking in the sunlight.

Sunlight? She looked at her watch. Five thirty in the morning! The Street was alive with market traders. And a song came to her, an old favourite, Katrina and the Waves, and she let rip, oblivious of the disapproving stares of the locals. 'I'm walking on sunshine . . . oh yeah! An' it makes me feel so good, yeah-yeah!'

She revved the Yamaha to a blue-clouded scream and took off.

At home, she showered and tidied up the place, for Jenny coming in from Barcelona tonight. She booked Orso for a table for two at lunch and called her best journalist *guanchi*, Sid Psmith, who worked for the *Independent on Sunday*.

'Orso's a bore,' he said, which meant it was too late in the month for his expense account.

'You want the story or not?'

'Who's paying for lunch?'

'You, when you hear what I've got.'

He paid for the lunch and left before dessert to call a photographer from Magnum Agency to meet him at Waterloo for the afternoon train to Bournemouth. Holly headed home on a high. Katrina wouldn't budge from her head, 'Walkin' on sunshine . . .' over and over, as she stopped by Camden Lock and bought a bunch of freesias, a bag of croissants and some freshly roasted Blue Mountain. Back upstairs she opened a bottle of Gewurztraminer, sloshed in ice cubes and mineral water, and sat down at the screen.

Turks and Caicos would be a nice place to spend the afternoon, do a little scuba, soak up some UV before building a driftwood fire and hollering a few beach bums over to partake of barbecued red snapper and icebox Red Stripe. Failing that, the computer screen and the modem would have to substitute. She accessed the local British Chamber of Commerce via the International Directory, reached a fax and phone number, and decided to shelve the electronics for the personal touch. She checked the time zones, put up her feet and dialled the morning sun.

In her most honeyed tones, Holly asked if there was anyone that end who could possibly help her in a little matter – calling from London, Whitehall actually.

The girl who answered spoke posh Caribbean. 'Mistah Redaway's naht in de ahfice raight now, mee ay be av sahm assees-tahnce?' she said.

'Gosh. Super. Would you?'

'Pleeshure. Mee ah intrahdeuce meeself, Mz Aidelita De Cruz, bot me frenz carl me Aida.'

'Aida. Wonderful. Now, there's a little something the people upstairs want to know—'

But Aida wasn't finished with her intro. 'Ay'm de BCC Poblic Relaightions Officur, ay'm arlso de President of de Prestige Toarstmarsters Interna-tion-al Turks an' Caicos Branch, Treasurer av de International Lai-yons Club av de Turks and Caicos, an' dis year's Gran Mistress av de Turks an' Caicos 'ash 'ouse 'arriers.'

'You're a Hasher? Super! On-on!' Holly had run the Jakarta Hash on a Micronet trip. Loved the jungle run, hated the beer-sodden, prick-exposing après ritual of

Down-downs. 'Ms Macpherson. Cynthia. OBE, actually,' she neighed. 'I'm a senior aide to the personal assistant of the Junior Under-Secretary, Foreign and Commonwealth Section, Export Division of the Board of International Trade, Department EQ 27. I've a little enquiry, on behalf of the powers that be, the junior minister, if you must know,' she confided *sotto voce*. A sharp intake of breath beamed halfway round the world. Aida was impressed.

'We need any background information currently available concerning King Strong Corporation. Perhaps you've come across them . . . socially?'

Aidelita certainly had. Why, her best friend Josephine worked as a company secretary for King Strong Corporation. How fortuitous, commented Holly. Well, to tell the truth, Aida intimated, like a lot of the companies registered in T&C, there wasn't much actual what you'd call day-to-day business transacted. Just a lot of phoning, faxing, E-mail and trips to the bank next door. Otherwise just replying to messages from the head offices and making sure the computers were kept working and dust-free. You know the sort of thing. Holly knew exactly the sort of thing.

So the head office in the case of King Strong would be where exactly? Oh, Hong Kong, of course, but then your boss would already know that, wouldn't he. Yes, yes, it had slipped her mind, said Holly. There wouldn't be the remotest chance of Josephine letting Aida have a couple of things she could fax over, like a company letterhead, a brochure, a list of the board of management? Holly would be most appreciative and in her capacity as a senior civil servant in Whitehall, London, would have no hesitation in putting forward Aidelita's name for possible consideration in the annual honours lists.

The faxes arrived a couple of hours later. Holly learned two things to her advantage. The first was that King Strong Corporation was wholly owned by a parent organisation, MacKinnon Hsiamen, which was registered in Hong Kong and traded as a blue chip on the Hang Seng index. The assets of Mac H, as everyone in Hong Kong referred to them, were estimated to be around three billion US dollars. Everyone also knew that MacKinnon Hsiamen, the venerable Scots trading house which had first set up trade in Amoy and Swatow in the early eighteen hundreds, had been acquired two years ago by the Taiwan family-owned company PANG. And if you hadn't heard of PANG, then you'd never picked up the *Asian Wall Street Journal* or bothered to peruse the odd back issue of the *Economist* when sitting in your dentist's waiting room. Providing, that is, your dentist was like Holly's, who'd just traded in his last year's Benz for this year's Lexus.

Holly knew all about PANG. They covered a lot of ground. It included shipping – they owned the second biggest container fleet in the Far East; a fast-growing Asian airline, Asiatica – Asian routes so far, but looking to merge with Aussie Mitchell Air for their global landing rights; leisure, hotels, resort complexes, golf courses throughout the region. They had just signed a deal with the Pathet Lao to help capitalism bloom via the Number Seven iron. Holly scanned her memory: textiles, factories all over greater China. Shoes, likewise.

Electronics – computers, integrated circuit boards, OED manufacturing, peripherals. And they owned the tallest building in East Asia, PANG Tower, on Tunhua South Road, Taipei.

Okay. So the first thing she'd learned was that Wendell Securities was nothing other than a point gnat for PANG. The second thing she'd learned from the T&C faxes troubled her greatly, and since she couldn't yet figure out its significance she put it to one side in her mind. Store and simmer, till time was ripe for comprehension.

She put on some summery evening clothes, white XL Captain Haddock T-shirt over black calf-length cotton. She had a date with Mother and the estate agent at the Bull and Last on Highgate Road.

'Market's slow, he said, 'but you'll get a good price. Parliament Hill's on the doorstep, families, fresh air, the walks. Lovely selling points.'

Holly didn't distrust the man, which was quite something. She thought he'd do a fair deal. As for Mother, she disconcerted Holly by flourishing a plane ticket. Her flight was in two weeks' time.

'Why the rush, Ma?' said Holly, after the agent had departed.

'*Shao-lan*, something in my bones says go now or else it'll be too late. You want to really know something? Something of significance?' The glitter in Mother's eye was one Holly had seen countless times since her childhood. It presaged apparently momentous events, usually connected with the supernatural, the occult, or Mother's much-quoted skill of prophecy. Usually good value, entertainment wise.

'Go on,' said Holly with her glass of beer hovering halfway to her lips.

'You'll be coming with me!' Ma cackled triumphantly.

The beer was gulped, nearly went down the wrong way. Holly knew better than to say another word. She just walked Mother home.

It was getting on for eight thirty when she arrived at the gym. Tommy Chen had asked her to sit in on his final selection for the female team to represent England at the European aikido championships coming up in Prague in a few weeks. She knew he had an ulterior motive: to fire up her engines enough to get her to put herself up for selection. But Holly-Jean had assessed herself thoroughly. Apart from the fact that, having taken on Wendell she was going to be far too busy, most likely unavailable, the toll of recent events, Su-ming foremost among them, had reduced her mental fitness way below performance par. Since the martial disciplines were as much a mental as a physical activity, she thus ruled herself out from selection. At international level the best was what you offered – all or nothing. So she sat on her haunches by the tatami mats and watched the trials.

Two ferocious black Liverpudlians who had trained together since early teens were straightforward first choices in Holly's estimation. In fact the standard had rocketed in recent years. Holly felt her age, figured she'd have been the oldest one in the team by far had she been selected. She'd have been the best, but still the oldest. Sombre thought. Soon she'd be too old – next year, or the year after that. Still, there was a while to go before senility set in.

It was late when the bouts finished and Chen *Lao-shr* had given his pep talk.

Holly had deliberately restrained from using the public phone to call the studio and see if Jenny had arrived yet. In the first place it would have been bad form to leave the tatami before the last bout was over. Secondly, she enjoyed both the exercise of mental discipline required and the luscious building of anticipation. Besides, on the tatami, her mind went to another place.

It was after midnight when she'd said her goodbyes and good lucks to the team and Tommy Chen and bestrode the Yamaha with a grin a yard wide. Anticipating Jenny.

Silly girl had left the front door unlocked.

Holly stopped mid-hallway. GiGi was marauling strangely, shimmying against the wall towards her, his fur spiked up, tail jerking nervily. Something was up.

Holly dropped her bag and raced down to her studio door. It was ajar.

Jenny.

She threw herself into the flat, slapping on all the lights, and came to a sudden halt as illumination flooded the place.

There began a scream, a scream without sound, without end.

Her mouth clamped, her eyes saw, her mind shut down. It refused to work. Not for a long while. Not while she picked up her beloved GiGi and began crooning into his neck, pacing back and forth. Not while she put him down and began punching the wall till her fists were mangled and bloody.

Not until she forced herself over to the bed and slowly knelt down till her head rested on the soft, cold belly. For this was Jenny, her love. Spread like a beached starfish as in that first dawn light, that first time. Only this was different. This was terribly, terribly wrong. For Jenny's beautiful hands and feet were bound with red silk cord to the four corners of the bed.

Her body wasn't. Four neat severings had untethered her.

11

She didn't do much for a while. Just sat at the table, watching the slap and flow of a black inner sea while the daylight grew outside.

When she was ready she didn't call the police. Instead she called the number the *Ju Lyan Bang* officer had given her. It took a while to reach him. But when finally his voice came on the phone, it was clear he was awake, occupied and expecting her call.

'It was reported to me earlier that your studio received visitors. I was given to understand you were not present, so no intervention at that time was felt necessary.'

Holly swore in Hakka at him. 'My best friend was slaughtered by shit-eating cowards!'

The BBC phonemes spoke on as calmly as if discussing the weather. 'And who have you spoken to?'

'Nobody. I called you first.'

'Could you explain why you haven't called the police?'

'The . . .' She couldn't bring herself to describe the horror at the other end of her studio. 'Looks . . . Chinese.'

'Is it, ah, wet?'

At that point Holly smashed the telephone onto the table and repeatedly punched her knees till the pain cleared her head, then she picked up the phone again.

'Calm yourself,' he cooed. 'I shall expedite matters. Stay put. Don't use the phone. Speak to no one, admit no one. I will call from the car phone to let you know when I arrive.'

It was a long while before he came. With him were the silent ones. On entering the studio, he took Holly's hand and placed a little silver grinder in her palm. He closed her fingers over it. 'Go to the bathroom, ingest a little of this in both nostrils. It will ease the pain.'

She looked at the ornate object and knew it for what it was. But then the men began shoving furniture about, tearing off black PVC bags from a roll and she couldn't face that. So off she went. Why not? she said to her swollen reflection in the bathroom mirror. Chinese traditional medicine.

As soon as the heroin hit her nasal passages, suffused the capillaries and entered her blood, her system immediately rejected the toxin and she threw up a great gushing, purging fountain of bile and half-digested food. She looked at it swirling down the sink plug hole and heard her own voice, cracked, distant: 'Let all my sentiment and sorrow be gone. From now on only anger will inhabit this body.'

Very shortly after that, things began to get a lot better, a lot clearer, and the black tide inside her skull ebbed and disappeared. She cleaned up, brushed her teeth, dabbed scent behind her ears, and went back out of the bathroom to face the world again.

She sat down at the table with her back to the proceedings, picked up GiGi and stroked him.

Mr Plum Blossom sat down opposite her, pocketed the silver grinder. 'Will you be needing more?'

'Nope. I've got work to do. I can't afford to waste time in the land of nod.'

Pleased, he bowed his head. 'Yes, I did not take you for an invertebrate. You wish to make a fight of this?'

'It's already begun.'

One of his men came over and placed something on the table.

Holly glanced quickly at it then away, before her eyes flickered back, dragged by the fascination of something she could only describe as the embodiment of evil. The red silk cords which had tied down her friend. Blood-spotted, a darker splash of vermilion.

She stared, filled her eyes, her head, with the image, entering her as rage.

The *lao-ban* picked up the silk cords, studied them carefully. Then pulling a piece of decorative material from his pocket he wrapped them up carefully, placed the oblong cloth object down on the table before Holly.

'Something significant?' asked Holly.

'Very. But nothing that concerns you. Just yet,' he added.

'What the hell do you mean? She was my best friend. I fully intend to hunt down those responsible.'

'And then what? Do you expect to fly off to Taiwan on the next plane? Do you think you, a single female, could take on the entire *Fei Ying Bang*?' But he was smiling. Goading her. There was far more to come, Holly knew.

'The *Fei Ying Bang*?' she said. 'Flying Eagles. Taiwanese triad.' Rae-Smith's fireside chat.

'Yes, these three.' He pulled three Polaroids from his pocket and laid them on the table. 'Mid-level soldiers. Left by private plane from Chigwell a few hours ago. I have just received reports of their boarding the KLM nightly Amsterdam–Bangkok–Taipei flight.'

Holly studied the faces in the Polaroids. Three shaved heads, with a single pony tail, contemporary fashion mimicking the loathsome *queue*, the shaved skull with single long plaited pigtail that the Manchu emperors forced the Han Chinese to wear as an act of obeisance.

'The society comprises ethnic Fukienese/Taiwanese. It is more than a hundred years old. Its headquarters are in Taipei, Kaohsiung and Hsiamen. Taiwan is their stronghold. They are our deadliest rivals on the island and from their base in Fukien Province throughout the mainland. Now it appears they also wish to defy us in the global diaspora.'

Holly didn't speak. Kept staring at the photos.

He went on, 'You recall mentioning Wendell Securities.'

She gave him her attention. Dear Jenny's incredulous joke about murderously lucrative English as a second language. Now maybe she'd hear the real motive behind all of it.

'Wendell Securities is a Luxembourg-registered trading company,' said the triad officer, 'whose majority shareholdings are owned by King Strong Corporation, a company based in the Turks and Caicos Islands. King Strong is wholly owned by a parent organisation,

MacKinnon Hsiamen, registered in Hong Kong and listed on the Hang Seng index with assets totalling well over two billion US dollars.'

'I know all about it. It's part of PANG,' intoned Holly.

'PANG is the grand achievement of Pang Chong-ts,' he continued.

'I know that too.'

'But what you may not know is that Pang is a superior *lao-ban* of the *Fei Ying Bang*.' For a second Mr Plum Blossom's composure slipped; under the mask Holly saw naked malice, and she recoiled as he spat out, '*Go-dr tong sying-lien!*' Dog-arse fucker! He composed himself. Brushed a hand through his hair. 'One of our most troublesome and persistent adversaries. The rivalry goes back to the early days of the *Kuo-ming Tang*, the KMT, the nationalist Chinese who until recently our society supported as the rightful rulers of China.'

There was a crash from the rear end of the studio.

He yelled, 'Take care, *go-pi nau!* Dog-fart brain!' Mr Plum Blossom's nerves were betraying him. Worse, his soothing narrative peppered with explosive foul invective was threatening to unravel the blanket of poppy sap. Holly closed her eyes and watched the glow inside her skull, half listening to the silky voice. 'Pang was a lowborn Fukienese, a turtle egg of Hsiamen/Amoy pirate descent on his father's side and a Swatownese concubine for a mother. He was shunned by the Sun Yat-sen clique, but the good doctor himself liked Pang. But when *Guo-fu* died, all that changed.'

Holly noted his reverence for Dr Sun, according him

the title Father of the Nation. It signified little, she'd never met a Chinese yet who didn't.

'The Chiang Kai-shek faction, the Whampoa Military Academy cronies, took over the Party in the twenties, and Pang was thrown out. From that moment he turned his full attention to crime and swore eternal hatred for the KMT and, by extension, ourselves. The result is PANG Corporation, always in the Forbes top fifty.'

'Cut the history.' Holly had had enough. 'Just tell me why Jenny was murdered.'

'My dear Ho *Shao-jye*, Little Miss, you can hardly expect to go poking your nose into Wendell without upsetting the corporate owners. PANG may be huge, but they keep a very tight rein on even their tiniest investments. Such as Oxbridge ELSI.'

That rang a bell. A steeple-full of bells in fact. Holly fished the name from the stored information on simmer. Oxbridge was the rival chain of language schools represented by Wendell Securities who'd wanted to buy out Ravensdale. Unbelievable.

'You mean to tell me Oxbridge ELSI are part of PANG?'

'A tiny off-shoot, but yes, it's PANG.'

Holly's mind whirred. If Oxbridge were PANG – but there was something else too. Something bubbling up from the simmering pot. Ding Hao Entertainments . . . who had made the booking with the Augustus Talent Agency that had sent Tracy Vinnicombe to Taipei. Ding Hao had an office on Tunhua South Road in Taipei and Tunhau South Road was PANG Tower's address too.

But if Ding Hao was part of PANG too, that made one neat coincidence too many. She'd always made it a rule to reject the vagaries of chance when dealing with the Han. Their reptilian brains headed off fate well before the creek.

'Ever heard of Ding Hao Entertainments?' she enquired casually.

Plum Blossom's eyes glittered for a brief second, but the signal was clear. 'You're maybe too smart for a Little Miss.'

So Tracy Vinnicombe's disappearance points east and the attack on Chen Ba-tsun were connected. But how the frock did the smooth-talking gangster sitting next to her know of her interest in Ding Hao and Oxbridge?

'Your mother is due to fly out to Taipei a week on Monday, correct?'

Hell's balls, thought Holly.

'You yourself have some pressing affairs in Taiwan. The missing girl Tracy and other matters.'

Holly flared. 'Would you mind telling me just how long you've been spying on me?'

But not even Holly's genetic tendency prepared her for his answer. 'On one level or another, since you were born,' said the perfectly shaved Chinaman.

She stared at him with mouth agape and a look of dementia.

'You have been under our protection since your English father impregnated your mother thirty years ago.'

Oh Mother, thought Holly.

As if he could read her thoughts, he nodded and said, 'The Ho clan has always been well represented in our society.'

She didn't know whether to feel comforted or repelled by this news of her criminal antecedents.

'You recall I spoke earlier of your debt to the society. As events have transpired, now would be a propitious moment to expunge the claim. My men have finished here. All traces of evidence linking the event to the *Fei Ying Bang* have been removed. They are now *our* concern,' he emphasised. 'I suggest you call the police within the next hour. I will be in contact with you shortly with details.' He got up to go.

'Fine,' she murmured, her brain handling the overload of new information. 'Wait!' she called. 'Details? What details?'

'Of your flight to Taipei, of course.'

'Excuse me?'

He picked up the cloth package and followed his men to the door.

'I decide if and when I go anywhere, pal,' she shouted after him.

He stopped, looked back at her with a bland smile, unable, it seemed, to dignify her outburst with a response. He closed the door behind him.

She heard their feet clatter down the iron staircase. Then silence.

GiGi mewed and banged his eyebrow against her shin. Absent-mindedly she reached down and swept her hand through his comforting fur. What would she do without GiGi? She continued to stare at the door.

Slowly the thought sank to earth. It's not as if I've got a choice here. You don't negotiate with the Bamboo Union. You just continued to live. Limbs intact.

Oh. *Jenny*.

She stood up, shook her head violently. Breathed deep. All right. She knew the rules. She'd read the book. She believed she had just got the goodbye look.

She reached for the phone and called the police. 'There's been a murder . . .'

Mick Coulson arrived just after the locals. She'd mentioned his name. He took one look and claimed the crime for ALCO. Metropolitan Police CID from Belsize Park arrived. Followed by forensics, the photographer, the duty doctor. Then suspiciously soon afterwards the press came, slavering at the gory rumours of ritual death, dismemberment. A rabble of nationals and North London locals snorting and squealing like stuck swine.

Mick came through for her, herding the scrum of flashlights and microphones back down the iron staircase. He called Marika to come and pick Holly up. Holly spent the rest of the early morning above the wine bar, drinking giant glasses of claret to numb the last brain cell into submission. When she lolled forward and her eyes closed, Marika and Charley the bartender, who had a room somewhere in the building, hefted her into a bed.

She woke mid-morning with a hangover crashing enough to suppress the formation of sentiment. Instead she took a breath, three cups of double espresso sent up from downstairs and faced the questions snapping like

Dobermans. Was the Bamboo Union officer really real? He said she was obligated, she would have to go to Taipei, but why? What was it that so involved her? Could all that guff about a lifetime's surveillance possibly be true? Or was it just emotional fabric softener setting her up for something else again? Something arcane as a Chinese set-up within a set-up? A merciless charade? The three men in the Polaroids could be anyone. An exotic lure with shaven heads and plaited queues with Jenny playing the sacrificial lamb? Or was that a mere case of mistaken identity? Her friend tragically being in the right place at the wrong time?

It boiled down to one question: why all that effort to lure one lowly female software piracy investigator to Taipei? She was no match for their male violence, their brain power, their incredible ancient skill at lethal power games.

Tamada! You addled monkey-brain! You should have known from the moment the old dragon started going on about Taipei . . .

Upstairs was Marika's private line, unconnected with the wine bar downstairs – that phone never stopped ringing with bookings. Mother was out or not answering. Holly's skin prickled, *chi-pi*. She'd best go round. Meanwhile a call to Margot. To break the news.

'Margot? It's me, Holly.'

'Holly, lovely to hear from you. How's everything?'

'There's no way I can say this without pain, so take three deep breaths. Right now. Do you understand?'

There was silence. Margot was unaccustomed to

taking orders; something in Holly's voice must have made her compliant and her voice came back tiny. 'Three deep breaths?'

'Yes, please, Margot. Now.'

Margot did so, while Holly counted. Then she told her the news. Margot whispered thanks and cut the line.

Janet Rae-Smith next.

'Don't go to Taipei, Toots,' she said after she'd said all the right things about Jenny. If anyone could handle news like that, it was Janet. 'Last place on earth you want to be. Far too dangerous.'

'But Taipei's *Ju Lyan Bang* territory. I'd be under their protection.'

'This ain't the movies, kiddo. Wise up. How in the hell do you protect anyone from a boy on the back of a Sanyang Vespa carrying a blown duck egg full of nitric acid?'

Holly thought about that one for a second. 'What do you know about PANG conglomerate's little offshoots?' she asked, needing confirmation that the Bamboo Union officer's story was solid on facts. 'Two small outfits. Ding Hao Entertainments, Oxbridge ELSI.'

'Easily done. I've got a friend at Dai-shuo Securities in the City, she's their Taiwan expert.'

Holly gave her both her mother's number and Marika's.

'I'll try and get back to you today,' said Janet. 'Just one thing, Holly. Right now you're acting under massive stress. You can hardly expect the old synapses to behave rationally. What I'm trying to say is, do you know why you're going? And don't give me any flim-flam about obligations, Chinese ancestry or any other excuse you can dig up. Because if the reflex is what I think it is, then I'm going to do everything in my power to dissuade you.'

'And what do you think it is?' said Holly.

'Revenge.'

Holly rang off. Her body had flooded with adrenaline and her lips tingled. Immediately the phone rang again. It was Mick Coulson. He'd notified next of kin, for which Holly thanked him. Then he went into a gloomy report on the police investigation. Complained that the Drug Squad heavies were trying to muscle ALCO out of the running. She got rid of him. She didn't mention Taipei.

She sat for a moment watching the embers of Marika's sandalwood log fire; the blue scent was a lovely affectation, but wrong for now when Holly needed to be alive, every brain cell hard, cold and marching. Maybe Janet was right. Maybe she was irrational. Maybe it was revenge. Who cared?

An awareness crept over her that she'd overlooked something. She reran the tape in her skull. Nothing percolated. Something . . .

GiGi! Damn it all, she'd completely forgotten Hopalong!

She let herself quietly out of the wine bar flat and found a mini-cab office on the corner of Barnsbury Road. Turkish pin-ups and not a razor blade in sight. A cherished 3.8 S-type Jag took her back to Camden Lock mercifully without too much leery chit-chat. She got down at the iron bridge over the canal and walked the last of the way.

Marow! 'Sorry, sweetheart!' The comforting fur rubbed her ankles as she climbed the staircase. She stopped at the front door and took a deep breath, then entered the changed place.

Police tape decorated her door. Minty emerged from across the way. 'Came up as soon as I heard from Coulson.' Bless him.

'Thanks. I'm going to be going away. Can you take GiGi down to Devon?'

'Going where?'

'Taipei.'

'*Taipei*?' Minty swore an exotic oath.

'Taipei.'

'When?'

'Day or two. Don't know exactly yet. Could you handle GiGi from now on?'

'How long are you going?'

'Don't know. Maybe a week.'

'Are you nuts?'

'Probably.' She dialled Mother again. No reply. She felt the sudden need to sweat.

While Minty sat at her kitchen table and talked about this and that, Holly skilfully managed to avoid full-face confrontation with her bed while she filled her sports bag with her kit.

'Right, I'm off to the gym.' With a last hug of grey fur and the hot whiff of anchovy breath, she handed her three-legged companion to Minty. 'Cat basket's in the closet. Be gone before I return.'

She unchained the Yamaha, very conscious of the concerned gaze of her two pals from the steps above her.

'Just don't say a word,' she said, without looking up. 'Please.'

They didn't.

At the gates to the lock she looked back and saw Minty holding GiGi's one front paw and wagging it in goodbye. She waved, clamped her jaws shut and rode like a banshee to Highgate, tears streaking her temples, cold on the night wind.

Tommy Chen was just finishing an advanced class when she arrived. The usual crowd of Armani yahoos of both sexes. She kept her head down and changed in the lee of her locker.

On the tatami she expunged.

Outside herself, she flew. Chen *Lao-shr* didn't have a chance. His handicap: he was Chinese, a man. Images unseen but conjured up from her studio acted as an ocean swell that pushed her *chi* on a tide of raw power. If you'd called it hate, you would have failed to understand the nature of the discipline invoked in this martial art. It was darker than that. From some other place.

Once or thrice Holly connected, unforgivably; she failed to feint at the last minute and nearly killed her teacher. The last time before he called the proceedings to an immediate halt, she was on the point of sliding her opponent's Adam's apple through the back of his neck.

'Enough!' shouted Chen, breathing hard, suddenly gripping her wrists in a vice hold. 'You are behaving intolerably!'

Holly stopped, stood back. '*Dwei-bu chi, lao-shr.*' She

bowed twice as she uttered the words of formal contrition and turned away.

They met at the juice bar after she'd showered. His first words worried her.

'I heard. So you are forgiven.'

'Heard what?' she asked.

'About your tragedy. Your friend. I am very sorry. Is there anything I can do?'

How could he know? Holly waved airily. 'No, no. It's over.'

'I sincerely trust you're not planning anything rash. I know you very well. It wouldn't be like you to lie down with the lambs.'

Holly looked at him but nothing was revealed in that teacher's mask. Still she dissembled.

'Maybe it's time to be a lamb for once. Really, there's nothing I can do,' she sighed. 'I'm thinking I'll just get away for a while, go down to Devon for a month in the country. Stay with Minty and Jane. Take a rest, breathe some fresh country air, regroup.'

'Good idea. You've been hard at it ever since you left Micronet and went freelance. You know, I was very hurt you left yourself out of the national team trials, but as your *lao-shr*, I can only be immensely proud. In fact, despite your tribulations, or maybe because of them, I'd say your fighting spirit has not diminished one bit.' He grinned wrily. 'You were like a bloody bolshie tiger out there.'

'Thanks for the compliment, *lao-shr*. Well, off to clotted cream land for me. I'll be in touch.'

'You do that,' he said.

Hard to fool Tommy Chen. Hard to know whether you fooled him.

With a formal blow, Tommy walked into his office behind the juice bar and closed the door. Holly picked up the guest phone sitting by a statue of Buddha at the end of the bar. She reached Mother and told her she was coming over. Then she dialled Janet Rae-Smith.

'Sorry, Stretch. Been busy. Any news?'

'Don't know whether I should be telling you this or not. The company addresses listed at the Ministry of Economic Affairs for both Ding Hao Entertainments and Oxbridge ELSI are one and the same, Number 291, Alley 67, Lane 285, Tunhua South Road, Section 1, Taipei.'

'No prizes. Rear end of the PANG building?'

'Bang on, Toots,' said Janet. 'Not only that but the MOEA has them registered under the same trading licence, a licence recently transferred from another company. No prizes for guessing.'

'One of PANG's.'

'All nice and cuddly under the paternal wing.'

Holly's intuition was slam-dancing. 'Far too bloody neat a coincidence if you ask me.'

'Maybe, maybe not. But does this mean you're on the next flight out? I sincerely counsel against it.'

'Dunno. But just in case, wish me luck and give me some friendly numbers to call.'

'On the record, I beg you not to go, Toots, but let me see.' She paused, presumably rummaging through her address book. 'Ah, here's one of the lads – Nick Mayo, English but works for Chemical Bank. Spook background,

228

I'd guess, spent a couple of years out of Oxford as an officer with the Gurkha Regiment in Hong Kong. What he doesn't know about Taipei sleaze isn't worth knowing.'

Holly noted down the number. 'Anyone else?'

'Yes, Stratton McMurtry, an ex-Jesuit missionary turned smart aleck consultant. Runs three-day seminars out of fancy Asian resorts. Part old-hand savvy, part mystic mumbo-jumbo, they try and teach the round-eye the art of negotiating with the yellow peril, at huge corporate expense but apparently results have proved worthwhile. At any rate, the big multis are queuing up to enrol. But that might be due to the lure of Club Med Ko Phangan.'

'Ta, Stretch,' said Holly when she'd got the number.

'Look, wee lassie, will ye nae listen tae reason? Ye dinna oughta go, hen.'

'Pilgrim, a gal's gotta do what a gal's gotta do.'

'Och, ye stubborn bitch.'

'True enough.'

'Nothing I can say?' said Janet.

'Nope.'

'Holly, Holly, Holly.'

'I know, I know, I know.'

'See ye's.'

Holly couldn't be sure whether she had imagined a click just after Janet broke the line, before she replaced the hand set. Probably just her paranoia, she said to herself climbing astride the Yamaha, revving high and wheel-spinning out into the night. Tommy Chen did love his gossip though, just as any Chinese good and true.

It was late when she parked outside Mother's. A cold

night wind came off Parliament Hill, carrying a familiar scent – an exotic hint of the far country in the heart of the city. This was the smell of her childhood. Our house. Our street. Where she'd played, grown up, gone through the mixer.

She pushed her key in the lock and entered. Home again.

She stood in the hall, drinking in the familiar currents and reviewing her decision. She'd pre-empt the bastards. Nobody told her when, where and what.

'Little Orchid! I was expecting you.'

'Sure, Ma.'

Mother's chicken soup was pretty superior. Unlike effete Westerners, the Chinese believed in using the whole chicken, including the head and feet, beak, beady eyes, claws and all. Mother's chicken soup swam with velvety abalone slices, winter-moth chrysalises, crimson seed pods, medicinal bark shavings, all soused in *mi-jou* rice wine. Heavy sopor. It made Holly drop her clothes and fall into her old bed. Tucked up under her Rajasthan mirrored bedspread, below Biba, Aladdin Sane and remembered fear of exams.

Mother came in to say goodnight, kissed and stroked her head, before turning at the door and switching off the light.

Holly propped herself up on one elbow. 'Ma, it's time you told me about Pang.'

Her mother's foul oath was followed by an endless silence. The bedroom was lit by only the dim landing light. Holly waited in a semi-intoxicated state of exhaustion and nerve-racking tension.

'Grandmother Chang-i, Dawn Fairy,' said her mother after an age. 'By golly, a first-rate woman, your dad used to say. Had to watch him when she was about. At fifty they said she was thirty. The famous gambler Lee Hong who lost a million kwai betting on how many times a frog would croak lost his reason trying to make her his *shao tai-tai*, but Chang-i would never agree. He struck her once in public and paid for it. She wouldn't accept that from anyone, no sirree. Came to a nasty end did Lee Hong.' She paused. In the darkness Holly held her breath. Her mother never ceased to amaze her, there was so much she'd never heard from her, so much there to hear. Given time.

Mother sighed. '*Ai-yo*. She was one of the great beauties of Taipei. The Japanese officers were sex-crazy about her!' Then she was silent for so long, presumably lost in memory, that finally Holly could stand it no longer.

'Ma, I've got to know. What's the story with Pang? Just who was Lee Hong?'

'Lee Hong? They were copulating, and just at the onset of Clouds and Rain my mother pushed an ivory chopstick clean into his ear.'

Holly digested that one. Mother turned to go.

'*Soy-ee?*'

'Didn't I say?' She stood in the light from the hallway. 'Lee Hong was the tycoon Pang's uncle and godfather.'

The door closed and after a long while Holly slept. Her night was filled with dreams of the restless dragon Cathay in days gone by.

Mother woke Holly at five thirty, her usual working

hour when after sipping tea she liked to walk up Parliament Hill to do her Tai Ch'i at the crest, looking down on St Paul's, Canary Wharf and, on good days, the Crystal Palace radio tower. But not today. Mother had a cab waiting to take them to Chinatown.

They walked through from Shaftesbury Avenue and entered the red doors of the Taoist temple. The place was busy as usual in the pre-dawn hours. Mother greeted her friends and bought incense and paper money to burn.

'Give the ancestors something to spend in heaven.'

'Any chance of coffee first?'

While Holly stood yawning, Mother spoke to one of the temple staff, an old man with an enormous bald copper head like a tea egg. He nodded sagely and pointed to the oracular batons. Mother came back and grabbed Holly's hand.

'First we pray, then we ask.' She made Holly *ker-tou* to all the various gods, then *bai-bai*, before placing the incense sticks in the urn. Since there were about five urns and seven gods, this took a while. Holly wondered if some forms of religion didn't keep the faithful bloody fit.

'Right,' said Mother when satisfied. 'Let's get on with it.' She stood in front of the baton container, bowed three times, tugging Holly down with her. 'Choose.'

Holly selected her baton. Mother read the inscription and handed Holly two fat wooden crescents. 'Number 51. I'll go and fetch the hexagram if you throw the *gao*. See what comes up, Little Orchid. Then we'll decide

232

whether you come to Taipei with me or not. Let the gods choose, far less trouble.'

Holly shrugged; who was she to argue with the awkward bundle of energy that was Mother? Whichever way the wooden crescents landed, both facing up, both facing down, or one up and one down – yes, no or maybe – Holly reckoned the decision had already been made, and not by the gods but by more temporal powers.

She got a 'Yes'.

Mother returned with a little scroll of paper tied with a red ribbon.

'What did you get?'

'A "Yes".'

'Right you are!' said Ma gleefully. She undid the knot and unrolled the scroll, then began to read the Mandarin explanation of Hexagram 51 of the Oracle of Change in dramatic tones, embarrassingly loudly it seemed to Holly but apparently ignored by everyone else milling about the temple.

'CHEN – Thunder,' she declaimed, holding the unfurled scrap of paper close to her glasses. 'AROUSING. Both trigrams identical. Arousing above! Arousing below! Sounds like fun, Little Orchid,' she said in a Hakkanese aside. 'Or vengeance,' she cackled.

'Mother, please,' said Holly, looking around, squirming.

'THE DECISION!' she declared in ringing tones. 'Thunder when it crashes will find her smiling! The noise terrifies everyone within a hundred miles yet she is unperturbed, approaching the temple with the cup of sacrificial wine held safely in her hands!'

What could one possibly say to that?

12

Flying forwards in time. Towards the red-streaked east, high above the purple sea of clouds. Wide-eyed, on the edge of her seat, while others slept on in the belly of the beast.

Holly's potion, the elation of motion. Nose against the porthole, gazing at the empty spaces of central Asia where the lights of occasional villages sparkled dimly up into the night. And Holly-Jean wondered whether someone down there was looking up in the sleepy waking dawn, fetching water, baking bread, thinking of the big bird as it rumbled across the sky towards the dawn.

Over China she checked Mother in the seat next to her and wondered for the umpteenth time what she was doing here. She went over it all again and knew it was because she had no other choice. Because she wanted a life after all this. Because to find that life she had to be there, in the seat next to her mother, heading east, towards the dawn coming up like thunder over the China sea. She had to take back her sanity, her life or, as the Chinese would say, her face through the act of retribution.

She considered this. Was her fuel revenge?

No. No image of bloody violence accompanied this emotion. She searched for but found no comforting pictures of three queue-tonsured decapitations. No imagined blows delivered, bludgeons swung. In place was the rosy-hued scene of Holly the heroine rescuing Tracy Vinnicombe from the maw of the evil Orient.

The stewardess offered her mineral water and her thoughts came down in the teeth-grinding morning of no-sleep. She fingered again the cloth package the young Chinese had given her as she and Mother had stood waiting at the check-in line at impossibly crowded Gatwick. She knew what it contained. She'd examined it in the rest room immediately after he'd melted into the throng. Holly was traveller enough to make sure she knew what she was carrying for others. But this was no ordinary contraband. The rolled embroidered cloth contained the red silk cords splashed a darker shade of vermilion and three Polaroid photographs. Holly felt like a diver approaching the edge of the high board. She was scared shitless and had never felt more alive.

They landed in grey sheets of rain at Chiang Kai-shek International Airport. The arrivals lounge was a zoo, with glass partitions holding the multitudes at bay.

Holly and Ma walked uncertainly across the concourse floor towards the exit doors. The doors swished open electronically and they stepped out into the wet heat and bedlam.

Bang-bang-bang!

Fire-crackers stunned Holly into momentary deafness, the white-fire strobes of countless detonations blinded her. She stood swaying like a drunkard, clutching onto cackling, shrieking Mother as the explosions rent the sauna-sweaty air and turned it blue with gunpowder smoke.

The Ho clan, with banners and headbands in the hot rain proclaiming the auspicious and joyous return of Mother.

Holly's ears were battered anew as kettledrums beat out, tin cymbals clashed, and ritual chants were yelled in her face by strangers with red spittle and the aromatic breath of betel nut.

'To ward off evil spirits!'

'Announce to the gods the happy occasion!'

'Ensure the deities keep a benevolent eye on the prodigal Ho *Tai-Tai*!'

One of their own. Come back home.

On the chartered bus, with all the din of fifty relatives talking in Hakka and Mandarin at the same time, Holly emerged from her trance-like state and started getting a strong feeling of Chineseness. She looked at her skin and felt the whiteness drain away, imagined the yellow tint getting stronger every crawling kilometre of the five-lane traffic jam to Taipei. Silly but real.

They crept past the belching flare stacks of Formosa Plastics, the world's biggest naphtha cracker, and into the mountain-ringed city as evening darkened and the city switched on its lights. The rainstorm had abated now. Taipei gleamed in the gloaming, blanketed in a purple haze of hot pollution. They crawled across the bridges of its two poisoned rivers which ran into the

Pacific where the sunset's augmented shades lit the sky as garishly as a first-run print job, and entered the city.

It was all and more that Holly had imagined it would be. Lovely and grotesque. Sugartown. Built on piles of cash. Architectural mayhem soaring to the sky. The priciest claddings available. Money, taste, sense no object, *face* the only stipulation.

Holly stared wide-eyed out of the window as they passed upturned pink marble ziggurats, stainless steel hanging gardens, copper-mirrored Legoland Chrysler Buildings, glittering visual gobbledygook. The bus stopped and she remembered the point of all this: Ma's moment, the returning heroine.

So Holly entered into the homecoming celebration. Four days of banqueting, lunch, afternoon and evening. Every relative securing face-giving visitations. Every meal twelve courses. All washed down with beakers of XO. *Gan-bei! Gan-bei!* Dry glass! Dry glass! Time passed in a blur of soused heartburn days and sweaty restless nights. Wearing the fixed grin of jet lag and sensory bewilderment, Holly did her bit for Mother. But underneath, the tiger was straining at the leash.

Discernible throughout was one constant: the hovering presence of a tall, handsome, silent man, introduced to her as she first stepped onto the chartered bus at Chiang Kai-shek as her third maternal cousin twice removed, but you can call him *Ye-ban i-ho sywe-je*. The name sounded good so Holly had paused to translate it mentally: the After Midnight Scholar. She'd looked at him sharply and from the lascivious twinkle in his eye received confirmation of her Mandarin ability. At first she'd forgotten him in the confusion of the bus ride. But after a couple of banquets, aware that he rarely left her presence, she understood. He was there for her protection. She didn't mind, he hadn't said a word since.

On the morning of her fifth day in Taipei, Holly woke with her now habitual brandy and MSG hangover and the beginnings of an asthmatic wheeze. She told Mother enough was enough. Today was hers, she had work to do.

She showered and sat down to a Hakka breakfast – a bowl of watery rice and various condiments – pickled ginger, pickled garlic, fermented *tofu* smelling like ripe Stilton, salted preserved duck egg, scalding fish soup. Ni-i-i-ce.

One of her cousins was announced.

'Mercury Chen.' He handed over his card in formal fashion, so she had to put down her chopstick and the bit of pickled ginger, stand, fumble for hers, present it, then study his for a polite while. It read: Captain, Bureau of Criminal Investigation, Ministry of Justice. She slid it into her already bulging card holder.

'Captain Mercury?'

'Call me Merc.'

'Merc. Call me Holly-Jean.'

She waited while he performed the ritual English Conversation Lesson One: Chit-chat. How do you like Taipei? Have you eaten? Would you care for a cup of tea, a cigarette, more food? And the last desperate effort as the whirlpool of face-losing embarrassment gathered speed: How is the traffic in London? As the deafening echo of 'It's not as bad as Taipei's' resounded into the squirming silence, Holly took pity and began to speak Mandarin.

'And what can I do for you, Merc?'

'Oh, but your Chinese is wonderful.'

'Thank you.'

'No, really. For a foreigner, excellent.'

'Okay, Captain, I'm a busy lady, so let's get it over with, what can I do for you?'

'On the contrary, Holly-Jean *Shao-jye*, it is I who am at your disposal.'

'With car?'

'Of course.'

'Day off?'

'Familial piety and excellent *guanchi* with my superiors.'

She waited till they were in the car, the After Midnight Scholar as usual sitting in the back, unbidden. 'But you're not a Ho.'

'My mother is.'

'From your job description I'm assuming you're not *Fei Ying Bang*.'

'My dear Holly-Jean *Shao-jye*, please guard your tongue. You must remember we Chinese are not so open-minded as you foreigners.'

'Hey, I'm family. Ho, just like him.' She jerked a thumb at the back seat.

'Yes, but you, er, I mean, your father, your education . . .' Mercury Chen spluttered as the Yue Loong Ford sedan wove in and out of the kamikaze traffic.

'Not quite yellow, you mean,' said Holly.

'No, no, that's not what I meant, you misunderstand.'

'Don't worry, Merc. I'm used to it back home. Now, I

want you to take me to . . .' She looked for the business card.

'My apologies, there's been a misunderstanding, Holly-Jean *Shao-jye*.' He was looking at his watch. 'I have to take you to my appointment.'

'Noooo,' said Holly. 'You have to take me to *my* appointment. At my disposal, right? And less of the "Little Miss" would be appreciated.'

'But I have arranged . . .' He glanced at Holly's face. 'Well, perhaps just a little later then.'

'Good. Two things. First, identify these three.' She pulled out the Polaroids from her pocket and fanned them in front of the steering wheel.

'I don't recognise them at first glance, but I'll run them through the computer back at the ministry.'

Holly was sure from the intense lack of expression following his quick glance at the photos that he certainly knew who the men were. In fact, he showed so little interest as he steered through the insanity that passed for downtown driving in Taipei it confirmed what she'd assumed: everyone hereabouts knew all about the Polaroids and, for that matter, everything else connected with her business, and had done from day one.

A funny phrase popped into her mind; she decided it was to be her Taipei motto: 'Expect the evitable, never assume the inevitable.' If she knew one thing it was this: she was in China. She'd already donned her Chinese thinking cap, growing mental gills to think underwater with the submerged rationality of the Oriental anthill. Sod 'em. She could handle a bunch of Chinese flakegots!

'Your kind assistance will be most appreciated in this

matter,' said Holly, practising a fixed smile bow.

He bowed back. There was a stifled snort from the back seat.

'And now for the second thing you can do for me. Take me to the law firm, Lee and Li.' She at last extracted the card from the recently acquired bundle and read aloud, 'Min-sheng East Road. Know it?'

'Of course, but we'll have to hurry. Our appointment is for eleven, and we can't be late.'

'You hard of hearing, Merc? *Your* appointment is for eleven, mine is for now.'

'You don't understand,' he muttered unhappily. 'You just don't understand.'

She kept hearing that phrase. It annoyed her.

Lee and Li's offices were in a vaguely convincing Graeco-Roman temple of moulded polymer. As Holly looked up, the thought recurred that Taiwan's Foreign Exchange deposits, eighty-seven billion US dollars at the last estimate, the world's highest, higher than Japan's, had done things for its skyline if not its taste. Then she beat a hasty retreat from the fission-like heat on the street, skipped up the marble steps and inside, thanking God for air conditioning as the plate-glass swished shut behind her and the uniformed doorman approached.

The sign in the icy elevator said, 'Accept the tyranny of fate.' Like frock I will, thought Holly.

Lee and Li were on the twentieth floor. The After Midnight Scholar picked up a magazine and took up his post in the lobby.

The Lee and Li lawyers had framed certificates from

242

dozens of American and European law schools on their walls, wore granny specs, flashy bow ties, cufflinks and patterned braces, only they'd call them suspenders. Chink yuppies, mused Holly, but they blew it with the white socks. Sad.

She announced herself. There followed Lesson 100, Advanced Chit-chat, sub-titled An Effusive Round of Vacuous Welcoming Wittering. She was getting to be an old hand. She watched the eyes. She understood the Orientals used the moment as an opportunity for covert psy-ops. But this morning she'd had one too many 'How do you find Taiwan?' so she replied, 'Turn left after Hong Kong.' (Lennon's old joke. Reaction: total incomprehension.)

'Would a seat be too much trouble?'

Sure, okay, why not, yep, right, defnily.

Finally she grabbed one of the slick young men and ushered him into the nearest office. Flushed with mingled delight and horror, he steered her to his own, closed the door on the assembled gaze of fascination, offered her a leather seat, lounged across from her, punched his keyboard, and gave her a smile of devastating smarm.

Holly reckoned this one would break like a twig, so she abandoned all pretence of politeness and went for the nuts.

'I gather you represent Ding Hao Entertainments,' said Holly in staccato Mandarin. 'I need to know what steps have been taken to locate the missing contractee, Tracy Vinnicombe. Moreover, I want you to understand that I represent the British Foreign Office in this matter, that your firm will be held accountable for any eventual outcome and that I need to know your answer right now.'

Sweat broke out on the gleaming forehead. 'Ah. Sure.' Tapped dialogue with the screen. 'No trace of Tracy, huh?' Attempted grin.

Holly's eyes did their trick, the grin disappeared. She switched to English. 'I said I was serious and I meant it.'

A lock of greased-back hair sprang up awkwardly. He smoothed it down, it sprang up. Back to the computer. More tapping. Then he relaxed suddenly; something had come up which made him happy. He looked up, composed now, fresh debonair smile of regret in place. 'Miss Ho, sure-ry you know dat Ding Hao has already cease operatioh. Der company has gone already into liquidatioh. To-toh.'

'Ding Hao has shut down?' Holly had expected that much, but she wanted this smart boy to think her a slow-witted, bungling half-breed female.

'Bust-er-loo. To-toh.'

His gilt desk plate read, 'Went to Harvard, made the Law Review.' Holly wondered if that was where he learned to speak in a cross between Chevy Chase and Charlie Chan.

'Listen carefully, my learned friend,' she said, flashing Mick Coulson's Metropolitan Police ALCO warrant card, the expired one she'd prised off him one inebriated afternoon in Gerrard Street. 'Tracy Vinnicombe's been missing for four months. I'm here in Taipei on behalf of Her Majesty's Government to find her. And find her I will. Even if it means staying right here and making an enormous amount of official trouble for you and your firm until I do. Is that clear?' She wanted him to think her an *official* bungling female half-breed halfwit.

More tapped dialogue. Finger and eye. Measured reply. 'Vairlious sectioh of Ding Hao deem' worse retaining hap been transferrl to der entertainmeh divisioh of der PANG Conglomera.' Tappity-tap. 'Not, unfortuna-ry, der departmen dearing wiv der Soli' Gol' Dance Troupe. See, dat 'as been shut dow.'

Holly said, 'So the dancers are just left stranded in Taipei? What protection under the law do they have? Where does the London agency stand?'

The lawyer looked confused. Consulted his computer screen. 'De Augustuh Talen Agency as of las wee has rescindee ow contractuah obligati-ohs. Compensatory monies have been pay, we understan. From a leg-oh poi-of-view, der matter is close.'

That rat Augustus; but turning tail was precisely what she'd expected of him. 'So how are you, Lee and Li, going to find Tracy Vinnicombe?' Holly asked.

The young man looked embarrassed, shrugged, gestured out of the window at the Taipei sky, coppery with exhaust emissions and summer monsoon. 'She coul be anywhere, I'm afrai, Miss Ho. De exten of de leisure industry in Taiwan is qui' inestimab-oh. I'd be more dan happy to help if I cou, personow speaki, but how cou I?' He gestured helplessly. Smiling all the while.

'What about PANG? Aren't they responsible in some way?'

He looked incredulous and extremely nervous at the mention of the almighty. 'PANG, Miss Ho?' His voice cracked. 'Untouchaboh. PANG is planetaly! Divine-oloonie!'

'So what you're really telling me is that it's PANG who's responsible for poor Tracy's predicament,' she said dramatically, letting the words hang in the air. Holly didn't doubt her movements with regard to Taipei had been known from the moment she checked in at Gatwick. She just wanted to ensure that whoever and their third cousin got the intended correct impression: idiot girl with official *guanchi*.

'No, no. I'm not saying tha a' all. You misunderstan me!'

'So, it's all down to PANG, huh?' she ruminated pensively.

The boy fingered his collar and tried to tamp down his nervy forelock. His pallor had a greenish tinge.

'Right. I need to see some people.' Holly stood up. 'I'll be back.' She spun out of the office. The lawyer jumped out of his chair and chased after her.

The After Midnight Scholar was waiting by the elevator doors. He looked cadaverous and great in his perfectly cut black suit with black collarless shirt.

'How bout dinner? You flee tonigh?' said the ex-Harvard man, his hand reaching round to touch Holly's lower back an inch above the plumb line. 'Tomollow nigh?'

Elbow to solar plexus. Connection. Holly jerked a thumb at the doubled-up, wheezing presence and said to the After Midnight Scholar, 'Have a word with this twerp.'

But one glance at the After Midnight Scholar was

enough and the yuppie shrank out of sight as the lift
doors closed.

Double-parked, Mercury Chen looked extremely
nervous. 'Please, hurry, third cousin.'

Her door was hardly closed before he sent the Yue
Loong Ford screaming into the traffic lunacy at a forty-
five-degree wheel-spin slide.

'We gotta bigger fish to fly!'

'Stick to Mandarin, would you?'

'Chi-lin Road is one of the most favoured entertainment
cores of the city,' said Mercury superfluously, hurrying
her out of the car and slamming the door. Holly could
hardly not have noticed the nonstop action.

'Entertainment here meaning pretty much male entertainment,' she observed.

They dodged their way across the street. 'You want to
know an interesting fact?' said Mercury. 'Taiwan has the
highest WPC in the world.'

'WPC?'

'Whore per capita. One for every six males of the age.'

'I shouldn't think many people know that,' said Holly.
'Taipei's nowhere near as notorious as Bangkok,
Manila, the other dens of sin.'

'Different. Here there is no foreign tourism, nil. So all
the trade is for that bastion of moral rectitude, the
Confucian family head, the local Chinese husband.'

'You don't say.' Holly was warming to Merc.

They stopped to let a bus go by. 'You wouldn't know
this,' he confided as they watched a spanking-new black
Fleetwood Cadillac glide to a halt while a tuxedoed gent

holding a cell phone stepped off the pavement, opened the door and ushered in what looked like a thirteen-year-old in full make-up and big heels, 'but every business meeting ends with a meal followed by a girl. Lunch, tea or dinner. Standard practice. You wouldn't do much trade if you didn't furnish your customer with the appropriate entertainment.' The Cadillac surfed away. 'I trust you're not offended?'

'Cousin Merc, I was born with a very thick skin, and not yesterday.'

They reached the other side of the road. A thunderclap rocked the sky. Holly looked up. Noon had turned dark and brooding. The intense burn had eased slightly, but the air was still thick and poisonous enough to cut and slice with a knife. Holly just had to stand an awed moment in the reflected glory of those gilded pleasure domes.

'Look, we're running late. Wait here a moment, I'll check with the man.'

The edifice they were to enter, vast and neon-lit in the strange dusky Taipei lunch hour, was named Rolls-Royce Garden. It was a metal-clad pyramid with glass apex. Next door was a Gothic cathedral done in some fossil fuel derivative. Across the road was a polymer-mâché Mayan temple. She smiled at that one. She couldn't help it, she'd begun to enjoy these follies. She saw that the whole strip was an architectural fantasy, thrumming with limos dropping off and picking up customers.

'Boys will have their fun,' said Holly, thinking, in the time of plague.

248

'Not fun for some,' said the After Midnight Scholar in one of his rare bursts of loquacity. 'The girls are mostly *shan-ti ren*, the indigenous aboriginal tribals of the Taiwan hinter mountain ranges. Sold into prostitution by their parents. It's a kind of tradition round here.'

Holly nodded. 'Same old song.'

Mercury was speaking to a doorman. He turned and gestured at Holly. Nearby two young men lounged against the wall watching carefully. Brush-cut hair, white socks: society soldiers. Whichever society ran Rolls-Royce Garden, Holly reckoned she was about to find out. The doorman spoke into a wafer-thin mobile phone and the three were admitted through the portals of Rolls-Royce Garden.

Their shoes were removed, to be replaced by chamois leather slip-ons. Female perfection and grace in a white silk toga and jewelled asp headband led them through a central atrium, open to the glass ceiling ten converging floors above. A fountain spewed coloured liquid from the mammaries of Venus and the peni of assorted well-hung Cupids. Translucent polymer palms swayed overhead, a chamber orchestra in white tie played Strauss and a real tiger paced a gilt cage. Glass elevators whisked them up.

'Funny if you saw Mother-in-law going down the other way,' said Holly.

The After Midnight Scholar laughed uproariously. Mercury Chen looked disapproving. Holly decided Merc was a Victorian. At any rate, a practising Confucian, a similar hypocrisy. She still hadn't figured out the relationship between the high-ranking detective and the family's criminal affiliation.

She recalled Janet Rae-Smith's fire-lit lectures at Hogmanay. The gangs are a fifth estate of the realm, she'd said. Utterly unlike the Western concept of crime. Like a quango, Holly had said. Yeah, Johnny Quango, Janet replied.

They had reached the highest level of the pyramid. Mercury stopped along the corridor and spoke into a door intercom. Doors gasped and they entered an inner sanctum.

Thick steam clouded the pink-lit room. Holly discerned the Sistine Chapel reproduced on the ceiling. She was beginning to expect nothing less than excess.

'*Wai-ying*, welcome, English relative,' a voice croaked from somewhere down by the pool. 'And to you, Maternal Great-Nephew Chen.'

'Our humble felicitations, Venerable Ho,' said Mercury, bowing as he led Holly down marble steps to where the voice originated in a crumpled body. For once the After Midnight Scholar was nowhere to be seen. Near the old man sat a giant whose naked torso was one unbroken tattoo of dragons and phoenixes. His ham hands were splayed on tree-trunk thighs. An incongruously tiny penis fronted an enormous dangling testicular sac. Holly could tell at a glance that under the jelly roll would be steel girders. Ex-Sumo. The *irezumi* tattoo: ex-Yakuza.

'You have come far to see us, we are honoured.'

'The honour is mine, Venerable Ho,' said Holly. She didn't need telling he was a superior *lao-ban* of the society. A chinese don. He was wafer-thin, skin a dark brown parchment; a pickled walnut. But Holly didn't miss the salamander eyes. Alive, glittering with energy. Evil-looking old bugger.

Mercury handed the guard the three Polaroids and the red silk cords. With a repressed snarl, Holly realised he must have filched them from her bag.

The three of them conferred without involving Holly. Then Mercury said to Holly, 'Please tell the Venerable Ho your purpose in coming here.'

'I want to find a missing English girl. And the men responsible for the death of my friend in London.'

More conferring.

'You have our good will,' said Venerable Ho, dismissing them with a wave. 'Go carefully, member of the Ho clan.'

Mercury bowed and scraped his way out. Holly, sweating in the sauna air, wasn't in the mood. She waved a jaunty goodbye and marched out to the air conditioning.

'Your wellbeing in Taiwan has just been assured,' said Mercury in the corridor. 'As long as you don't act irresponsibly and without consultation. This is very important. You understand?'

'Listen, it's very nice of you, but I have work to do.'

'Yes, yes, we know, we will help you.'

'The royal we?' said Holly. 'Trouble is, I work alone.'

Mercury clucked disapprovingly as the After Midnight Scholar rematerialised and they entered the glass elevator.

On the street they found a lunch counter and ate rice,

fish, vegetables off styrofoam plates, washed down with help yourself watery Oolong from the giant urn.

'Though you don't know it, Holly-Jean *Shao-jye*, you are important to us. You can play an historic part in the drama to unfold.'

'Look, Merc, we'll get along fine just as soon as you stop taking me for a halfwit. I didn't think I just happened to be here in this place, this street, this town by chance. I know this whole thing has been engineered.'

Mercury looked uncomfortable.

Holly put down her chopsticks and pointed her finger at him. 'I'm patient. I can wait. Up to a point. But I won't do a thing further till I know why. Why me? You start to give me some satisfactory answers and I'll see what I can do for you. Till then, forget the "we" bit. If you want co-operation, you co-operate, got that, Captain Mercury Chen?'

Mercury stayed silent till they finished eating. 'I have office work to do,' he apologised. 'I will also check your photos against the records. Expect me to pick you up at eight tonight. I apologise but please make your own arrangements for eating dinner.'

'Uh, no, actually. I've got plans, thanks.'

Mercury shot the After Midnight Scholar an intense look and drove off. Holly and her escort hailed a cab. She looked at her watch. Two in the afternoon. She had a couple of hours to spare. 'There's something I've always wanted to do.'

The After Midnight Scholar gave the driver instructions for the National Palace Museum, the world's greatest collection of Chinese art and artefacts. It had been looted, some say preserved, depending which side of the fence they're on, from the length and breadth of China during the last days of the civil war against Mao by Chiang Kai shek and the Kuomingtang.

Holly spent the afternoon mostly in ecstasy and sometimes in consternation at the paintings, the china, the porcelain, the jade and other precious stone carvings, the embroideries, the carpets, the scrolls, the ancient divining tortoise shells and more. But it was the miniature carved ivory, jade and nutshells that really fascinated and repelled. These testaments to mental torture were displayed under magnifying glasses so you could see, for example, through the open windows of a half-inch-long carved pleasure boat the cups of tea and *mahjong* tiles on the table inside.

The insanity of the art form was confirmed when she came across a solid piece of ivory the size of an orange, carved into thirty-three concentric spheres. She read that upon being presented with the gift, the Emperor had blinded the artist and broken his fingers to prevent him from making another and thus to preserve the uniqueness of his prize.

She walked away from the displays feeling confused and angry, *chi-pi* running over her skin, pricklingly aware of the Chinese half of her.

From the museum car park, she wielded her mobile phone and called the banker Nick Mayo to confirm dinner. She chose a brand-new Toyota cab, for the airconditioning, and pre-empting the After Midnight Scholar confidently told the driver, 'Ho-ping West Road, intersection with Hsiamen Street. Number 101.'

Holly was getting a vague idea of the layout of the city. Unfortunately all the maps available had been printed long before the convulsions caused by the building of a subway, the second freeway, the straightening of the river, the relaying of the railroad underground. Taiwan, like all newly fabulous rich, was into 'remodelling'.

They got home before the evening rush hour. Holly showered off the fetid grime of Taipei and lay on her bed under the mosquito net, air-conditioning turned on full blast. Mother was out with the Hell's Grannies, as Holly, with an affectionate RIP nod upwards to Benny (she'd always loved his show, despite the universal disapproval of everyone at Camden), had dubbed the gang of widowed relatives to whom her mother had instantly gravitated. Later she dressed in silk-cotton and slipped out of the house via the back alley. Poor After Midnight Scholar would lose face, but she would lose the nerve-grating constraint of his eternal hoverance.

The bar was way out in a suburban mountain valley. It was called the Pig and Whistle, complete with fake Tudor beams and bottles of Bass ale at just under six pounds.

'Stick to the best!' yelled Mayo, dressed in running gear and, judging by his sweat-drenched condition, just returned from an evening run. 'Taiwan *pi-jou*! Brewed from fermented rice and rat shit! Nectar of the gods!' He upended the 75cl bottle and drained it in one go, to howls of 'Down-Down!' from his similarly athletic chums.

This was the China Hash Thursday evening run, the most notorious of the worldwide Hash House Harrier drinking-running clubs. Patronised and matronised – Holly noted the fit, American women in sweatbands and similarly clutched bottles of Taiwan beer – by ex-pats the world over, but especially virulent in Asia.

Holly was welcomed enthusiastically, forced to drink copious quantities of beer very quickly with the result that at some vague, later juncture – she'd lost all sense of time about twenty minutes after arriving at the pub – she found herself supine on a rotting wooden bench surrounded by bamboo and tropical jungle. It was a Chinese watercolour lit by suspended paper lanterns, complete with a spectacular waterfall and, closer, the contents of her stomach.

She lifted her head. 'Ouch!'

'You all right, old bean?'

She sat up and looked round. Nick Mayo had come out of the pub which was some fifty metres back along the lantern path. He handed her a bottle of mineral water and a roll of toilet paper.

'Thanks.' Holly drank gratefully and cleaned herself up.

Nick stood a few feet away, at the edge of the sharp incline, gazing at the waterfall, moonlit and milk-white against the dark forest.

Holly stood and joined him. She felt refreshed. The air was delicious. The night dew opening up the jungle's secret breath.

'Was slamming those beers normal for a Thursday night in Taipei? I couldn't handle it.'

'Well, you know. Ex-pats. Pressure cooker days. Alcoholic nights. Luckily us lot run like dervishes three or four times a week. Gives our livers a bit of a chance. You must come on the Sunday run. Now that's an eye-opener.' He laughed and pointed up at the gaping tropical moon. 'Serious moonlight, that.'

'You see Bowie?'

'Yep. Milton Keynes Bowl.'

'I was there!'

They were silent for a second. Shared place and time. Different photos.

'Got a call from Janet Rae-Smith. Told me you're interested in PANG.'

Holly guardedly confirmed.

'Did Janet tell you the bank handles a fair bit of PANG's foreign transactions?'

Holly told him Janet had only said he was a good friend and would be as helpful as he could. Nick accepted that and went on to say that he, personally, had been working with the conglomerate for more than eight years. He knew a lot and filled in many gaps. Holly didn't tell him what she'd heard of Pang's triad connections. Another time.

As they were walking slowly back to the pub, following the lanterns through the bamboo grove, he said, 'You know, of course, the man's a gangster. But then they all are. Right up to the honollable plesident.'

A few steps before the pub back door, he added, 'Better go carefully there, me dear.' Pushed open the door and roared, 'Where's the beer for *fuck*'s sake! Where's the *sleaze*!'

Holly got a ride home much later and was let into the house on Ho-ping East Road by an extremely worried and embarrassed After Midnight Scholar. Holly chucked him under the chin. Poor guy'd lost major face.

Next morning, Holly and Mother had a long chat. It seemed that Ma was ready to move to her intended new home, a few hours south of Taipei, mid-island in the county of Miaoli, up in the mountains. It was where she'd spent her infancy before moving to Taipei for schooling.

'Of course, you and your young man will want to stay here and get better acquainted.'

Holly stared at her, ice-cold can of Mr Brown coffee midway to her lips. 'What did you say, Mother?' she asked with equal frigidity.

'Well, of course, there's always the After Midnight Scholar, but on the whole he's rather secondhand, to put it politely. No, Third Cousin Chen. A much better prospect. After all, he's got his position at the Ministry of Justice. Already a captain at his young age. There's no telling where he's headed.'

'I can tell you exactly where he *isn't* headed,' said Holly caustically. 'And that's up a garden or any other kind of path with me.'

'Now, now, Little Orchid, no need to be hasty. Let love take its time,' she trilled, snapping the lock shut on the last of her suitcases for the journey south. Holly looked at her. Either the woman was senile, or . . . no. No. Not that, surely. She shook her head.

'Mother, you need the rest. Go off to your new home, get settled in and enjoy yourself. I'll come down and see you in a few days when I can get away.'

'Oh, don't worry about me, daughter. I can take

care of myself. I'm home now. Everything's just about perfect. The only thing left to consider is you and your future. The family's future.' She eyed Holly. 'The next generation . . .'

'Mother, if you partook in this fiasco, wittingly or not, just in order to get me back to Taiwan and married off, I'd find it extremely difficult to forgive you.'

Mother busied herself stacking her cases by the front door.

'My God, my best friend was murdered!'

Mother looked at Holly with eyes full of maternal devotion. '*Ai-yai-yai!*' she sighed and slumped down onto the cases. It occurred to Holly for the first time that the fight had nearly gone out of the old hen. An image of her mother, shrunken, wizened, preparing for death came unbidden. She ran over and picked up the old lady in a gentle hug.

Mother spoke into the crook of her daughter's neck. 'I know nothing about these big affairs, believe me, *Shao-lan*. But every day I pray for your friend's happiness in heaven. Little Orchid, your heart was broken. For that I'm sad. Then I think, it could have been you, *Shao-lan*, and my heart turns to ice, and I give thanks. Yes, I am grateful that you are alive and she is dead. Try to understand. I'm just an old Chinese widow who wants the best for her only daughter,' Holly felt the twig-like body stiffen with resolve, 'and only lineal descendant.'

13

The apartment building was a brand-new, copper-mirrored stack halfway down Jen Ai Road, a tree-lined avenue where some of the most expensive real estate in Taipei, and thus the world, could be found.

Chen Ba-tsun's mother reacted with extreme indifference, which in the context of Confucian rules of etiquette amounted to open hostility, when Holly was introduced as somebody connected with the Ravensdale English Language Schools. Holly was shown the door, after the briefest of conversations, by the Filipino amah.

As she stood at the elevator, Chen Ba-tsun slipped out of another door down the corridor.

'I'm really sorry about my mother's rudeness. It was very kind of you to drop by. But as you can imagine, it's been a very difficult time. My mother took ages to come to terms with what happened. She cannot bear to be reminded of . . .' The girl shrugged.

Holly said, 'And I'm really sorry to rake up all the pain again for you. But I wanted you to know, I thought you might find some degree of comfort in the knowledge, that

259

the outrage you suffered was not directed at you personally.'

'What do you mean?' asked the girl, the fingers of her left hand worrying her wooden Buddhist prayer beads.

'Yours was just part of an orchestrated series of such attacks by organised crime, aimed not at you personally but at the owner of the school, Ms Ravensdale, who has since been murdered.'

'*Wo-de tyan!* Oh, poor, poor Miss Ravensdale. She was really very kind. A genuine friend to all of us students. The reason I went back every year was because of her. I miss her. I thought perhaps one day to return, after all this is history . . . I guess then that I will always miss her.'

'You and me both, kid,' murmured Holly.

The After Midnight Scholar emerged from the elevator but Holly gestured him away and he took up his usual post at a respectful distance.

'About my mother's reaction in there,' said Chen Ba-tsun. 'She's absolutely terrified someone will find out what happened. The loss of face, the . . .'

'I know, I know,' said Holly. 'It's hard sometimes being a Chinese daughter.'

'Kind of you. But of late, my *ku-chi*, my bitter tears, have turned acid.' She looked at Holly with old eyes. 'Oh yes, I feel deep sympathy for her predicament, she'd have great difficulty in finding me a suitable Chinese husband if word got out that I'm *used goods*.'

Holly left after promising to keep Chen Ba-tsun informed of the eventual outcome, if any.

Just as she was stepping into the elevator, the girl

asked, 'How was the funeral? Were many there?'

Holly kept her finger on the Doors Open button, breathed deeply. 'It was immediate family, I wasn't invited – they didn't know about me . . .' She smiled at the girl. 'I did hear there were plans for a big memorial service in Bournemouth to be organised by all the schools. Sometime later this month. I don't know if I'll be back in time. I'll try and find out when and let you know, if you like.'

'Please do. I would want to send some flowers.'

The doors closed and as the lift dropped in silence without physical sensation, Holly felt mildly comforted by the encounter. But she quickly squelched that line of thought: time for mourning would come later. Right now she had to keep moving. On and on. Ride this roller coaster wherever it led.

Stratton McMurtry Consultants' Taipei offices were a few blocks away, near where Jen Ai Road intersected with Tunhua South Road. The walk would take her past the PANG building, visible now towering over the other high-rises. She couldn't resist the chance to peek, despite the fact that walking in Taipei was a hazardous activity. Where the pavement existed it was occupied either by motorcycles and scooters parked like a row of sardines or by illegal food vendors with mobile gas kitchens, stools, tables and bundles of chopsticks. 'Pavement' was something of a misnomer for the cracked and detritus-strewn roadside, complete with odd open sewer and dead cat. Within a few paces her shoes were squeaking with goo. Luckily today was cooler. The sky was darkening again, but this time there was a hint of chill on the sudden slamming gusts.

'*Tai-fong you lai*,' observed the After Midnight Scholar in an uncharacteristic conversational opener. There was hope for the handsome dummy yet.

'Ah yes, Typhoon Jeremy,' said Holly. 'Just what we don't need.'

'Ah, but the typhoon always scoops the shitty air out of Taipei and dumps it on the mainland.'

'In that case, lay it on, Jeremy, and suck away PANG while you're at it.'

They crawled ant-like past the soaring obelisk, yet another post-mod variation on the Chrysler classic. Genuine Art Deco went with Manhattan like farmhouse clotted cream with freshly picked raspberries, but the glitzy Asian version looked plain stupid. PANG, however, by virtue of its giddying height, was impressive, Holly grudgingly admitted.

The address of the McMurtry Consultancy was a gaping hole in the tree-lined avenue. The building to the left was ten numbers lower. In the other direction lay only the tallest building in East Asia.

The After Midnight Scholar nipped back and asked the liveried doorman parading outside PANG. Holly watched as he was directed to the rear of the building. He waved and gestured to her to follow.

Not another frocking unlikely coincidence. Who was directing this Charlie Chan movie? She considered her next move. Ducking out of the appointment would look strange. Besides, now her gander was up. On-on.

She wove her way back through the pavement throng of city-suited types eating lunch of steamed dumplings and noodle soup, round to the back of the vast building. The After Midnight Scholar was waiting by the Palladian entrance to the Taipei Shangri-La Hotel which formed part of the east wing of the huge complex.

The consultancy was in a leased suite on the thirty-third floor of the hotel. Holly reckoned either business was exploding or someone else was footing the bill. She had a fair idea who.

She said she had an appointment; the gorgeous receptionist told her she was expected and sent her right in.

McMurtry, fancy haircut, fancy Mandarin silk suit, skin and bones as befitted an ex-Jesuit, offered her lunch but she declined. She explained that she was merely calling by to convey greetings from Professor Rae-Smith.

'So what else brings you to Taipei at typhoon times?'

Her cover story was genuine. She really was a delegate of the Software Intellectual Property Rights Association attending next week's Electronics Trade Show at the Taipei World Trade Centre. It had been a simple matter of flashing her associate's card at the show organiser's office on her second morning in Taipei to get an official guest invitation.

'It's a contemptible situation and getting worse,' said McMurtry, oozing sincerity. 'I always emphasise at our workshops that software piracy is a crime. It is theft, pure and simple, no different to bag snatching. I doubt my words make much impression,' he sighed. 'The Chinese believe that since we the imperialists exploited them for so long, we have no right now to complain. The spiked boot is on the other foot, so to speak. At times I am inclined to agree with them.'

'What about swamping the market with virulent infestations?' Holly told him about the Dragon Boat Day virus that had all but destroyed Archie Ross's reputation.

'Yes, there's that too,' he nodded sympathetically. 'And that is precisely why we try to inculcate the holistic principle as a life-role model transcending mere commercial activity but with built-in guarantees of success.'

Ah yes, success, the magic formula at last. Holly had him tagged now. He was a New Age Greabo. Ex-Jesuits, ex-hippies, they were all the same; once a zealot, once a shyster.

They chatted idly about London and the coming handover of Hong Kong. He went on casually to mention that he was due to fly south after lunch, heading down the unpopulated, undeveloped east coast to check out the first international hotel to be opened there as a potential workshop venue. Why not join him and some aides as their guest at the five-star hotel? French management, he added. 'Check out the speculator ocean cliff scenery then fly back early Saturday morning?'

Put like that, it sounded rather tempting. The trouble was, Holly-Jean reckoned hers could well be a one-way ticket. Destination: Pang Chong-ts. Return: unspecified. Class: terminal. Her mind whirred. After all, she still had no firm clue as to motivation. So far, she'd been served up a soup consisting of hearsay and gossip, both historic and hysteric, plus a great deal of Oriental mumbo-jumbo.

Time for two reality checks. First, somebody had murdered Jenny, either by design or by mistake; if by mistake, then the intended victim was herself. Second, Tracy Vinnicombe was still missing and everything pointed to the fact that Pang was somehow connected to her disappearance. So either this was an innocent invitation to see some amazing scenery or it was a lure into the den of the enemy. In which case it was the perfect opportunity for . . .

She left the preposition dangling. She hadn't quite got as far as an actual *plan* yet. She'd just have to dust off her old fall-back strategy: walk right in, step right up, baby let your hair hang down.

She agreed to meet McMurtry and aides at the Sungshan Domestic Airport, a mile or so up at the end of Tunhua North Road, in an hour's time. Departure time for Tai-dung was three fifteen. Check in at the Far Eastern Transport Desk.

Holly taxied back to Ho-ping East Road, showered, changed, and called Mercury Chen. She argued with him for a few minutes, and then told him she was going anyway. In desperation he blurted out, 'But we think we've found Tracy!'

'Surprise, surprise,' said Holly drily. 'Don't think I didn't figure you lot have known her precise whereabouts all along. After all, you've been at such pains to tell me how all-powerful the Bamboo Union is on this bastion isle. What was it you said: "Nothing breathes the air on Taiwan that we don't know about." I told you before, pack in the games, Mercury, and I'll roll over and play Miss Overseas Chinese for you. Are you ready to move tonight?'

'Ah, not quite yet. We have to devise a suitable MO.'

'Well, when you're ready, let me know. I'll be back in the morning.'

'*Go-pi!* It'll be my neck if you're not back! At least tell me where you're staying the night.'

'Le Meridien Formosa in Tai-dung County.' She hung up.

She made check-in with minutes to spare before they closed the flight. That was at twelve minutes past three. The twin jet-prop took off on time at three fifteen. Twenty-seven minutes later it began its descent. By four they were in Le Meridien's air-conditioned minibus heading along a stretch of beautiful coastline, the blue Pacific whipped into white-topped frenzy by the coming of Jeremy.

In reception she spotted the After Midnight Scholar climbing out of a taxi just as they were being assigned their electronic card keys.

The flying visit proved to be nothing more than just that. She enjoyed the aforementioned spectacular views from the vertical cliffs in the last of the eastern light, getting there by way of the death road hewn by Allied POWs during the war. Dinner wasn't bad; French cuisine with an Oriental slant, a nice couple of bottles of Aligote.

Apart from which, she made two dreary discoveries. First, that Stratton McMurtry was a self-obsessed bore who was either a brilliant actor or definitely not *au fait* with any PANG inner circle. Second, that the ex-Jesuit was a randy goat.

Holly-Jean quickly dissuaded him from any further steps in that direction. In fact, he was finding it hard to step in any direction when the After Midnight Scholar paid a courtesy call to her room.

'Saw him go in, didn't see him come out.'

'He's all yours,' said Holly, watching as the Chinese politely helped the doubled-up McMurtry wheeze his way back to his own room.

Mercury Chen arrived promptly after breakfast and made a jackass of himself pretending a surprise encounter with Holly as they were all standing in reception waiting for the luggage to be brought down.

'When are you heading back?'

'Next flight. Nine twenty.'

'Wow. Coincidence. Me too.'

'I thought you'd just arrived,' said McMurtry.

'You know how it is. Change of plans.'

So on the plane Holly was able to look back from the tiny first-class section and see not one, but two guardian angels seated in economy. The flight was extremely bumpy. The wind was gathering in fury somewhere out over the ocean. Jeremy was working out, building muscle.

Queasily she said goodbye to McMurtry and his group at Sungshan. She waited till their taxis had been swallowed up in the traffic before walking back behind the row of concrete pillars where Mercury and the After Midnight Scholar hovered.

'Right then, the plan. Let's have it.'

'The plan?'

'To rescue Tracy. You said you'd found her. Remember?'

Mercury looked at the After Midnight Scholar who remained as expressive as an Easter Island grey-neck.

Holly sighed and signalled for a cab. She'd have to take this lot by the scruff of their scrawny necks.

Holly had dressed in baggy jeans, T-shirt and trainers. It was evening and they were standing outside the house on Ho-ping. Strong gusts rattled the windows and tossed the cryptomeria trees to and fro.

Mercury looked approvingly at her apparel and said, 'We have definite confirmation of the location of the missing girl. Tonight we make reconnaissance.'

'Great work,' said Holly caustically; it would have been impossible to hide anyone from the Bamboo Union on Taiwan, let alone a blonde-haired foreign girl. She wondered how long they'd known. Probably since the demise of the Solid Gold Dance Troupe.

Mercury sent the Yue Loong Ford up onto an elevated highway leading northwards, out of the city, towards the Pacific coast. Taipei at night was dazzling. Lasers were commonly used to highlight the available entertainment. Here a ten-floor karaoke establishment, there an all-night indoor prawn fishing pool and golf range. Every business had a neon sign. Every floor had a business. Every building had plenty of floors. The place was ablaze, like a glittering dragon chain-smoking firework bongs.

'How about the three Flying Eagles? Did your computer come up with any names?' asked Holly.

Mercury considered his reply. 'Look, Third Cousin Ho, forget those three. They were just mid-ranking soldiers doing their job. Following orders. You have to think of it as war. You have to aim for the generals, the leaders, not the enlisted men.'

'So how am I going to get to General Pang Chong-ts, one of the world's richest men and thus a semi-deity here on Taiwan? By the way, would you mind putting on your headlights.'

Mercury complied, with a hiss of lost face.

There was silence for a kilometre or two as they pulled out of town. The weather had definitely changed. Jeremy was only a few hours away. Rain was para-diddling the Yue Loong roof now, thunder and lightning strobing the sky out over the ocean. Occasional gusts rocked the car with a whump and a perceptible lift.

'*Tai-fong yo lai*,' said the After Midnight Scholar.

'Very astute,' muttered Holly.

The road narrowed, another one hewn from the cliff face by Allied slave labour. Only a low sea wall sepa-rated them from the wind-whipped frenzy of the big waves. Now and then a high roller would lunge in from the swell and hit the sea wall with a burst of milky spray that clattered on the bonnet of the car.

'Your man Pang,' reminded Holly. 'It's time, you know. Time to talk or I'm out of here. You wouldn't want a loose cannon like me running around Taiwan, now would you?'

Mercury shrugged, seemed resigned. 'All right.'

'Good. I want to know what the motivation is. Why me?'

'I'll try to make sense of it for you,' said Mercury, thinking for a while. 'You know, third cousin, that for us

Chinese, face is the most important commodity. It embodies honour, power, prestige. Without face, all achievement, all acquisition, turns to dust. Without face, there is no meaning. Without face a Chinese cannot survive, you see?'

'So to hurt the man, lose him face,' said Holly. She'd always understood the concept of face but not the ridiculous extent to which it was practised in China. After a few days on Taiwan, however, she was starting to get the picture. She supposed it was to do with living like ants on the anthill. So many billions, all trying desperately to get ahead yet slave to a tyranny of conformity. The only thing to make sense was face.

'Maybe you have a vague idea of it,' said Mercury, shaving the spray off a scooter. His driving was erratic to say the least. 'Anyway let us agree that face is the route.'

'So to reach someone as high up as Pang we must somehow make him lose face.'

'Precisely.'

'Which, I assume, is where Tracy comes in.'

'Correct. We know she is currently being held against her will by the *Fei Ying Bang*. If we can help get her off the island, the society, and by extension Pang, will lose face.'

'And your lot will gain face,' said Holly.

'Again correct. All the more so if the person seen by everyone to have done the rescuing, to have stolen the face, is a mere girl, moreover a foreigner.'

'Even sweeter if it's the granddaughter of the famous concubine Chang-i who murdered Pang's Uncle Lee Hong with a chopstick through the brain.'

270

Mercury braked involuntarily and the car went into a nasty skid. In the back seat the After Midnight Scholar let out a yelp, whether in response to Holly's revelation or Mercury's driving, it was hard to tell. Mercury glanced at her nervously.

'Now I understand.' She was very angry. 'This is why I'm here, right? Why Jenny was killed – to win points in the face wars. I wouldn't even be surprised if it turned out to be you lot who killed her!'

Mercury looked sick. 'N-no way. Far more important elements. Worldwide containments. Maybe Jenny was a mistake. We still think it should have been you who was . . . e-er . . . murdered.'

'You think, do you?'

'At this point we're pretty sure it was you they were after. It's the only reasonable explanation. The blood-feud to avenge the death of Pang's uncle.'

'You call any of this reasonable,' spat Holly. 'Frankly I doubt you are telling me the truth.'

Mercury pouted. Holly went on, 'So then. What explanation can you come up with for the gang-rapes of oriental students?'

'Extreme terror is the traditional weapon of Chinese gang society,' said Mercury. 'The gang-rapes were the bullying tactics necessary to forcing Ravensdale to sell out to Oxbridge.'

'But why was Pang's Oxbridge ELSI so desperate to acquire Ravensdale? What is it with these Language Schools?' Mercury looked at her as if she were a simpleton.

'Of course they needed full control of the Language

school business in order to expand their alien-smuggling, drug-couriering, money-laundering enterprise. Particularly the money-laundering. What better way to shift cash than through thousands of language students legally travelling the globe?'

'Sure, Mercury.'

The ride, like the rest of that night, was memorable for many reasons. Due in part to her cousin's lack of lateral vision or thinking and in part due to the awesomely precipitous coast road, Holly-Jean sat in bilious expectation of an imminent encounter with her maker from either a head-on collision or drowning at sea. Her cousin took every narrow hairpin too wide, entered it too fast, and left it braking and thus drifting uncontrollably on the rain-slicked surface. Added to which there was plenty of traffic in both directions. In the end she gave up bracing herself against the constant close shaves and near misses. Instead she closed her eyes and went into meditation, silently chanting her mantra.

Some forty minutes of vehicular nightmare later, Mercury Chen swung the Yue Loong Ford into a parking lot built on reclaimed ocean. Holly stepped out into the furious blather of Jeremy.

Considering the weather, the parking lot was oddly full, with crowds of people coming or going up the narrow road, leaning into the wind and rain. Up ahead, through the sheets of rain, Holly could see coloured lights. As they got closer, she saw it was a temple, built into the rock wall.

'Why so many devotees in this crazy weather?' she yelled against the howling wind.

'Auspicious day,' shouted Mercury. 'This is the Dog Temple. We're in the Year of the Dog, the Month of the Dog and this weekend is the Dog's birthday.'

Skirting the rock wall and the road were hundreds of twinkling vendor's stalls, canvas awnings flapping wildly in the sudden gusts off the ocean.

'Tomorrow will be much worse, being the Sunday; it is the climax of the festival. People will travel all day from all over Taiwan to pay their respects to the Dog God.' Mercury tugged Holly along, gesturing at the exotic food on offer. 'Fancy a snack? Cock testicles, deer-antler wine, tiger-penis soup, stir-fried crickets, snake blood, stinky tofu, it's all here!'

'Don't show off, cousin,' said Holly. 'You forget I'm half Chinese. This stuff doesn't shock me. Though why aphrodisia should be served at a temple is a puzzle, I'll admit.'

Nearer the entrance were incense sellers. Some sticks were as tall as Holly and as thick as a thigh. 'They cost an arm and a leg,' said the After Midnight Scholar.

'How much?'

'Two thousand US each.'

There were gold-leaf paper money stacks, cartons of imported cigarettes, cases of beer – offerings to the gods or ancestors, to be consumed later.

Something else was puzzling Holly. Most of the devotees looked rough. Razor-cut gangsters, heavily painted women. All chewed betel nut, their teeth red-stained, which Holly had learned was a sure indicator of low class on the island.

'Welcome to the Temple of the Eighteen Princes'

Dog, *Shr-ba Hwang Gong*,' said Mercury.

'Why all the lowlifes, the gang-bangers, pimps, whores?' said Holly, following along.

'This temple is special for these people,' explained Mercury as they pushed by the many shrines built into the sweating black rock. 'They feel unwelcome in other temples, feel the gods will look down on their misdeeds and hence refuse their requests. But being dedicated to a dog, they feel comfortable here, offering up their intercessions, their guilty secrets. Besides, there have been some spectacular results in recent years, so the Dog Temple has a good reputation for granting favours.'

'So the losers come to the Dog. God written backwards,' mused Holly. 'What's this mutt's story?'

They stood watching a striptease unfold on a garishly lit stage, to the accompaniment of deafening karaoke speakers. The girl was left wearing a diaphanous nightie and black high heels. Holly was shocked to see tiny children gawping up at the lustrous black fur between her ivory legs.

'It's a famous local legend,' said Mercury, dragging himself away. 'A couple of hundred years ago, eighteen fishermen from Fukien just across the Taiwan Strait were caught in a storm, wrecked and washed up dead on these rocks. The sole survivor was the ship's dog who refused to leave his masters even after they were buried and stayed on to guard their graves. Local villagers admired such fealty and fed and cared for the animal. Then someone for some reason asked the dog for advice when throwing the oracle. The results were good and word spread. After the dog died, the outcome of prayers continued to be excellent, so the dog became a god. We Chinese are practical people, especially when it comes to religion. Everything comes down to results, or at least perceived results.'

They moved with the throng up the steps and into the cave temple.

The enclosed space was unpleasantly clammy. The smell of incense was overpowering, sickening, the press of bodies claustrophobic. Holly hated crowds, confinement. The interior was lit by thousands of candles and their heat and scent added to the cloying atmosphere. Chanting and wailing relayed by speakers hung from every corner. Statues of demonic guardians glared down from every angle.

The After Midnight Scholar was helping her down dark steps, going underground, deep into the rock. They pushed their way through the jam of bodies until they were forced to a halt.

Holly looked up to find herself face to face with a stone foreleg. Her gaze travelled up and straight into the jewelled eyes of a black stone dog papered with gold-leaf offerings.

'Stroke it! It brings luck,' Mercury said.

Holly did so, feeling the gold-flecked skin warm and damp from the touch of countless palms, the gold leaf seemingly breathing and pulsating.

Did she imagine a small charge entering her skin? For a moment she stood rooted to the spot, the countless superstitions Mother had drummed into her childhood flooding back in a wash of supernatural imaginings.

Then she was shoved on by the press, down into the darker recesses of the temple, deep into the mountain where the crowds thinned out. There was less candlelight here, fewer supplicants, murmured chanting. The walls were narrower, the ceiling of rock lower. Menacing deities stood in rough niches. This was most definitely not Holly's cup of tea. Far from it. She stumbled in the gloom, reached out a hand. Touched something – hair? 'Eek!' she screamed involuntarily.

Mercury's pencil light beamed towards her. Holly saw she was clutching the human hair of a bright red face with huge bulging eyeballs. An angry god.

'Chung Kuei, the Exorcist,' announced Mercury.

'Bully for him,' muttered Holly, unnerved, releasing the hair. 'How far are we going? Are you telling me Tracy's down here?'

Mercury didn't answer.

They reached a dead end. Holly looked around the dimly lit space. There was now only a mere handful of pilgrims moving along the cave path. For the first time she became aware that there were only male devotees in this section of the temple.

Mercury produced a baseball cap printed with the words Puerto Galera, Republic of Philippines, and some lightly tinted sunglasses. 'Put these on, please, he said. 'You'll be taken for either a young man or one of the occasional *tong-sying lien* females who come to this place.'

She did so. He and the After Midnight Scholar donned similar hats and glasses.

'Remember, tonight is merely reconnaissance. We

must be careful not to bring attention to ourselves.'

'Get on with you, Sherlock,' said Holly. Mercury hissed her silent as a couple of passers-by glanced sharply in her direction.

At the end of the wall there was a turnstile and light shone from further up ahead. They joined the shuffling queue, Holly in the middle. Money changed hands – wads of purple Taiwan thousand-dollar bills. Then they were through a narrow passage and into a vast open space, a casino from hell.

Holly looked up. The roof was half rock, half polymer sheeting and bolted steel built onto the rear of the cliff wall. Giant Tiffany lamps hung suspended, lasers flickered. The panels of the hall were painted red and gold. Leather booths with tables lined one wall. Card games and mahjong were in progress. Piles of cash, overflowing ashtrays and bottles of XO brandy and *Kao-liang* sorghum spirit littered every table.

About thirty partitioned cubicles lined the other wall. Girls in bikini tops and mini-skirts stood at open doors with the stoned faces of junky prostitutes everywhere. The place was crowded with punters, wandering about watching the action, chatting with the girls, gobbing their betel juice into spittoons. A karaoke TV was blaring near the bar, and a man wearing a white shirt open to his waist sang drunkenly.

Mercury strolled along beside Holly, the After Midnight Scholar on her other side as they made their way through the crowds cruising the short-time rooms. At the far end were twin glass doors guarded by tuxedoed bouncers. People were coming in and out and Holly glimpsed the headlights of cars.

'That the main entrance?' she murmured.

'Yes. There's a private car park, well hidden from the coast road. Of course, everyone knows about it.'

'Tracy's in one of these cells?' asked Holly as they passed by the many closed doors.

'That is our information, yes.'

She stared angrily at a red-faced, sweating man who emerged from one of the cells with a lascivious yell to his mates who were waiting to go in. Inside, she glimpsed an electric fan, a mirrored wall, and a Chinese girl straightening the bedsheet with one hand, hairbrush in the other. So this was Tracy's fate. She had a sudden urge to barge right in gouging and kicking and find the girl there and then, but as if sensing her rising indignation, Mercury grabbed her elbow hard and steered her on towards the other side and the exit doors. 'Cool down, please, Ho *Shao-jye*!'

'Soon, then. Very soon.'

They moved on past the bar. Holly noticed a giant condom machine offering all colours and variations. At least there was that.

'Seen enough?' said the After Midnight Scholar to Mercury. 'It's not too healthy to stick around here. People are beginning to notice our cousin.' Indeed, some men were pointing and making ribald comments, grabbing their crotches.

'Okay, let's go. We'll walk very casually out of the doors. Don't hurry. Remember, you're just one of the crowd,' said Mercury, handing each of them a can of Taiwan beer.

'Come again, *sirs*, and you too, Madam *tong-sying lien-dr shao-jye* – your type is always welcome with a fat red envelope!' Nudge-nudge, wink-wink, and they were ushered out by the bouncers into the rain-lashed night.

'So they realised I was female. Do they know about me?'

'Probably,' said Mercury calmly. '*Go-pi!* This typhoon's a damned nuisance! Come on, let's run!'

The slippery jog across shellac path and sand dunes back to the coast road and then the half-mile or so to the car park was an exhilarating battle with the elements. They finally made it to the car, drenched to the skin.

'So why the brothel in a temple? Even by Taiwan's standards that's a bit over the top, or is the Dog Temple host to some arcane sex cult?'

'Ah, not exactly but . . .' Mercury was obviously uncomfortable. 'One or two such temples offer this . . . ah . . . service. There's the belief, held by some, that powerful energy, a special *chi*, is generated by the, ah, confluence of . . . er . . . sexual fluids.'

'Go on.'

He was using paper tissues to wipe down his dripping hair. 'The girl, Tracy, being a white-skinned foreigner, blonde and blue-eyed, was a major attraction. Her customers would pay an enormous, ah, donation to the temple—'

'The red envelope stuffed with cash.'

'Precisely. For the privilege of, ah, how to put it . . . draining the white girl's *Yin* energy into their *Yang*.'

'Under the auspicious male *Yang* eyes of the dog deity.'

'Quite. At such a moment they consider a massive boost of power would flow into their bodies, thereby granting desires, bringing luck or solving problems. It's all about sexual energy and the *Yin-Yang*.'

'And male fuckheadedness.'

'Er . . . I suppose so.'

'Does this place belong to the Flying Eagles?'

'Not the temple itself. That is sacrosanct. But the *Fei Ying Bang* have been running the brothel concession behind the temple for quite a few years now. It's a highly profitable business, as you can imagine. When your friend got put on the books, it set the underworld buzzing. Soon the rumour was going around that a short time with the white princess at the Temple of the Eighteen Princes' Dog brought amazing fortune, not to mention all sorts of health benefits. Someone claimed to have won the lottery after Tracy mumbled the winning numbers during intercourse. Another reported being cured of baldness, yet another said his cancer had cleared up. Others reported that their businesses had turned round. All sorts of miracles were bandied about.'

'Poor Tracy might unwittingly have done some good,' murmured Holly.

'It's not much of a comfort but they're no doubt keeping her massively dosed with tranquillisers and heroin, so she probably isn't aware of too much.'

Holly said nothing.

'You've got to remember it's a different culture over here. Completely different. Values, reasoning, logic, everything.'

'It doesn't make it right.'

'No.'

'I suppose we couldn't just go to the police. She's a foreign national, after all.'

'Don't be silly, I am the police. Besides, we're out in the wilds here. This is Taipei County jurisdiction, and the law in these parts is applied in direct proportion to dues paid.'

'I could go to the British Trade Office.'

'This is Taiwan, third cousin. We have no diplomatic relations with the outside world, no extradition treaties, nothing but massively profitable two-way trade. No one would be prepared to rock the boat and make an international incident out of it. Besides, these things happen all the time. Always have. Look at Shanghai.'

'Well, I might just stir things up a little.'

Mercury looked at her nervously, 'Please, don't. We will work together. We have made our reconnaissance. Now we must make our move and without too much delay. They will be expecting something since you've been on the island for a week now.'

The After Midnight Scholar said something Holly didn't quite catch.

Mercury said, 'I think the opportune time to effect a rescue would perhaps be the middle of next week. Say Wednesday night, when the temple should be very quiet. We must also create an elaborate diversion.' He conferred with the After Midnight Scholar in a mixed Hakka-Taiwanese local dialect she didn't understand.

'Yes, I think that's an excellent suggestion from our scholarly friend,' he said in Mandarin, turning back to Holly. 'There will be a grand reception honouring your mother's return home. You will be the guest of honour. We'll invite some local dignitaries, maybe the mayor if we can apply enough squeeze. Perhaps some of the British trade people. You will be in the public eye, until we can slip away. The Hyatt would be best, I think. It's got the most face in power circles. Also they've got plenty of banqueting suites available at short notice.'

'Assuming we rescue Tracy, then what?'

'Off the island the same night. It would be far too difficult to guarantee your long-term safety. After all, third cousin, you are the vital element in all this.'

'So I gather,' Holly said acidly, wincing as they passed an old Hino truck on a blind hairpin and by a miracle missed a rearing Yamaha.

On Sunday Holly-Jean ran the China Hash.

'What about the typhoon?' she'd wondered earlier.

'All the more excitement, me dear!' yelled Nick Mayo down the phone. 'Pick you up in ten minutes!'

The start was more than an hour out of town, high in the mountains. In deference to the day, T-shirts were handed out at the start with the words, China Hash, Dog Day, and a graphic cartoon of the beast.

Holly was surprised by the large turnout, especially the number of locals; she'd thought it an ex-pat thing. 'Why all the yellow taxis?' she asked. She'd had a sudden fascinating idea.

Nick Mayo, hash name Mijo Slut, explained that because Dog Day was a special day, the Taipei Hash – a men-only Saturday Hash, mostly locals, some taxi drivers – had been invited to participate in the China

Hash. Consequently there were about one hundred and fifty runners. And a beer truck. Mr Piss.

The run was staggeringly beautiful and hard – through a bamboo grove, up a vertical mountain jungle path onto high-ground buffalo pastures, on up above the timber line, all the while slogging through Typhoon Jeremy which had hit landfall two hundred miles to the south-east. Two hours after the hares set off, Holly dragged her muddy, bleeding limbs back to the start and the drinking ritual known as 'Down-downs'.

The physical exertions of the run had all but incapacitated her body; the alcohol finished the job. Empty stomach. Rapidly empty brain. Holly was showered with beer and formally given a hash name, Yellow Brit Ho. By the time the race of drunk drivers, Sand-Crab the Taiwanese taxi driver in the lead, careered round the narrow tropical forest roads 'on-on' to the 'bash', a bacchanal at the bemused local eatery, Holly was in a state of agape delirium which not even the ritual of 'Burning Arseholes' disturbed. This was a motley contest during which drunks of both sexes climbed up onto the tables, lowered their pants and endeavoured to drink a whole 'down-down' mug of beer while rolled newspapers inserted in their rear orifices were set on fire. Quite what the landlord or the other guests enjoying their Sunday evening out thought of the spectacle remained a mystery. 'Lads will be lads,' Holly slurred to Sand-Crab as he gingerly sat down beside her.

When much later – Holly had lost all track of time, for the second time in a week – Mayo dropped her off on Ho-ping East Road, she managed to arrange a meeting for Monday morning at the bank.

She rolled under the mosquito net and slept a delicious sleep of dark ocean depths.

Mayo was chipper at 10.00 a.m. Monday morning.

Holly, feeling pretty good herself, came straight to the point, 'I'd like to know anything you're prepared to tell me about the Oxbridge ELSI chain.'

Nick looked at her with a grin. 'I'll tell you one thing, if I didn't have my job in the bank I'd certainly look into the three hundred and fifty million pound English language business. You'd be amazed to know how much Oxbridge turns over. Obviously I can't divulge real figures, but there's got to be some laundering going on there. Perfect set-up, after all.'

'How so?'

'The thing is so fluid. Schools are set up all over the English-speaking world. UK, USA, Canada, Australia, New Zealand. Others in resort locations: the Alps, Caribbean, all the south-east Asian resorts. Just move the paper around. Floating foreign exchange.'

'How did it get started? Hardly the thing for a Taiwanese company to get into, is it?'

'They bought two or three established large organisations lock, stock and barrel, retained all the expertise and then let them get on with it.'

'But you reckon the profits look too good.'

He plied his keyboard and the printer began to zap off a spreadsheet. 'If that bottom line is generated by the jolly old ABC, then I'm in the wrong business.' He smiled at her and said, 'If you'd excuse me a moment I have to visit the little boy's room.'

Holly slipped round behind the desk and checked the figures. When Nick came back she was seated demurely in her leather chair.

'Do you usually compute in thousands or millions?'

'This is Asia, me dear, how could you ask such a thing?' he said in mock outrage. 'Millions it is. And a very nice commission for the bank, every step of the way.'

Holly changed the subject. 'They told me on the hash that in the twelve years you've been living here and all the down-island runs you've put together, you now know the hinterland mountains better than anyone on the island, including the army. True?'

'Probably.' He gestured out of the window down at the traffic gridlock below. 'I get out on average three times a week. You can't rely on their maps. They purposely don't publish accurate ones in case the mainland communists get hold of one. Ignore what you hear about the thaw, the prevailing mentality is still we're the bastion isle under constant threat of war.'

Holly left after half an hour's earnest discussion, taking with her copies of Nick's own hand-drawn maps, and diagrams.

She called Mercury Chen and had him meet her at the World Trade Centre where he and the After Midnight Scholar accompanied her as she made her official guest visit to the electronics show.

'What does your bureau know about PANG's Oxbridge ELSI? I've evidence the money involved is astronomical. Heard of a crime tie-in?'

'As a matter of fact, I have,' said Mercury *sotto voce* as they passed by the booths flogging peripherals – motherboards, mice and modems. 'Owing to its convenient worldwide location, Oxbridge ELSI is a front for a wide variety of criminal activity, the obvious one being smuggling: illegal aliens for the bonded labour market, individual narcotics mules, and prostitutes, all travelling under the guise of English language students.'

'You say you want to hurt PANG, so why don't you shut it down?'

'If we had hard evidence of the type your friend Nick Mayo could provide, we might. But then again why should we? Taiwan has an export-based economy. As I said before, nobody, from the President down, wants to rock the boat. Besides, the international bodies shun us. We pariahs have to make our living where and how we can.'

'Nice speech for a lot of spurious crap. The same hypocrisy used to justify the trade in endangered species, rhino horn, tiger bone, bear paw. Well, since your lot aren't going to do anything about Oxbridge, maybe I can.'

'Now don't go doing anything rash, third cousin.'

After lunch at the Hyatt where they also booked the banqueting suite for Mother's official reception on Wednesday night, Holly dumped Mercury and the After Midnight Scholar and paid a visit to the British Trade and Culture Office. She talked to the education officer, a pleasant woman from Godalming whose job was to promote and arrange educational visits to the UK. She was aghast when Holly explained to her why she should take extra special care when vetting all Oxbridge visa applicants in future.

Next, she walked across the corridor to the visa section and applied for a temporary travel document in the name of Tracy Vinnicombe. Passport missing, believed stolen. She handed over three copies of the passport photo Mrs Vinnicombe had given her, the fake police report courtesy of Mercury, and was told the temporary travel document would be ready for collection in twenty-four hours. Finally, she formally invited the trade relations officer to attend the reception at the Hyatt on Wednesday night.

On the ground floor there was an international card phone booth under the palms in the building's central atrium. She checked her watch. Three in the afternoon. Seven in the morning in the UK.

Mick Coulson was still in bed.

'Listen up, buckwheat. Here's your promotion to inspector.' Holly filled him in on Oxbridge ELSI's extra-curricular activities.

He was ecstatic. 'Oh boyoboy! If this is as big as you reckon, it could mean, well, the sky's the frigging limit!' he gushed like the overgrown school lad he was.

Well satisfied with her day's work, Holly returned to Ho-ping East Road to find the After Midnight Scholar in a double-parked 4x4 Nissan Patriot.

'I'm going down-island to take some things for your mother. I intend to bring her back with me tomorrow morning so she can attend the reception. She thought you might like to accompany me for the drive. Also to visit her new home.'

I bet she did, said Holly to herself. Nice cosy little jaunt, just the two of us. On the other hand, she did want to check on Mother, see the place where she was apparently going to spend the rest of her days. From what she'd heard, the ancestral home was a beautiful spot, set high in the mountains in an area just off the *shan-ti ren*, an indigenous tribal reserve. Better than twiddling her thumbs in Taipei. Besides, she'd be back the next day.

'Why not? But first let me get showered and pack a bag.'

They left the poisoned clag of the western coastal plain with its factories, paddy fields and cities, one of the most densely populated strips of land on earth, and drove up the mountain tracks. Here Ilha Formosa, the beautiful isle so said the Portuguese, can still be found. Holly found it.

Mother's home was a stone, three-winged traditional house built round a courtyard. That evening the locals came by and a feast developed round the big bonfire with dancing and carousing till the early hours under the waning moon.

From her bed, Holly could see down the steep valley to a lake. Titanium in the moonbeams. In the forest, the thousand instrument symphony endlessly tuned up in anticipation of the curtain rise at dawn. It was so beautiful she could hardly bring herself to try and sleep. She wanted to savour the night, etch it upon her mind for recall some wet November teatime in Camden.

A soft tap on the door. The After Midnight Scholar paying court.

Intoxicated by the beauty of the moment, Holly reached out and slowly lifted the mosquito net.

14

Typhoon Jeremy was working its way up the western coastal plain, wreaking destruction and emptying the paddies onto the chemical stacks.

On Ho-ping East Road, as the neon signs came crashing down to explode on the street and the government declared it officially a Typhoon Day, they had a final briefing. It was Tuesday afternoon.

Sitting round a never-ending pot of Oolong *cha*, Holly wanted to know if there'd be guns.

Mercury Chen assured her that there'd be 'hardly any'. 'They won't be necessary. Our men will already be inside the place as customers. We'll create a diversion to block access from the temple. One canister of tear gas should suffice. The devotees will think it's a fire down below. Meanwhile, the rear main entrance will be completely sealed off. These things are ritualised. They'll hit us somewhere next week in retaliation. No one should get hurt. Of course, if some joker starts pulling a pistol, he'll get what's coming.'

'So let's have it again. While you lot secure the temple, Tracy and I are to be taken by jeep down-island

291

and shipped off the island via snake-head boat to Hong Kong.'

'Correct.'

'Who's doing the driving?'

'Naturally the After Midnight Scholar will continue to be responsible for your personal protection till you are safely off Taiwan.'

'What about the typhoon?'

'According to the latest reports, it will be north of Taipei by Wednesday night. You'll be leaving from a beach two-thirds of the way south down-island. If it's too rough to put to sea, you'll wait out the storm in shelter near the beach. Remember, the typhoon's your best friend. No one wants to go chasing around the island in those sort of conditions.'

'And you honourably promise that all the girls will be released into the care of the Candle-light Halfway House Charity Organisation.'

'If you insist, yes.'

'I do insist. Without your solemn word on this, I won't take part.'

'You have it,' said Mercury, grim-faced and clearly not pleased with what he plainly saw as Holly's unwarranted interference.

'What guarantees do you have that Mother will be left in peace?' she asked.

'No one needs a war involving widowed grandmothers. I told you, this whole thing is about face. No one wants the streets flowing with spilt blood. Besides, after you've gone, your mother will be under the constant protection of the After Midnight Scholar and his men until the dust settles.'

Holly glanced at the tall, thin presence who merely nodded without expression. Since his silent withdrawal Tuesday dawn, he'd been utterly discreet, for which Holly was very grateful. The last thing she needed was a triumphant Mother cackling her head off. Still, she'd been hyper-sensitive to nuance and gesture but no one had shown the slightest hint of awareness. Not even the tiniest glint in the eye to indicate that anything had occurred. So much so, that it now seemed to Holly the stuff of dreams. Yet the Chinese night has a thousand eyes.

They went over the plan one more time.

The reception at the Hyatt on Wednesday night was a great success. True to his boast, Mercury had managed to get the mayor, up for re-election in a month's time, to put in a showy ten-minute appearance. He raised a toast to a returning prodigal daughter, and joked, 'Such a valuable import will surely help to lessen the trade imbalance with the United Kingdom.'

As the guests were beginning to cha-cha-cha to a Filipino combo, Holly went to the rest room, changed into her travelling clothes and slipped out of the hotel.

They reached the Dog Temple about ninety minutes later. As planned, she entered via the temple's underground passage in a group including Mercury, the After Midnight Scholar and about a dozen men. As they passed through the turnstile, tear gas was released back up the passage. They all wrapped wet scarves round their faces and on the count of three burst through the doors and charged into the casino.

Without warning, the men around her whipped out guns and started firing. Beside her, Mercury produced a Uzi, yelling, 'Thirty-two-round magazine!' and began spraying the air.

The After Midnight Scholar threw her to the ground behind a pillar and stayed close in the deafening bedlam. Within seconds the air was thick with burnt cordite.

It was over quickly. Holly poked her head up as the smoke cleared. The opposition, obviously taken by complete surprise, could be seen herded with heads down and hands held high in abject surrender. A few of the tables full of bottles of beer, mahjong tiles and poker chips had been overturned. She could see no casualties apart from one man holding a bloody forearm. It really was more ritual than true battle, she thought as the After Midnight Scholar helped her to her feet.

Mercury's men were emptying the cubicles. The girls and their customers tumbled out in various states of undress and dishevelment. One or two tough ones screamed and cursed defiantly. A prod from a weapon quickly quietened them down.

'You promised no guns!' hissed Holly as she pushed by Mercury and began to search the cubicles.

'Merely a stage effect.'

'*Gong-chi! Gong-chi!* Congratulations!' people kept saying, coming up to her one by one and touching her briefly or bowing. One fellow dropped to his knees and kissed her feet.

Holly ignored them as she went along the line banging open doors. Those still cowering inside the cubicles were frightened and shocked; some were tiny and terribly young. Halfway down the row, Mercury stood and beckoned. She ran over, took a breath and opened the door.

Tracy Vinnicombe, naked, lay tied to a dirty soiled mattress, obviously drugged to her eyeballs.

'Your friend?' asked Mercury.

Holly nodded. The After Midnight Scholar pushed past and sliced the ropes tying Tracy down. Someone handed Holly a plain white kimono which she used to cover the pliant, bruised body. She couldn't help but notice the cigarette burns on the girl's breasts and thighs, and she struck out wildly at the nearest person, swearing incoherently at the men around her in Hakkanese. 'You pig-men should be castrated and torn in two!'

The After Midnight Scholar tried to help her lift Tracy, but Holly pushed him away. Gently, she hitched the skinny body over her shoulder in a fireman's lift.

'Get me some water, tea, anything!'

'No time!' yelled Mercury, shouting orders at his men and tugging her along at a run. 'Go now! Others will be coming! My men and I will stay till you are safely clear.'

Mercury hustled her out of the double doors into the stormy night where a number of open trucks were waiting.

Something was wrong. Holly stopped and stood her ground in the buffeting wind and rain.

'The other girls! You aren't going to leave them, are you?' she hollered. 'You promised me!'

Mercury shouted back, 'We can't possibly take them. It will mean a cycle of violence and vendetta.'

'You already have that cycle. I demand you release them!'

Mercury looked desperate. He shook his head, rain streaming off his forehead. 'Third cousin, try to understand. I have to follow orders. Besides, the girls . . . they know no other life.'

Holly shook her head contemptuously. 'Then we'll give them a life.' From her pocket she drew out a small personal protection siren and hit the button.

Whoop! Whoop! Whoop!

Despite the blather of the typhoon, the noise split the night. While Mercury looked on disbelieving and the After Midnight Scholar threw his head back into the lashing rain and roared with laughter, a phalanx of yellow taxis came thundering out of the sand dunes. Within moments the combined China-Taipei Hashers under the direction of Sand-Crab and Mijo Slut began shuttling the dazed girls into the waiting taxis. One or two refused to come and were left behind.

Within moments the taxis began racing away. Holly laid Tracy gently down inside Mayo's Telstar and the After Midnight Scholar climbed in after her.

She wound down the window and looked out at Mercury, 'You did a great job there, Captain Chen! 'Bye now!'

Mercury stared at her for a moment, then with a wry grin raised his hand in salute. 'I'll miss you, third cousin!' He brought his hand down and banged the roof of the car. 'Go!'

The After Midnight Scholar slapped the dashboard and Nick Mayo, the Mijo Slut, gunned the motor and with a screaming wheel-spin they went skittering over the sodden sand dunes into the typhoon night.

A mile or so ahead, the procession of taxis split into three directions, two electing to go for the north and south sections of the coastal road. Nick Mayo headed inland across country away from the ocean.

An hour into the howling ride, dim lights behind them indicated they were being followed, but a series of double-backs and U-turns quickly shook off their pursuers.

They bypassed Taipei and the big cities of Taoyuan and Chungli. Keeping to the mountain roads, they meandered down the spine of the island till they reached Mother's new home. The sun was just coming up.

Inside the house, they washed a now conscious but silent Tracy. She was in a state of shock. It would be about now that she would begin to experience the first shivers of cold turkey. The local shaman was summoned and brought some evil-smelling broth.

The After Midnight Scholar had come well prepared. After some discussion during which he pointed out over Holly's objections that the girl was far too weak to handle both cold turkey withdrawal and a boat ride in a typhoon, he turned Tracy over and with deft skill shot her upper thigh full of morphine followed by a vitamin booster.

Nick and Holly filled up on hot food and rice wine and slept an hour or so till noon. Then it was time to move on.

They stayed on the mountain roads till they reached the latitude of the evening rendezvous where they turned right and headed west, down to the coast. Stopping only to fill up with petrol and buy drinks, they arrived at the beach as dusk fell. They parked the car in a thick copse of pine trees overlooking a scrubby wind-blown beach.

They climbed out of the car and stretched their legs. The sky spat needles of rain into their eyes.

Holly looked out at the maddened sea and began to doubt the wisdom of the plan. Risking herself in the night crossing was one thing, but with a sick and weak Tracy to carry along it was all but suicidal.

What the frock! She'd come this far on the roller-coaster ride, it was too late to turn back now. Besides, what choices were left to her? She looked back at the car where Tracy lay in damp dreams. Could she leave the poor kid behind after all this? After all, what had been the point of it all? To expunge her guilt over Jenny? No, it was to put up and shut up and do something, for God's sake! And she'd done it! She wasn't about to turn coward at the last hurdle.

She stepped onto a section of high dune and looked out for the signal. The ocean was frothing and slamming about as gigantic waves reared up and crashed down onto the shore. The vague tourist map showed they were exactly on the Tropic of Cancer, and darkness fell as quickly as a stage curtain.

They had to wait another half-hour before the twin lights of the snake-head flashed. With the After Midnight Scholar on one side and Nick on the other, Holly lifted Tracy out of the car and stepped onto the sand.

15

'You're looking halfway human this morning,' said Minty as they met in the yard about a week later.

Holly stepped over the chickens who were busy trying to pry worms from the cobbles and GiGi who was looking askance at the sharp beaks and claws peck-peck-pecking.

'Feeling halfway that or something,' she said, reaching down to pick up her three-legged friend and nuzzle his grey fur.

'Leaves will be turning soon,' said Minty. 'You should see the heather up on Exmoor. This is the time of year I like. Colours to drive you insane out there. I feel as if I'm standing in one big pot of paint. Gets the ju-ju going, I need a ten-league paintbrush.'

'You said you were going to do the bees today.'

'Yes. I think I'll take off a couple of racks of honey, leave the rest to feed them through the winter. Want to help me?'

'You bet.'

Jane came out from the cottage. 'Call for you, Holly. From London.'

Holly exchanged looks with Minty and went inside the cottage.

She came back out into the Indian summer sunshine ten minutes later with a bounce to her stride that hadn't been there before.

'Mick Coulson,' she announced.

'What happened?'

'They just arrested thirty illegals working in a sweat shop in Edmonton. All had false passports with student visas issued on applications by Oxbridge ELSI. Coupled with the bust last week of eighty Ks of coke at the Rustington branch school, Mick reckons that will be enough to close down the whole show.'

'Brilliant,' said Minty. 'Bloody well excellent work, Holly-Jean Ho.'

Holly looked around at the Devon countryside, the big sky above, the thatched cottage, Jane and her old friend the artist.

'I've had enough of this country life, Minty. High time I went back to work.'

Minty grinned and nodded. 'Attagirl.'

That evening, sitting by the log fire with glasses of wine, homemade bread and dripping honeycomb, Minty said, 'You finally ready to tell me all about it? I've been waiting with bated breath for more than a week now.'

So Holly-Jean told him. She paused from time to time to drink more wine, lost in the recall. They all cheered when she got to the point where they'd rescued Tracy and set free the other caged girls. This was the part that gave her pride. The part that healed the other losses. Jenny, Su-ming, Sharon.

Holly shook her head in the firelight, ridding herself of the remembered faces. She slurped wine and pushed back what she knew to be massive guilt. Survivor's guilt.

More wine while the others waited in silence for her to resume the story.

'A riot, that was. And all the time, looking over our shoulders expecting a bullet or a machete, or an egg of nitric acid . . .'

'An egg of acid,' repeated Minty, mystified.

'*Ai-yo*, enough,' said Holly, draining her glass. 'Suffice to say, we managed. The escape was possible only because of the fact that there was a raging typhoon and most sane people were staying indoors while he blew over. Not us.'

'Not you, no ladyee!' They clinked glasses.

'So where was I?'

'You'd just arrived at a beach on the west coast as evening fell. The rendezvous.'

'Now that was something else. Waves as big as arctic icebergs pounding down onto us as we tried to get Tracy on board the fishing boat.'

'What about the After Midnight Scholar?' asked Jane. 'I do love that name.'

Holly was amazed to feel her face burn with remembered something or other. 'He insisted on staying with us for the night crossing to the mainland.'

'A smuggler's vessel? A watchumacallit?'

'A snake-head. It smuggles anything from people to heroin to dried fancy mushrooms. We landed at a little beach on Mirs Bay in the New Territories. A Rolls-Royce, believe it or not, was waiting to drive us into

Hong Kong. That's where we said goodbye to the After Midnight Scholar.'

'Unbelievable. A latter-day Lochinvar,' said Jane, eyes twinkling.

Holly looked at the glowing embers and smiled. 'Yes. Didn't say much, but a good man to have around in a pickle.'

Minty poured more wine. 'What about passports and stuff? I must say there's no one quite like you, Holly-Jean, for making something as wild and dangerous as a night crossing by heroin boat in the teeth of a typhoon sound routine.'

'Do I? Well, I can assure you it wasn't,' said Holly, accepting the wine. 'In fact, I've never felt more seasick in my life. I'm sure parts of the Yellow Sea are just that since I crossed the ocean.'

'Yeeuch!' said Jane and they all laughed.

'So then you're nice and cosy in the Roller,' Minty prompted.

'Yes. The Bamboo Union put us up in a fabulous suite at the Peninsula Hotel. They had room service bring up the manager of the basement mall fashion boutique. Hong Kong wealth demands real designer lines only. We had a private viewing with a live model. Money was no object, I was assured, so I said, thanks very much, don't mind if I do!'

Again they laughed aloud. The sound of healing. It was a good sound to hear, a long time coming.

'I chose a Rifat Ozbek for my sins.'

'And how was Tracy coping during all this?'

'Coping,' said Holly. 'Just. Oral methadone. On the

hour. The After Midnight Scholar saw the turkey off till we reached Hong Kong. From there the society supplied her.'

Jane asked what fashion Tracy chose from the hotel boutique.

'My suggestion: a Romeo Gigli silk ladies' business suit.'

'Why all the lavish care and cash handouts?'

'Yours truly,' said Holly. 'Crazy, isn't it? I'd apparently achieved a major victory by being present at Tracy's rescue.' Holly went on to explain to them the concept of face.

'You mean you were set up from the beginning?'

'We'll never know exactly when it all began,' said Holly. 'But hell, I must be some kind of mechanical doll. Those frocks manoeuvred me all the way from Camden Lock to Taipei.'

'Just in order to make this Pang Chong-ts lose face, it's unreal,' said Jane, wonderment in her voice.

'But wait a minute,' said Minty, getting excited as his thoughts veered off.

Holly sat and waited, in silent dread of the place his reasoning was bound to lead.

'Where's the beginning to all this? At what point did happenstance become a set-up?'

'Don't ask,' said Holly.

But Minty was relentless. 'I mean, surely they couldn't have known what was going to happen with you and Jenny? I mean it was purely chance that Jenny asked you to help in the investigations of the attacks on her students, right? But then how did they know?' he reasoned, his voice rising.

'I told you, we'll never know,' said Holly. 'I think we might be able to trace some of it back to the point when Margot Silverman opened her big mouth, totally innocently, during one of her trips to Hong Kong. But then according to Mr Plum Blossom, they've been watching me ever since birth.' She gestured helplessly.

'How in the hell did they know Jenny was going to be killed?'

Jane tried to hush Minty. To no avail.

'Come to that, how did they know you wouldn't be in the flat that evening, or that you would . . . Oh shit.' His voice dropped as the implication hit him. 'Oh, fucking hell,' he said, his voice old and tired. 'Jenny killed. Tracy sold to the Flying Eagles. No, it's too farfetched, right? Tell me it's too farfetched, dammit!' He was shaking with anger.

'For God's sake, Minty!' cried Jane. 'It's over!'

The silence was split by sudden howling. The baby had woken upstairs. Jane went up to tend her.

Holly stood staring at the fire. In the long, charged, quiet moment, neither of them moved. They could hear Jane cooing and singing a lullaby to calm the baby.

'God, I'm sorry, Hols.' Minty moved close and put an arm round her, saying, 'I'm the clodhopper, aren't I?'

'No, you're just too damned smart sometimes. You see that's the stuff I've been trying to deal with,' said Holly. 'If it's true, it means I am solely responsible for it all. Jenny, Tracy, the whole thing.'

'Nah. Forget it!' said Minty. 'It's fantasy. No one is that diabolical. I should never have even suggested such a thing. What a fool I am to even think it.'

'Oh, don't worry, Minty,' said Holly, with a bitter grin. 'I saw it, you saw it, anyone who knows the story can see it.'

This time the silence took a long while to break.

'The Chinese are something, aren't they?' said Minty finally.

'The Chinese are something,' agreed Holly.

'Let's go for a walk,' suggested Minty. 'We get shooting stars this time of year. The equinox and all that.'

They donned boots and went out into the night.

Up on the moor behind the house, Minty said, 'So you were staying at the Peninsula.'

'Cor, you don't quit, do you?' said Holly.

'It's a damn good story.'

'Right,' said Holly, deciding it would be best to enlist the aid of her tag-teamster. Get someone else to help wrestle her demons. 'So there we are in the Somerset Maugham suite or whatever. Tracy's looking very skinny-chic in her Gigli suit with her runny nose and the shakes. The temporary travel documents are all in order. One last bottle of champers and we caught the nightly BA to Heathrow, first class. I hired a car at the airport, drove Tracy home to Poole. Stayed for lunch with her mum during which we dried our tears and got smashed on claret. When I felt ready, I called you and set off for Devon. The rest you know.'

'Amazing, Ms Holly-Jean Ho. You really are bloody well amazing.' They walked on a while, the Exmoor night air crisp, pristine.

'GiGi was waiting in the lane when I drove up. I never told you that, did I?'

'No, you didn't.'

'There I was, trying to remember your directions – third gate on the left after the Sportsman's Inn, down the lane with the grass growing in the middle – and suddenly I see my darling Hopalong crashing through the hedgerow. Nearly ran over him. He knew, you know. He knew it was me. He came out a mile or so to greet me.'

'Cats, familiars . . . scary. Arroooohhh!' He bayed at the moon.

'I tell you, I'll never see a better sight in my life as that old moggy of mine. Three-legged bugger damn near broke my heart. I opened the car door and he sort of flip-flopped in, you know how he does. Drove the rest of the way up your lane with him on my lap peering through the steering wheel, dribbling all over me.' The tears were streaming down her face. 'Sorry. Can't help it.'

'Healing stuff,' said Minty, hugging her.

Later, when they were back inside, he asked, 'How's Tracy doing now?'

'I spoke to her mum yesterday on the phone,' replied Holly. 'As well as can be expected is the verdict.'

The next morning she packed GiGi into the wicker basket and sat beside Minty in the old Saab back to town.

It didn't take long for business to pick up again. People had heard she'd been away, but not much else. She'd acquired a mysterious reputation, not such a bad thing for an investigator, though she wasn't sure what effect it would have on her good will in the nerd world of software. She'd even got her name in the papers.

306

There'd been a flurry with the toilet-paper press when the story of Tracy Vinnicombe's rescue first surfaced, thanks mainly to the self-publicising and quick-buck-turning efforts of John Augustus. By the time Holly got back to the studio and work, it had all but blown over.

On her return, Marika threw a Gravadlax and aquavit party at the wine bar, with Holly as guest of honour. She invited Mick Coulson who filled her in on the latest. Oxbridge ELSI was coming under heavy investigation on all fronts, headed up by Serious Crimes with special assistance from the Drug Squad, the Fraud Squad and the Inland Revenue. She also asked Janet Rae-Smith to come, but she had accepted a guest lectureship at the University of Wisconsin at Madison and was getting ready to leave the next day.

'So soon!' Holly complained.

'It's only for the academic year,' replied Janet. 'Maybe you'd like to come over and visit. Beautiful place, all lakes and forests.'

'Sounds as if I'll have to.'

Marika had a new lover, a bass player in a women's jazz rap band. Holly liked her on sight, and they knew they would all be good friends. It was a nice bash. Friends, music, food and booze. The staff had stacked the tables in the garden room and they danced on Marika's gleaming wood floor.

That night for the first time Holly felt truly at home, her adventure behind her.

'Bit tame after the China Hash,' she told them to fits of laughter at the descriptions of the ex-pats' insanity.

The old routine of life began to come together. Sort of.

Perhaps it was the coming of winter. Early November in London was not the most uplifting time of year. Or maybe it was the absence of Mother who by all reports and telephone calls was perfectly happy in her new home.

Whatever.

She found after a few weeks that she was going half-heartedly after her old software customers. She accepted only a few new ones here and there. She wasn't very enthusiastic, not by Holly-Jean's standards. Couldn't get a handle on it really. She began to wonder if the condition might be terminal.

But then the other kinds of assignments and requests began to trickle in. People who'd heard about the rescue. Stories about gangsters and Taiwan. People who needed help in locating missing persons. Errant husbands, clever mistresses, cheating business partners. Some specialised courier work was offered her. She farmed that out to reliable girls who worked for Margot or Marika.

Without any effort on her part, the thing began to grow. She decided she needed a full-time assistant to handle the office work. Minty came back to town and volunteered his services.

'I think I like your new line of work. Got a bit of the hard, the real. Good for my painting.'

Holly, meanwhile, looked on it all with detached amusement. So she had turned out to be a private clit after all . . .

One night in late November she decided to call the gym

in Highgate. It was high time to get back to the tatami. But Tommy Chen was out of town.

Of course, she'd forgotten. The World Championships at Den Haag. He'd be away for a week or two.

She went for a run on the Heath. Back in the studio she showered and cropped her hair back to its habitual inch. Then she put on Cassandra Wilson's 'Blue Light till Dawn' and laid her deliciously tired body down on the floor. The music was good enough to send her spine ashiver.

She thought about Tommy Chen. It occurred to her that she'd missed her last chance at the European title. She was definitely not getting younger. Some of the kids competing today were in their teens. She'd never be able to match their *chi*. Perhaps it was a part of her life that had passed on. Like so much else.

The light was blinking on her answerphone when she came out of meditation. There was a message to call a number she didn't recognise. She dialled anyway. It was the lady from the telephone company.

'I've been trying to get you for days, so I tried nights. We've nabbed Mr Tentpole!'

Holly didn't understand for a moment before she remembered and let out a shriek of delight.

She was bopping to the music when the doorbell rang. She looked at her watch. That would be the signwriter. He'd promised he'd drop by that evening.

She unlocked the door. But it wasn't the Rasta man. Tommy Chen stood there with a big bunch of white chrysanthemums.

'Tommy, what a delightful surprise!' Holly hugged him, accepting the flowers.

'White?' she joked. 'Has anyone I know died?'

'All I could get,' said Tommy looking away with a little shrug.

'But aren't you supposed to be in Holland at the championships?' she said and added with genuine concern, 'If you don't mind my saying so, you look terrible. You sick?'

'I feel terrible, and I am in Den Haag,' said Tommy, closing the door and reaching out.

In one single lightning movement he had Holly prone on the floor with her carotid artery between his thumbs and had already brought enough pressure to prevent blood from entering her brain. She knew that without the oxygen supplied by blood from the artery she'd be brain-dead within a few minutes.

'*Lao-shr* is a *Fei Ying Bang?*' she managed to croak. 'You're one of Pang's boys, Tommy?'

Teacher Chen looked unutterably bleak and sad. Tears began to well out of his eyes as he stared down at Holly. '*Yi-wu.*' He lessened the pressure perceptibly as he spoke.

Keep him talking, thought Holly.

'*Yi-wu?* The code?'

'The code of honour: total and utter obedience. Unbreakable, my dear Holly-Jean. Vowed in blood when I first joined the society.'

'I never took you for a Flying Eagle gangster, *lao-shr.*'

'Don't call me that, Holly dear. Please. Try to understand. My father held my arm for the burning of the induction brand when I was fifteen.' He showed her the mark on the inside of his forearm.

'Always wondered,' she whispered, weakly.

'I am a very senior officer of the *Fei Ying Bang* here in Europe.' He tightened the vice-hold again.

Holly instantly felt her consciousness sliding. Life at a tilt. A redness creeping into her vision.

'I have been resisting the termination order since you returned. But now the word has come direct from Pang Chong-ts himself.'

Holly struggled to move her limbs but all she felt was leaden weakness, a towering urge to sleep. With one last effort she put all her training into practice and summoned all her *chi*. Her body rose a few inches from the ground, but Tommy Chen simply pushed her back down with a tiny tweak of his thumb.

Twilight. Dreamlike. No matter how hard she tried, she couldn't make her limbs move.

'You foolish child,' the voice was saying in the distance. 'Why did you think you could go against someone like him? Why, Holly? Why did you make this happen to me?'

She forced her eyes to focus, one last effort to break the stranglehold. But all she could see was the face above her. Tears were streaming down Tommy Chen's cheeks.

'This is the worst moment of my life,' he said, tightening his thumbs one last time.

Holly's vision closed and she saw only black ink inside her skull. The voice travelled from far away.

'You were always my best . . . My favourite student . . . Goodbye, dear Holly-Jean, dear *Shao-lan*, my dear Little Orchid . . .'

The black wave broke and rushed up the beach towards her, the water engulfed her and the darkness overshadowed . . .

Sudden strange hiss. Caterwaul marow!

Teacher Chen loosened his grip for a milli-second.

It was all Holly got. She took it.

Survival instinct shook her mind awake. Forced her instantly up and out from underneath the crushing weight. The grip released, she flew upwards, opened her eyes and saw Chen struggling with both hands behind his neck.

GiGi! Three paws worth of claw embedded in Tommy Chen's nape!

Holly lunged and a vicious liver kite half felled Tommy. She grabbed GiGi's fur and ripped him off, skin, hair, shirt and all, as Chen screamed in agony.

The Master's foot windmilled and knocked Holly and GiGi flying back towards the kitchen table. She picked herself up and forgetting all her training in her blind rage, she charged full tilt, head first, maddened.

It was the one move he could never have foreseen. The one clumsy graceless flailing he wouldn't have taught her in a thousand years.

Wild as some demented beast, Holly-Jean's forehead butted his chin. His guard came up too late to prevent her sickening contact but caught her in the temple. They were both stunned in the clash. Holly shook her head, channelled every cell, every ounce of energy from the soles of her feet to the tallest hair on her head.

Howling, she charged again. She crashed into him, tangled him in her arms and with her momentum

312

unbroken, bundled him through the window to fall on the cobbles below.

'All right, Missus?' said the Rasta, stoned, looking up at her a few feet away from the crumpled body.

'Not really,' croaked Holly.

The Rasta came up the iron stairs and in the door. 'Wha' you mean? Dat some self-defence!'

Holly paused. 'You see he made one fatal mistake. He broke his own rule.'

'What dat?'

'His heart wasn't in it.'

'Besides,' said Holly, stroking GiGi a while later, after the ambulance had gone and the police had finished questioning Holly and the eye-witness Rastaman. 'It was two against one.'

'Say wha' now?'

'Me and my man.' She nuzzled GiGi's velvet fur. 'My secret weapon.'

'Sweee-yeet!'

She poured wine for both of them.

'I guess you'll be needin' a new pane a glass 'fore I cain start me work.'

'Can you fix it tonight?' said Holly.

'Course, missus. Knows a yard in Chal' Farm. Twenty-four-hour emergency plumbin' an all. Just ride me bike. Five minutes, I'll be back.'

'Did you bring your paints?'

'Sho did, missus, all here.' He toted his bag on the floor. 'Same saign feh me wrait agin?'

'No,' said Holly, stroking GiGi. 'That's why I called

you over. This time there's a change in the wording.' She took some paper from the strewn floor, found a   scribbled. Satisfied, she handed it to the Rasta.

He read it out loud. 'Holly-Jean Ho and Associates. Private Investigations.'

'That's right.'

'Owabout de colour, missus?'

'Oh, same again, I should say, wouldn't you?' said Holly. 'The purple and silver certainly looked . . . boss.'

'Dat look boss, missus,' the Rasta agreed.